LETTING LOOSE

Joanne Skerrett

KENSINGTON PUBLISHING CORP.
http://www.kensingtonbooks.com

DAFINA BOOKS are published by

Kensington Publishing Corp.
119 West 40th Street
New York, NY 10019

All Kensington Titles, Imprints, and Distributed Lines are available at special quantity discounts for bulk purchases for sales promotions, premiums, fund-raising, educational or institutional use. Special book excerpts or customized printings can also be created to fit specific needs. For details, write or phone the office of the Kensington special sales manager: Kensington Publishing Corp., 119 West 40th St., New York, NY 10018, attn: Special Sales Department, Phone: 1-800-221-2647.

ISBN-13: 978-0-7582-1424-9
ISBN-10: 0-7582-1424-3

First trade paperback printing: August 2007
First mass market printing: December 2009

10 9 8 7 6 5 4 3 2 1

Printed in the United States of America

For both my grandmothers—who, like Dominica,
were sweet and fair; rich and rare.

Acknowledgments

Thanks to the Almighty for creating such an amazing place and all the blessings that come along with my heritage. Thanks to my family, friends and colleagues for your continued love and support. And, of course, my most talented editor, John Scognamiglio, and my agent, Frank Weimann.

Chapter 1

"Ms. Wilson takes it from the back!"

I whirled around from the chalkboard. What the . . . ?! I knew that voice and its owner was going down today! I'd had it with these little brats.

"Who said that?" I wanted to scream, but I'm the adult here, the professional.

The classroom of thirty ninth graders rippled with repressed giggles, but no one was going to answer my question. They looked at me, none trying to appear particularly innocent or guilty. They knew and I knew that Treyon Dicks said it. Since he came back from his third or fifty-ninth stint in juvenile detention hall, Treyon's been cruisin' for a bruisin' from me. Sometimes I think I'd like to let him have it, jail sentence be damned. But listen to me; who says "cruisin' for a bruisin' " anymore? That's the problem right there. These kids don't respect me. I'm just not "down" enough.

I could walk into any of my colleagues' classes right now and there'd be a lovefest going on. They'd probably be sitting in a circle, holding hands, and reading Proust out loud. But that never happens in Ms. Wilson's class. It's like my kids can sniff the eau de wannabe public school teacher that

I wear every day. I'm supposed to be a refugee from a posh private school who doesn't really want to be in this vast urban educational complex. But I do. I really do. Sometimes. Yes, I miss the genius students at my old school, the two swimming pools, lacrosse games, landscaped grounds, parents who care—at least the normal ones. But I don't miss the awful incident that brought me to this place. And I shouldn't even think about that right now. I need to just fit in and do a good job. Shape up or ship out, like my father used to say.

The rows of chairs and desks facing me were beginning to rock with laughter. I searched their faces, trying to affect my most serious warning face. No one would speak up.

Speak to me! But I got only averted eyes and giggles because I was freaking Amelia Wilson, lover of Shakespeare, Milton, Donne, Morrison, Hughes, Walker, Countee Cullen, Nella Larsen. I don't get Donald Goines or Jay-Z. I keep misspelling Ludacris. It's ludicrous. And I'll never gain my students' respect although I've been in this school for over a year. I'll just keep getting dissed (do people still say that?) day in and day out. But I can fight back!

"Okay, Treyon." I put the eraser and the chalk down on the desk. I'd give him a chance to apologize. If he gets suspended again, God only knows what kind of trouble he'll get into. The last time he pulled something like this—he drew a picture of two people having sex, doggy style—he was kicked out of school for three days. It was three days of relative calm and serenity for me; my twenty-nine other kids come with their own myriad problems. But I did worry about Treyon. I worried that he might get into a fight because he wasn't in school. That he might get hit by a bus. That he would come to some violent, tragic end and it would have been all my fault because I had gotten him suspended. But I just didn't know what else to do with this kid. . . . I didn't tell him, but I was quite impressed with the quality of the drawing, though.

"You can apologize or you can go to the principal's office."
I tried to smile, mainly to mollify him. What I really wanted to do was leap across the rows of desks and chairs, grab his skinny neck, and throw him out the window.

"I ain't apologizin'." His head lifted in defiance. "I ain't said nothin'."

Okay. This was how it was going to be. I had my instructions from Mr. Bell and I would follow them. This was last period and I was not going to make the last few minutes of my day go up in a plume of angry smoke.

"Fine. Go to Mr. Bell's office then."

He got up from his seat, grumbling as he gathered up his heavy goose-down jacket. He's lucky I didn't have the burly security guy escort him out.

"Bitch!" he mumbled, slamming the door hard.

The rest of the class went silent.

I took a deep breath and went back to writing down the homework assignment on the chalkboard: Read the first four chapters of *The Grapes of Wrath.* I didn't care that they thought it was too much. I didn't care if they hated me and were plotting my death at the bus stop every day. I didn't care. I didn't care. All I knew was that when I was in ninth grade, my teacher would assign us the whole book, not four measly chapters.

"We go'n have a quiz or sum'n?" asked Tina, a pretty girl who was actually one of my better students but who also thought her street cred was more important than maintaining her B average.

"Maybe. Maybe not. Just be prepared."

They groaned and rolled their eyes. "Ms. Wilson, you so mean," one of them said.

I didn't answer. I'd heard it all before. Then the bell rang.

Chapter 2

There seemed to have been a blizzard since lunchtime. My little Beetle was completely submerged under what looked like a foot of snow; I couldn't see the lime green paint. I considered the white mound and weighed it against my aching back. That same back I'd almost put out after a murderous spin class at 6:30 this morning would not hold up to all of this shoveling. I looked around the parking lot. Maybe there was some student I could pay. . . . But the few boys who I saw walking toward me had nothing but hate in their eyes. They must have gotten the memo: Ms. Wilson is not cool, and she is mean. I sighed.

As I started brushing the snow off the top of the car, I saw that Miguel, Mira Gutierrez's live-in boyfriend, had driven up and was cleaning off her car. Hmmm . . . Well, isn't that nice. Five minutes later, Lashelle Thompson's scary-looking boyfriend pulled up in a huge SUV, a Ford Expedition or something equally awful, thumping some bass-heavy music (Ludacris?), and started shoveling around her car. What the heck? I'm Amelia Wilson and I'm a loser who shovels out her own car, while my colleagues have their significant others do theirs.

In a high school parking lot, full of cars belonging to students and teachers and God knows who else, I seemed to be the only woman shoveling. Could this be real? Was there some implicit genetic code, like a computer command, that I was not aware of that automatically prompts men to show up to aid women whenever there's heavy snowfall? Or if I were one of those women who possessed such a thing as a boyfriend, would I have to call him and order him to my place of work for shoveling duty? Was that how it was done? And would I ever get to participate in this ritual? From the looks of things, it was highly unlikely. And that was especially sad for all the men out there because, according to Treyon, I would "take it 'from the back.' " The memory of the Treyon debacle prompted me to stab my shovel into my back tire a little too forcefully. He'd gotten sent home for a week. And this time I wouldn't lose any sleep over it. As a matter of fact, I was hoping that he'd be buried in a snowbank. Well, not fatally.

I have to get rid of this snow before my back breaks, I told myself. I was panting and huffing, and that really came as a disappointment. For a whole month—it was number one of my New Year's resolutions—I'd been going to spin class three times a week. Granted, I could only make it through a half hour of the class. But I was trying! I shouldn't be all out of breath because I was doing a little shoveling. I was actually sweating. Then panic hit. I remembered the news stories I'd read about people who'd had heart attacks while shoveling after snowstorms. Oh my God! I'd better slow my pace!

I was so tired, but I had to keep going. I told myself: *You're taking one for the team—the big girls' team. You're a strong, independent, smart, single woman. You can shovel out your own darned car. You don't need a man to do that.*

But then Lashelle's boyfriend waved at me with an apologetic smile that said, Sorry you don't have a big, strong man like me to do this for you. Then he went back to shoveling her spot. I felt exposed, cold, wet, and depressed. But I dug my shovel in, inches to go before I sleep.

Thirty minutes later, Lashelle, Mira, and their men in waiting had all left and I was still shoveling when the tow truck rolled by.

"Hey, sis, you need some help?" It was my brother, Gerard, who rarely did anything right, except for right now. Driving a truck with a snowplow was one of the many short-term jobs he'd managed to keep for the past two years since he'd gotten out of prison.

"I'm almost done, Gerard. Where were you a half hour ago?" I held my aching side with one hand, the shovel with the other.

"I just did a couple of driveways down Melville Park." He showed me a roll of bills. At least he wouldn't be asking me for any money for another week. "I'll plow around you so you can pull out this space," he said.

I waited in the car as he cleared the snow around it. It felt nice and warm and toasty. Even the little daisy on my dashboard looked happy. My back was sore, but I would live. At least it was Friday. I'd have all of Saturday to recover. Oh, and this half hour of shoveling meant that I was off the hook tomorrow. No spin class. Yay!

My cell phone rang just as I waved good-bye to Gerard. I popped it open and my heart vaulted over some invisible inner crossbar.

"Amelia. How are you?"

It was my bête noire. My one indiscretion in life that had cost me my cushy private school job, the respect of my students, and most of my self-esteem. I would also like to blame him for my weight gain, though admittedly I've always had a weight problem. But maybe if I'd never met him it would have already ceased to exist. . . .

"I'm doing just fine."

"Can I see you?"

"No."

He sighed heavily, like he was expecting me to say something different. We've been having this same conversation for the past year!

"I really hope you can . . ."

"I really hope you can work on your marriage and leave me alone," I said and hung up. I held my chest. *Good girl. Good answer. Now breathe easy. I am not a loser. I deserve more than he could ever give me.* But I had to hear it from somebody else.

"Whitney," I wailed to my best friend, "he called again."

"Jeez! Amelia, why don't you use the block on your cell?"

"I don't know how!" This was true. I was no good with technology.

"Whatever. If you really wanted ol' dude to stop calling, you'd find out how."

"You never showed me!"

"I didn't show you how to screw him either, but you managed to learn all on your own."

"Thank you, Whitney. What are you up to?"

"It's snowing so I'm actually working late. . . . That lawyer guy is coming over later."

"What lawyer guy. Duncan?" Whitney's dates were as interchangeable as pop stars and usually almost as pretty.

"Yeah, Big D is what I like to call him."

Of course. Whitney had an endless supply of Big D's in her life. "Well, have fun. I'm going home."

"Tell your roommates I said peace and love."

"Very funny." I hung up. At least she'd taken my mind off bête noire briefly. Ugh. Good sex, bad times, bad memories. Not going back there.

Chapter 3

My roommates Kelly and James were back from another of their two-week "research" vacations. I could tell that before I even pulled into my parking space in front of our apartment. Their van, which I liked to call the peacemobile because of the assault of bumper stickers launched on every available space, was out front, and they had shoveled a space for me behind it. I loved those two, even though they were strange. Not that I had the right to be calling anyone strange.

The apartment was a cluster of warmth and comfort. Yummmm . . . Kelly was making chili. I sniffed the air for meat. No. Kelly only made vegetarian chili, or no-guilt chili. When I make chili, there's plenty of meat. And guilt.

"Ames? That you?" Kelly called out from the kitchen. Like all the white girls I've come into contact with in my 27 years, Kelly found a way to shorten my name. My college roommate at Simmons, Wilhelmina Williams (yes, her parents did do that to her), called me Amy the first day we met and so did every professor and every other person I knew on campus over those three years. Even in graduate school and in the one year I flailed around in a doctorate program, I was called Ames, Amy, and Amester. I never objected. It's not that big of a deal. I prefer Amelia but I'm not militant about it.

Kelly and I met in the doctoral program at Boston College. I quit to go back to teaching and she stayed. I would have finished, but from what I've read in my extensive self-help book collection, I have a fear of success. Anyway, I love to teach. It may not show when I'm facing a roomful of angry ninth graders, but I really think it's my calling to get kids to fall in love with great books the way I did when I was a kid. . . .

"Come in here, see what we brought you," Kelly said.

The smell of the chili overpowered my will to do anything but follow its scent, and my aching back was now forgotten. All I wanted was a bowl of the stuff. If I did not eat now, I would surely die. I felt like Esau at this point. I would have given up my birthright, if I'd had one, for just a taste of this chili.

I hugged Kelly. "Welcome back, girlie. Gimme a bowl of that stuff. I'm starvin' like Marvin." The first time I'd used that expression, James (Kelly's husband who is also in the same doctoral program) had asked very genuinely, "Who's Marvin?" But then he'd started saying it himself later on. It was funny that they thought *I* was hip and in the know. My students could set them straight on that.

As I settled down at our kitchen table with a bowl of almost-done chili, I listened to Kelly talk about her and James's trip to yet another sunny hotspot. They were researching primary education in former colonies, thus the frequent exotic trips. This time it was to Dominica, a tiny Caribbean island that supposedly had a boiling lake and some great hiking trails. That was the type of thing that Kelly and James did. After the tsunami hit South Asia, they promptly booked a flight and flew down to volunteer with some relief organization. They brought back some great pictures of themselves on the beach, looking tanned and happy with some brown-skinned, black-haired children. They believed in causes and lived for big political issues, unlike me who was just willing to let things slide as long as they didn't affect me personally.

James and Kelly hated gas-guzzling vehicles, George Bush (father and son), consumerism, designer clothes, and right-wing Christians. They loved to feed the hungry, clothe the naked, uplift the downtrodden, extol the virtues of diversity, discuss ways to improve urban education, write poetry and smoke weed, and have noisy sex on the weekends when they thought I was asleep.

"Oh, Ames, you really should go down there! You'd love it! Lots of cute guys, great weather, and great food! You know, when our plane landed in Boston this morning and they said how much snow was going to fall, I thought, James and I need to move to somewhere warm. Permanently!" Kelly said as she stirred the pot.

"Ummm . . . mmm . . . mmm . . ." Oh, this chili was so good.

"But, here's what we brought you," Kelly said, turning to me.

I looked at her hands and save for the chili-covered ladle could see no gift.

"James, she's ready for her, uh, souvenir!"

James came out of their room, looking his tanned and rangy self, his long brown hair wet from the shower. I sometimes wished he were my brother, too.

"Okay, dude," he said. "Now keep an open mind." James called everyone dude, even his mother.

They both wanted to be professors, and I could see it in Kelly, but James was such a stoner. . . . At least he was rich, so if he failed at this it wouldn't be the end of the party for him. He was from California. His parents were both in the movie business. Kelly, on the other hand, came from more humble beginnings in Weymouth, Massachusetts, and had been a high school teacher just like me. It was how we ended up getting along so well and being roommates for the past five years. James entered the picture later; I tolerated him at first for her sake, but he managed to grow on me after a while.

Anyway, I agreed to keep an open mind.

"We were hanging out with this dude, and Kelly thought you might like to talk to him. . . . Smart dude. I think you guys might have a lot in common."

I looked from James to Kelly and then back again. The last time they set me up it had been with a guy from their program at BC. The guy was the most boring person I'd ever met, and coming from me that says a lot. I mean, I may struggle with how to spell Ludacris, but at least I KNOW who Ludacris is. His name was actually Tom. No kidding. Tom. Tall, skinny, uptight, nerdy Tom. I took one look at him and thought, "This kid has never been with a sister before and I'm not going to initiate him." The date ended after I told him that I had a headache and needed to go home and lie down. He looked so relieved my feelings were hurt.

So who was this smart dude whom I would have something in common with?

James handed me the picture. It was a picture of them—James, shirtless, with Kelly, camouflage tank top and khaki shorts, and a big, tall brother (my favorite type) wearing a T-shirt that said MOREHOUSE, baggy cargo shorts, and Jesus sandals. Okay. This dude was no Tom.

"Isn't he cute?" Kelly sang.

"Ummm . . ."

"We showed him your picture, too, and he sent you his e-mail addy," James said, smiling.

I sighed. This could go quite badly or quite well. . . .

"You gave him my e-mail address?" Did they cross a

boundary? Did we have boundaries? Had I spelled out my boundaries to my roommates? And in this case, would that count? Because this guy was F-I-N-E.

"Your work e-mail . . . at the school," Kelly said, searching my face for signs of "boundaries crossed anger."

I shrugged. "It's okay. I guess. What's his name?"

Then James walked away to answer the phone, leaving Kelly and me to chat. This was better, because with James out of the room Kelly could give me the real dirt without fear of injuring James's fragile man-ego.

She sat in the chair next to mine. I had already forgotten about the half-eaten bowl of chili in front of me. And I was still holding onto that picture of not-Tom and glancing at it every few seconds.

Apparently, not-Tom had a name, a rather pedestrian one, Drew Anderson. I looked at his picture and he looked as if he should be named Ramses or Spartacus or at least after some African warrior. Am I losing my mind? Here I was building up this guy in my head to be a warrior and I hadn't even met him yet. Was I that desperate? Well, yes I was. I think.

"Oh, he's so sweet," Kelly was gushing. They'd met him while they were hiking up Mount Diablotins. (I decided not to ask why a mountain was named after the devil.) Drew was leading some high-school students on a hike, teaching them how to identify different plants and flowers, and James and Kelly decided to tag along. Once they'd stopped to eat lunch on the side of the mountain, James detected a slight American accent as Drew talked to them. Turns out that Drew had been educated in America but had moved back to his homeland after his father, who was the former prime minister of the island, died. He had lofty ideals, from what Kelly was saying. He was a sometime math teacher, a developer, and budding politician who was building schools out in remote villages with his own money. Own money, I asked? Apparently he'd worked in the U.S. during the Internet boom and had left the

U.S. before the crash. Lofty ideals, rich, smart. What was wrong with him?

"He had a lot to tell us about the education system down there. Ames, I'm thinking of focusing my dissertation on how the British system is unsuitable for educating kids in the former Caribbean colonies."

I looked at her. Oh. "That sounds interesting."

"So are you going to e-mail him?"

"I thought you gave him my address?"

"Well, yeah. But I think he might want you to make the first move. He seemed kind of put off by the whole matchmaking thing."

"Who wouldn't be, Kelly?" I rolled my eyes. "This guy must have his pick of beautiful island girls. What would he want with someone two thousand miles away?"

"Well, from what he said, he doesn't really have a lot of time to date. And besides, this is the information age. Distance is all relative. . . ."

"Uh-huh." I went back to the chili. Two thousand miles was not a relative I wanted to visit. Sure, this guy was cute and sounded near perfect, but he was so far away. I thanked Kelly for her efforts, but I couldn't entertain any African warrior fantasies. But he is fine. And the son of a former prime minister. Who has lofty ideals. But two thousand miles away? Was I really that desperate? Was he? And if he were some kind of royalty down there, how would he see me?

"I'll think about it," I told Kelly, as I helped her clean up the kitchen.

"Are you and Whitney heading out tonight?"

"Nah, too snowy. Besides my back hurts. I think I'll curl up with a book and some Häagen-Dazs."

She shot me a look that was kind yet reprimanding.

"Okay. I'll curl up with just a book."

"Sure you don't want to watch a movie with us?"

"Nah," I said. I always felt like an intruder when the two

of them got all cozy on the couch and I had to sit there with my eyes too embarrassed to do anything but stay glued to the screen.

So later I lay on my bed reading and thinking while the wind howled outside. I wished I were somewhere warm. I wished I had a date. I wished I could have some Häagen-Dazs. Butter pecan. That was my only addiction. Besides shoes. And I couldn't even indulge it just slightly because I have no self-control; I could inhale a pint of ice cream in five minutes flat. Yes, I've timed myself. It really isn't my fault; it's all genetic.

I come from a family of drunks, and that is why I never touch alcohol. Never once did and never will. My father died of cirrhosis of the liver when I was thirteen. My brother, Gerard, has been through so many programs that I think he's now well qualified to start his own drug and alcohol rehab business. My mother is a nondiagnosed alkie. She's not dangerous, just pathetic. It may sound harsh, but you have to understand what I've been through with this woman. She was drunk at all my graduations, teacher conferences . . . I try to stay away from her as much as possible.

When I think back on my childhood, I have to laugh sometimes. There was never a time in my childhood that there wasn't a drunk adult in charge. First, my dad, who loved me and my mother, but hated Gerard because he didn't believe that Gerard was his son. So he beat Gerard every chance he got but treated me like a little princess. The two of us went to the movies every Saturday afternoon, or if it snowed we would rent movies from Blockbuster and make popcorn and just spend the entire afternoon in front of the television. He dropped me off at the Boston Public Library when I told him I wanted to read more books. On Saturday nights, he gave me money and sent me to the liquor store on Seaver Street to get him his Tanqueray and Johnny Walker; the store owner always winked knowingly at me. Back then my mother would only have “a taste” on her way to prayer meeting or bible study. But then my father lost his job as a transportation supervisor at the Massachusetts Bay Transportation Authority and he began to drink his unemployment checks away. When those checks stopped coming, my mother found work as a secretary for a big law firm downtown. Then they started to fight. Loud and hard. And she started to have more than a taste.

When my father got sick, it got worse. I was in private school on scholarship and I didn’t want to come home. I was too scared to see him wasting away. So I made excuses as to why I couldn’t come home from boarding school on weekends. I had extra studying to do. Or tennis practice. Or some other lie I could think up. Gerard called me an ungrateful bitch. But the sicker my dad got, the more time Gerard himself spent on the streets, getting into trouble. It was 1993, and there was a lot of trouble available at the time in Boston.

I was forced to go home when the chaplain took me out of calculus, solemnly telling me that I needed to go home because of a family emergency. I knew what the emergency was, yet on the way home in the backseat of my English teacher’s Subaru I still prayed that it was anything but my father being dead.

My mom and I were the only ones who were crying at the funeral. Gerard was sullen. My aunts, uncles, and cousins seemed more glum than anything else. My dad owed them money. And in my family that sometimes was more important than life itself. Even now, my mother would sooner ask me for money than she would ask me how I was doing.

Once my father was in the ground, I put him out of my mind. I lost myself in books. I talked to no one for about a year, and everyone at my boarding school understood what I was going through because it was a touchy-feely kind of place. Then I came home to go to high school at Boston Latin. I felt as lonely there as I’d felt out in woodsy Concord.

Everyone studied so hard and cared so much about what college they would go to. I only knew that I wanted to be far away from my mother. But when that time came I didn't have much of a choice. I had picked UC Berkeley, but my mother had other plans. She said she couldn't have me "all the way out there where she couldn't keep an eye on me." So I went to Simmons instead, three miles away from where I grew up.

Had I been angry then? Yes. But now that I'm an adult, or at least now that I think I'm an adult, I've mellowed out some. I'm not as intense anymore. I certainly don't spend most of my time listening to A Tribe Called Quest and De La Soul, fancying myself some type of street-smart bohemian black nerd. I'm over all that. I don't hate my mother, Grace Wilson, anymore. Sometimes I feel sorry for her. We've had our fights, our blowouts, even a few shoving matches. But I'm staying on the sidelines as she crashes and burns. My new motto is like a doctor's: Do no harm. I will not give her any money to drink herself into oblivion. But I will continue to buy her groceries every week because she is my mother and that's just the way it is. And I will let her call me and berate me every week because that's just the way it is, too. But I don't internalize that stuff anymore. I'm so over it. I just wish I could have ice cream.

Chapter 4

On Saturday, the snow had mostly melted. The temperature struck up to forty-five degrees during the day, leaving gray slushy puddles everywhere. I spent the day doing what I love to do most on Saturdays: spin class, despite my aching back. Then an almond decaf latte at Starbucks with a croissant. Then I ran errands and made sure that I got myself something nice for going to spin class. This week it was a pair of chandelier earrings from Macy's. I walked by the MAC counter, keeping my eyes straight ahead. Oh, the longing for more makeup. There was no bad mood that a Viva Glam lipstick could not cure. No fat day that a Blunt Matte blush couldn't lighten. With MAC all things were possible.

Later, Kelly and James had gone out to meet some of their other hemp-loving friends in Cambridge, and I was glad to have the apartment all to myself. I planned to cook a healthy dinner, maybe spinach with chicken and marinara sauce. No pasta. God, I missed pasta. And bread. And pizza. And Snickers bars. But as my former Weight Watchers leader once asked me: "Do you love chocolate as much as you would love being thin?" That was a terribly cruel question to ask someone who had never been thin, I thought. But each time

I was tempted, I rephrased the question: "Amelia, would you love a Snickers bar as much as you would love to be thin?" It wasn't always an effective deterrent because depending on my mood the answer could be a toss-up.

But it was only four o'clock, at least two more hours till dinner. I needed a diversion. I went online.

My little virus-infested Dell laptop is so slow sometimes I think it's intentionally giving me enough time to really consider whether I want to spend my minutes in that vast and empty time waster called the Internet. The only upside to going online was that if I could somehow lose myself in fantasy on the Neiman Marcus Web site, then that would be one less hour I would spend obsessing about whether I was truly hungry or whether I was seeking emotional comfort in food. I almost fell asleep as the computer crawled its way over to my Yahoo mail.

As I waited for my in-box to load, my cell phone rang. "Hi, Ma."

"Amelia, where you been?" She sounded exasperated.

"I was out running errands all morning, Ma." What was her problem!

"I tried to catch you . . . I need some . . . I'm broke . . ."

She's not broke. Her disability check (I forget which disability it's for) came this week. My guess is she wants attention or she just wants to hassle me. Find out what I'm doing tonight.

"I don't get paid for another week." But what did that matter? If she truly needed money, I'd give it to her. But she doesn't. The house is all paid off; she's got a closetful of clothes and a refrigerator full of food. I've done my duty.

"Amelia, don't do this to me, okay? I just need a twenty. Something to buy the girls a beer tonight."

"Ma! I'm not giving you money to go out drinking. How many times do I have to . . ."

My in-box loaded and the first unread e-mail message

was from a Drew@hotmail.com. My heart skipped a beat. What a time to be having a fight with her.

"You're not GIVING me anything, Amelia!" she snapped. "I'm your mother, don't you forget that. If it hadn't been for me you wouldn't be where you are today."

"That doesn't work on me anymore, Grace," I said.

"You know what? You know what? You probably just gonna stay home and stuff your face tonight and it's making you sick that I'm having fun! You're an ungrateful little witch," she snarled. "Ungrateful!" She slammed down the phone. I gently pressed the end button on my cell phone. Funny how my family always resorts to calling me ungrateful any time I don't give them what they want. Moving on. I had an e-mail to read.

> Hello, Amelia, or is it Amy? I hope James and Kelly told you about me by now else you must think I'm some kind of lunatic. Anyway, I was kind of intrigued by what I heard about you. As you may have heard, I'm a former math teacher and I'm truly committed to improving the education system in my country and I'm always interested in talking to other educators. Drop me a line if you can. If not, please look me up if you ever find yourself at 15 25N 61 20W.

I didn't do that well in geography! Thank God for Google. Oh, those coordinates would point to Dominica.

Funny how corny his e-mail came off, I thought. As if he'd written and rewritten it, and then gotten so frustrated that he'd just latched on to the last thing he could come up with. I could tell because that was the M.O. for most of my students. Speaking of which . . . I had a Steinbeck quiz to prepare for Monday, and if those little urchins weren't prepared they'd feel my wrath . . .

Should I write him back? And if so, what should I say?

How should I sound? What did I want him to think of me? Well, I was a smart, independent, curvy . . . Oh, help me somebody. I need to just be interesting. That's all there was to it. So, since he used to be a teacher, I'd have to come up with some math joke or some math line to reel him in. That sort of thing worked in Nora Ephron movies all the time.

Then the phone rang, breaking my concentration.

It was Whitney. "Girl, what you doing?" She almost always had a conspiratorial tone to her voice, and that was for a good reason. She was always up to something or about to be up to something.

I've known Whitney since Latin. She was the smartest girl in the class, also the nerdiest, and she made me feel good about myself—being the fattest. While I cried about my mother's meanness, she complained about being placed with yet another greedy foster family that was only "in it for the money." While I complained about being fat, Whitney blocked me out by talking to herself about math equations and wishing for cuter glasses. MIT had been a good place for her until she fell for that Korean guy who later killed himself. I don't think he killed himself because of her; kids kill themselves at MIT all the time. But she sure thought that. That had brought a breakdown and a short stay at McLean Hospital, but she was all over it now. So she says.

"Oh, you can probably help me," I said. If anyone would know math nerd jokes, Whitney would.

When I told her about Ramses, er Drew, she sighed.

"Listen, don't screw with this bull, okay? The guy's probably just trying to get his green card off you."

"Whitney, he's not trying to get his green card! He lived in the U.S. for ten years before he went back to his country."

"That doesn't mean anything. He's probably some drug dealer or something. What are you going to do? Have a long distance relationship with him?"

It was my turn to sigh. "You sound like my mother. Listen, I'm just making a new friend, is that wrong?"

"It's not wrong. I just don't see the point. Those roommates of yours are turning you into freaking Bridget Jones."

"Gimme some credit, Whitney. I'm home. I'm bored. Can't I indulge my little tropical fantasy?"

"Go ahead and indulge. Just don't forget to join the rest of us in reality when you're done. So what're you doing tonight?"

"Me? Nothing. I've gotta make up a pop quiz for Monday."

"You're so mean."

"It's the only way I'll know they're doing the reading assignment."

Whitney snorted. "You know they're not doing the assignment."

I knew she was right but still . . . I didn't mind ragging on my kids, but it bothered me when other people did.

"Screw the quiz. Let's go to Milky Way. It's salsa night," she said.

"Salsa as in dip?"

"No, Amelia, salsa as in dance."

I groaned. "I dunno, Whitney. What kind of people are gonna be there?"

"What do you mean, what kind of people are gonna be there? You live with two stoner hippies and you're worried about the crowd at the Milky Way?"

"At least they're familiar stoner hippies."

"Come on, let's go out. You'll probably meet a cute guy. Either way, it's better than staying inside."

"Where's Big D?"

"Ugh. I think he's starting to catch feelings. He asked me to go away with him for a weekend."

"Really? That was fast."

"I'm, like, a whole weekend? With you?"

"What's wrong with him?"

"Too smooth. Too clean-cut. Not spontaneous enough."

"Oh," I said, "no edge." That was the next requisite to breathing when it came to Whitney's taste in men: lots of edge, meaning a bad boy.

"Right. So, you coming or what? I can almost hear the music; I gotta shake something tonight."

"Fine. Fine. I'm coming."

I couldn't say no to her. Whitney and I were practically sisters. She'd spent her childhood being shuffled from foster home to foster home and had been through so much family psychodrama it was a miracle that she'd ended up so successful. She was a scrapper, unafraid of anything or anybody. I couldn't imagine my life without her. I saw her living out all the things that I was afraid to do, and most times all I could do was shake my head in wonder. She was the big sister who I was always trying to keep up with. So I almost always found myself going along with her. Even now when I'd much rather stay in my warm room and reread Drew's e-mail again and again. I wondered what the temperature was on Dominica. Probably a balmy eighty-five degrees, the moon was probably full, stars big in the sky, and waves lapping at the shore . . .

Chapter 5

A couple of hours later, I was in my Beetle, the gauge read thirty-two degrees; so much for the temporary warm-up. My tires swished over the slushy side streets that led to Whitney's house.

Whitney worked for Microsoft, but she hardly ever left her apartment. She telecommuted to Redmond, Washington, and traveled there a few times a year. Her life, when she was deeply involved in a project at work, was actually quite stable. It was when she was in love that things went haywire. I was praying that she would not meet anyone new tonight. There hadn't been anyone to speak of for about a year and things had been relatively calm. Somehow, she'd vowed to be celibate for a year, and miraculously she'd almost pulled it off. Then that Duncan guy came along. But she'd been threatening lately to get back on the wagon, or was it off the wagon?

She looked pretty as usual. She'd dyed her dreads a light, light brown, and against her caramel skin it added a touch of exoticism to her prettiness. Whitney, petite and slim, could eat like a linebacker and it never showed on her hips because she worked out like a freak. I'm talking two hours of hardcore cardio six days a week. She wore tight, tight jeans and a pretty pink camisole top with a black leather jacket. I wore my slimmest size 14 black pants and a black ruffly georgette top. I topped it off with a funky necklace I'd bought from Banana and my new chandelier earrings from Macy's. I felt tall and glamazon-like in my favorite snow-proof three-inch heels.

I actually felt cute tonight. Those pants actually felt comfortable, and my thighs were not screaming against the seams as they were when I first wore them. Maybe those spin classes—that I could never finish—were working after all.

"Look at you, girl!" Whitney said, looking me up and down as I stood in the doorway of her Hyde Park house. "You losing weight?"

"You think so?"

"Yes, I can definitely see the diff," Whitney said.

Well, if Whitney's critical eye could see the diff, then there must be a diff. My mood soared.

I looked at myself in Whitney's mirror in her gigantic but spare living room. Yes, I did look a little bit smaller than, than, than, what? Than I'd felt since I don't know when.

"When you gonna get rid of that perm and go natural?" she asked, pulling at one of my shoulder-length locks.

"Girl, my mother would kill me!"

"You're a grown woman, Amelia. Besides, isn't her hair natural now?"

"Yeah, but she said that look wouldn't work on me because I don't have fine features like her. You know, I took my daddy's nose and some of his color. . . ." I was mocking Whitney, but those were Grace Wilson's words to me, verbatim.

"See, that's why I'm glad I don't have a family. I don't need anybody talking to me like that."

I shrugged. "Let's go."

I played Amel Larrieux in the CD player and Whitney snorted. “Why do you listen to that neo-soul crap? Why don’t you just go all the way and listen to jazz?”

“It’s the same thing; besides, I like to hear people singing.”

“Amelia, it’s not the same thing. And Billie Holiday can sing better than any of those chicks out there today.”

“Thanks, Whitney. If it weren’t for you I’d probably never have known that.”

She rolled her eyes at me as we pulled into the dinky parking lot. The Milky Way was just a neighborhood hangout for the most part, nothing fancy. There was a pool table, billiards, a few other game kiosks off to the side, but on Saturdays those were mostly abandoned for the dance floor. I hadn’t danced in a long time and I was feeling the urge.

Before we had even put away our coats, a tall, green-eyed guy with dark hair approached us. He looked Mediterranean. Well, Whitney did tend to date the rainbow. She gave him her killer smile. *Here we go,* I thought. If only he knew what he was in for, he’d run in the other direction. Of course, that was my envy talking.

I ordered a Diet Coke from the bartender, who I could have sworn gave me a dirty look. Sheesh. Sorry I won’t be adding to your bottom line tonight, dude! I had gotten through half the tiny plastic cup of watered-down liquid when I felt a tap on my shoulder. He was a bit short—and old. He was also very Latin-looking, which meant that he would probably know what he was doing on the dance floor and I wouldn’t.

Did I want to dance?

Okay. Proceed at your own risk.

The music was fast and it took me a few seconds to get on the beat. But this guy was good. He was leading and quite well at that. I just let go, and it felt so good. The room was getting hotter, but I was having so much fun. We laughed when one song ended and another came on and we didn't want to stop. About an hour later, Whitney tapped me on the shoulder.

"I'm leaving," she mouthed over the loud music.

NO! my mind screamed. Don't leave with this guy. But he was standing there looking at me quite impatiently. He knew he was getting laid tonight and I'm sure he didn't want to delay the action.

I asked my dance partner to excuse me and I grabbed Whitney's arm.

"Are you sure?" I yelled into her ears.

"Yeah, chill!" she yelled back. "I think I know him. He's a doc student at MIT. From Tunisia."

As if that made everything okay. Oh, Whitney!!!

But all I could do was wave as she walked her crazy self away with her Tunisian, who happened to look like a Greek god. I didn't much feel like dancing anymore, but my dance partner was waiting for me as soon as I turned my attention back to the dance floor. I just couldn't. Besides it was almost one A.M. I said good-bye to dancing guy without even asking his name and hightailed it out of there. I just hoped Whitney would be okay.

I tried to be quiet as I entered the house, though I knew that James and Kelly would probably be up. I turned on the computer again. Amid all the fun I'd been having I couldn't get the picture out of my head, and there it sat on my dresser. I'd left it on a MAC compact as I'd put on my makeup. No doubt he was a good-looking brother. While I'd danced with that nameless guy at Milky Way, I'd thought of some things to say. I remembered one thing that someone had sent me in an e-mail and I searched for it. Yes, it was about algorithms. Okay, that was a start. After four or five tries, I sent him this.

Hi Drew. Greetings from 38 00N and 97 00W, at least the part where the temperature's only slightly above freezing. It was nice to read your e-mail. I'd love to know more about you—and to tell you more about me. As you may already know, I teach English literature to unwilling students, but I mostly love what I do. I'm terrible at math, but I do know that the word "algorithm" comes from the name of a ninth-century Persian mathematician named Abu Abdullah Muhammad bin Musa al-Khwarizmi. Are you impressed now? Just kidding. Hope to hear from you soon. What made you decide to leave the US and go back home to Dominica? Sounds like you could have stayed if you had wanted to.

I pondered over this for a few moments. Did I sound pretentious? As if I were trying to sound smart? Or did I just sound corny? But this had been the last of four or five tries. This was the thing I hated about trying to make an impression via e-mail. I didn't want to sound sappy, too interested, eager, or any of those god-awful things. I just wanted to sound like a teacher who was glad to know someone from another part of the world. That's all. So this should do? I wasn't too sure but I hit send anyway and bit my nonexistent nails; that was another New Year's resolution in its embryonic stage.

Chapter 6

I begged off when James and Kelly asked me to go skiing up at Wachusett Mountain. For one thing, I had work to do. For another thing, I didn't know how to ski and I didn't want to learn. It was bad enough that I had to endure this cold weather, why would I want to go play in it? Besides, Sunday was my day to mentally prepare for the week ahead. I decided that I'd be kind and not spring a quiz on my ninth graders. Let them have their fun. But they would have to write me a paper on the Joads at some point before their little behinds graduated.

I made coffee and tried to read the *Sunday Globe* at the kitchen table, but I couldn't concentrate. I wondered about the e-mail I'd sent to Drew. I'd woken up at four A.M., panicked and convinced that I'd called him Ramses instead of Drew. Luckily, I'd cc'd myself a copy. Now, I wanted to log on to see if he'd answered. But it was only nine-thirty on Sunday. He was probably hungover from the night before. Those Caribbean people liked to party. Or did they? There were a couple of Caribbean teachers at my school and they seemed a bit too serious and uptight, except for one who was just a little too out there. But maybe they all had a wild side. What was wrong with me? Why was I generalizing about a whole group of people just because I was stressed about some dude I'd never met? I tried to make sense of the blurry newsprint in front of me.

Then the phone rang.

"Amelia, I just wanted to say I'm sorry about yesterday."

Huh??? Was that Grace Wilson? Apologizing?

"Ma? Is that you?"

"Yes, it's me. I wanted to tell you I'm sorry for calling you ungrateful yesterday."

Okay, she must really want some cash.

"Uh-huh," was all I could think to say.

She sighed.

"Amelia, I want to . . . I want things to be better between us."

Was this some kind of joke? Was I in the Twilight Zone?

"You want to what?"

"You heard me, okay? I just been thinking. All this fussin' and fightin's not doing me any good. I'm not getting any younger."

"Ma, you're only fifty years old, and you look forty." It was true. My mother was a beauty, a red-boned, voluptuous beauty with thick black hair she wore proud and natural once my father died. She got hit on all the time by men who were much younger than her. It bothered me much more than I was willing to admit. And, no, I didn't think it was the source of the tension between us. She was a madwoman. That was enough.

"I don't feel fifty, Amelia," she said. I put my coffee down. I hadn't heard her sound this down in a long, long time. The last time had been when Gerard had gone to prison for two years for armed robbery. Then she had almost hit rock bottom.

"Ma, what's wrong?"

She sighed. "I just want us to be friends, okay? Don't let

me get into how I feel and all that jive. Let's just be mother and daughter. Like old times. When your daddy was around."

Like old times when my daddy was around? I don't think I wanted to remember that far back. But she sounded sincere.

"All right, Ma. No more fighting then."

"Okay, Amelia." She paused. "You heard from Gerard?"

Here we go. "No, why?"

She sighed again and my antennae started chirping wildly.

"Well, Ms. Parker and them found him passed out off Columbia Road last night. If they hadn't found him he probably would have froze to death."

I grit my teeth. Gerard!!!

"Where is he?"

"He's here. He's fine. He's laying down. Says he don't want to go to the hospital."

I didn't want to go over there. I wouldn't go over there, I told myself. I left all of that behind. If she and Gerard wanted to go on living like this let them, but I would not be dragged into it.

"Ma, Gerard is twenty-five years old. . . ."

"Don't start with me, Amelia. What am I supposed to do, kick him out when he's down? He needs to go see a doctor, but he won't listen to me."

"He's not down. He's a grown man. If he doesn't want to go to the hospital tell him to go stay with D'Andrea!" D'Andrea was Gerard's longtime off and on, long-suffering girlfriend.

She ignored me. "Are you gonna come talk to him or what?" Her furtive tone told me that she knew full well what my answer would be.

"No, Ma. As long as you say he's fine, then I'm not coming over there just to get dragged into another fight. Gerard doesn't need me to tell him he shouldn't be drinking."

"All right then, Amelia. I love you, okay?"

I rolled my eyes. She knew how to lay the guilt trip nice and thick. "I love you, too, Ma. Take care of you."

I felt awful after I hung up, but that was the way of things. I had to leave it, them, behind. They were not me and I was not them. If I really knew what was good for me I would have applied to Berkeley's grad program and moved to California, far away where none of this could touch me. I don't know why I stayed. No, I knew. I was afraid that something catastrophic and awful would happen and they would have no one else to save them. This sucked. Why couldn't I have a nice, adorably abnormal family? Kelly's folks were bad, but they weren't this bad. At least they didn't call her at all. They knew they didn't get along and didn't pretend to with a bunch of perfunctory, useless communication.

I was getting depressed and I refused to get sucked into it. It was another phobia of mine. I saw what that did to my mother and my brother and I didn't want it to happen to me. First, the depression comes and then the drinking, or was it the other way around. Either way, it wouldn't happen to me. Better to lose myself in a good book or gourmet chocolate, or even better, a nice juicy fantasy.

I went online.

No mail from the islands yet. I browsed the *New York Times* Web site, lingering on the Sunday book review.

I checked my e-mail again; nothing but the usual junk. So, where was this Dominica place and what was up with it? And why would Drew give up America for a speck of a place in the Third World few people have heard of?

According to the CIA World Factbook's Web site, which I would take as an authority on the subject since its powers extend so far beyond that of most mortals, Dominica sounded like a pretty nice place: Last of the Caribbean islands to be colonized by the Europeans, mostly because the Carib Indians seemed to put up a really good fight. The island changed hands between the British and French a few times until

1805. . . . Oh, wait a minute! Dominica! Jean Rhys. How could I have been so dense? One of my favorite authors was Jean Rhys, a Dominican. But somehow I just couldn't put white Jean Rhys in my fantasy of me and Ramses on our deserted little island. She just seemed so white and French. But I still made a mental note to reread *Wide Sargasso Sea*.

The CIA had some great facts and some not so great ones, including the fact that the island was basically a huge volcano waiting to erupt. And that the unemployment rate was as high as, as, well, as my family's unemployment rate. One thing that really got me all excited was the fact that Dominica in 1980 had the first female prime minister in all of the Caribbean. Dame Eugenia Charles. This got me thinking that the title Dame was so outdated, especially for a woman who'd accomplished so much. Would anyone call Condi Rice a dame, even if she had been given the title by the Crown? But back to Dominica, whose population was a little bit under seventy thousand. That wasn't even half the population of Dorchester! And for a country four times the size of Washington, DC, that seemed to leave everyone enough space to move around and have a nice uncluttered life. *I want to go now!*

Oh! New mail. I took a deep breath before I clicked on it.

"Hi Amelia. Wish I'd known you'd written sooner. I've been busy all day working with an architect on the school we're breaking ground on in a few weeks, so I haven't had time to check my e-mail. I didn't know about that algorithm fella—thanks for that bit of info. *(Was he being sarcastic here?)* I'll have to remember not to lay any complex mathematical concepts on you as long as you don't force me to read any Shakespeare. *(Done!)* So, tell me more about you. What makes you laugh out loud? What makes you angry? Do you have siblings? Are you close to your family? What's important in your life right now?

Now that I've given you the third degree, I'll answer your questions: I moved back to Dominica because I felt a sort of responsibility to my homeland. The migration rate here is unbelievably high—understandably, most of the young people want to be in the UK or US, where there is more opportunity. But I guess the way I see it there are never going to be any opportunities here if our best and brightest never return. This may sound a bit egotistical, but I'm hoping to start a trend, a mass homecoming, if you will. I think if we can just get some more talented folks here, then the country would be a better place for future generations. *(Awww . . .)*

OK, I'm done with my political speech. As you can tell I'm passionate about this stuff. I enjoyed living in the US, but I got bored with making and spending money and not making any real difference. So, while I do miss Falcons games, the Hawks and Knicks, Burger King Whoppers, etc., I'm happier here and definitely more fulfilled. *(How fully evolved!)*

I may have asked you this before, but here I go again. Anytime you're in the area, come down and visit. I'd love for you to come talk to some of the high-school students here. They absolutely idolize American culture and I think they'd be really impressed with you and would most likely listen to you more than they would me or any of their other fellow Dominican teachers.

I read and reread it several times. Yes, he does sound like someone whom James and Kelly would hit it off with. He shared their idealistic view of the world. But he didn't sound like a protest freak. I mean, he was using his money to improve his country. It wasn't like he was spreading communism or building a madrassa. He just sounded like a good guy. A good, solid guy. And I liked that. I mean, he was great-looking, smart. Okay, I've gone over this list way too many times. There has to be a flaw. He knows I'm, er, Rubenesque. He did see my picture. There has to be a catch. But I decided to put that out of my mind. Why did there have to be a catch? I remembered the words of a famous preacher whose book I'd snapped up at Barnes & Noble. He said that if one doesn't expect great things to happen, then great things won't happen. There. I will put this into practice. I will expect something great to happen from now on.

So what to do? I couldn't write him back right away. That would seem too eager. But I wanted to know more and tell him more. But I had to wait. The way I felt now I'd probably pour out my heart to him. Telling him how much I wanted to escape my life and just live in someone else's for a while. No family. No roommates. No students. No freezing cold, snowy winters. I logged off instead.

The thing is, I kind of liked my life. Improvements were possible, but if it stayed this way forever it wouldn't be too terrible. At least I wouldn't end up like my mother, drunk, angry, and afraid to face the world, or Gerard, who seemed to be staggering onto the edge of some metaphorical cliff. I was better off than a lot of people I knew.

It was time to make dinner. Maybe I'd make deep fried chicken and oven-baked fries. Heck, I'll fry the fries. Why fake it?

Chapter 7

My last period class was angry with me again. I'd been so preoccupied with Drew on my mind and trying to drown out their insolence that I'd forgotten that I was the reason their beloved Treyon was suspended and would not be providing the entertainment this week. A part of me felt sorry for them. They had me right after History with Lashelle Thompson, who always gave them the "black perspective," regardless of the assigned text. One of the kids, Tina, I think, had asked me once why we didn't read more books by black authors. That had really hurt because more than half the books were by black, Asian, and Hispanic writers. But she didn't consider García Márquez relevant to her experience. How could I explain to her that I wasn't Lashelle, and more importantly, that the education that would take her to college was not necessarily the one that would bring her the most satisfaction or vindication. Instead, I gave her a list of books that she could borrow from the library and read on her own time, but I suspected that she would never follow through. Why did I give up so easily? I didn't know. Sometimes I thought that I didn't care enough anymore to be doing this.

These kids were wearing me down into an apathetic, disillusioned mess.

I asked if anyone wanted to discuss *The Grapes of Wrath*. Not one hand rose. Twenty-nine resigned faces glared at me. I couldn't take this today.

"Okay, guys. Let's talk about anything you guys want to talk about for just ten minutes. Just ten minutes, then we'll go back to the book."

At first there was silence. I'd been warned against doing this, it could backfire in so many ways.

"Why you ain't married?" This from Shanae, a cute but obviously nosy girl, with the most insanely multicolored braids I'd ever seen.

I cleared my throat. "I haven't found the right person yet."

"You got a man?" asked David, a 6'3" jumble of awkwardness who's one of my better writers and known to be one of the school's best rappers.

"Not really. I'm too busy. Listen, let's move on. Has anyone read anything lately they'd like to talk about?"

"I read about Beyoncé and Jay-Z on vacation in St. Tropez."

I cringed; celebrity gossip was not really my forte.

"Where St. Tropez at?" Tina asked.

Oh, God. Where was St. Tropez again?

"All right. Let's find out," I said, looking on the worn-out cabinet for an atlas. There wasn't one. That really irked me. The freaking globe was broken and there was no atlas at all in a freaking classroom. It was bad enough that I found myself bringing in my own supplies . . .

I had no idea where St. Tropez was and there was no atlas in the room to at least make it look as if I was trying to teach the class a lesson. I cursed the stingy Massachusetts Department of Education and racked my brain. I'm not stupid, I'm just scatterbrained. The entire class was looking at me as I stalled in the cabinet, pretending to look for something that I knew wasn't there.

Then I focused. I pictured a map of the world in my head and started mentally drawing in the continents. Okay, I thought. St. Tropez must be warm, and since Beyoncé and Jay-Z, those two paragons of ostentatious consumerism and hedonism, went there, it must have been expensive. Hmmm . . . South in some European country, France or Spain or Italy. Tropez. Lord help us, but I'm going to go with France. Okay, here we go, class.

They were nonplussed by my answer; they had already moved on. My performance thus ended, I decided to stop trying to be super teacher. Back to the text.

Everyone hated me again when I asked about the Joads. It was sad that our little rapport had ended so abruptly. But I couldn't take the chance of them asking me another question I couldn't answer. So, I was back to being Mean Ms. Wilson. The world was back in balance.

I couldn't wait till I got home. I hurried, ran, really, to the teacher's lounge to use one of the computers there. I had broken down late last night and written him a reply as long as a *New Yorker* short story. I gave him the family history—just the facts without too much of the ugly truth. Told him that I liked to read, cook, and watch movies; that I wasn't too athletic, though I did like to dance and was beginning to enjoy my cycling class (that was stretching the truth a bit); and that there wasn't much more to me than that. It sounded spare but I had to be honest because that was me. I wasn't like James and Kelly, who had ten billion hobbies and interests. You would not catch me climbing a mountain in New Hampshire on any given Saturday afternoon, nor would I be running any five-mile races or 10 K's. Give me a good book and a cookie recipe and I'm happy for a week. At least until I weighed myself again. Then I'd answered his questions. What made me truly happy? When my students show some interest in literature, spring, memories of my father before he got sick, great shoes. What made me laugh out loud? My brother's dirty jokes, though he makes few of them these days. What made me angry? The fact that poor kids got so little from public education in one of the richest states in the country. That my relationship with my mother will always be full of conflict. That I can't seem to bring myself to care about much anymore. Or did that last one just make me sad?

At the time I'd clicked send, I realized it had been too much. But I'd been feeling melancholy. I'd eaten too much at dinner again. Pasta with shrimp in marinara sauce. Three plates of it. And then Healthy Choice chocolate chip cookie ice cream for dessert. I could hear James and Kelly going at it in their room and I felt lonely and a little sick from overeating. So I poured my heart out. Now I had to do e-mail damage assessment. Either he wouldn't write back or he would with some reason why he suddenly became very busy and probably wouldn't be able to write much anymore.

There it was, his e-mail, at the top of my in-box, right on top of one from Whitney with only exclamation marks in the subject field. I didn't really want to know what that was about, though I knew it would be something that ultimately would involve Max, her Tunisian.

Here goes, I thought, as I opened Drew's e-mail. It was long, as long as mine.

> Wow, it's really hard to find a woman who'll admit to liking to cook in the 21st century. You're part of a dying breed. *(Okay, he has a corny edge to him that needs to be shaved off.)* I have to say I'm enjoying getting to know you. You sound like such a down-to-earth person. *(Oh no! The equivalent of a woman describing a guy as "nice.")*

And so on and so forth. He didn't understand why I didn't get along with my family. That's probably because I left out the part about our little drinking problem. He also liked to read but prefered history books and biographies. *(Hmm . . . only really smart people read stuff like that.)* He said he was angry, too, at how the American government tended to "misallocate its vast resources" when it came to educating its youth. Yeah, I agreed with that, though I couldn't have said it so eloquently. He wanted to talk, he said at the end of his e-mail.

It would be nice to have a voice to match with the picture and e-mails.

I had been thinking that, too, though I worried that my little fantasy could blow up into a thousand pieces if he ended up sounding like Pee-Wee Herman or that rapper who yelled all the time. But what if he sounded like Mekhi Phifer? Oh, then I'd be in big trouble. Then I'd have to get on the next American Airlines flight to that little twenty-nine-square-mile island.

He'd left a number and said to call collect. What kind of a person did he think I was? I would wait as long as I could. Maybe all week if I could stand it. In my heart, though, I knew I wouldn't make it through Wednesday—unless someone managed to destroy all the phone lines that got into my path.

"What you up to, sis?" a voice came from behind me, and I jumped in my chair. I'd forgotten where I was.

"Hi, Lashelle. How's it going?"

She smiled and sat next to me. Lashelle was cute. But she had a huge butt. All the male students loved her because of it, plus she loved to show it off. But that ghetto booty just bugged the heck out of me. It was always up in everybody's face. I mean, she wore tight skirts and too-small pants and her behind just hung out there. I didn't think it was cute. Not that I have anything against big butts. I have one myself. But in relation to the rest of her, Lashelle's butt was just proportionally disturbing. But what do I know? Whitney has told me time and time again that I can be a self-loathing sister. And Whitney, with her perfect size 4 butt, is up on those things much more than I am.

I minimized the screen. I didn't want Lashelle to see Drew's e-mail. She was more plugged in to the gossip network than I was, and I didn't want to become the subject of it.

"So, I heard you and Treyon got into it on Friday."

"Nah, it wasn't all that. You know he's got a mouth on him. I just wasn't in the mood for his crap."

She laughed widely, exposing her silver fillings. "Girl, you gotta learn to ignore those boys. They're gonna act that way, you know."

I liked Lashelle for the most part, but she tended to be a teacher in and out of the classroom, even when she was around other teachers. I didn't need her telling me how to interact with my students. I certainly did not tell her that she needed to be less familiar and friendly with hers. So I ignored her advice.

"Anyway, a bunch of us are thinking of going to Mexico, Cabo San Lucas, for spring break. I just realized that we forgot to ask you."

Oh, give me a break! They didn't forget to ask me. I was the newest teacher there, and I was still being hazed, it seemed, a year later. I'd been snubbed at lunches, ignored in hallways, you name it. The principal, my only ally, said that was the way they broke in the newbies. I guess I should have felt relieved that she was asking me on this trip. Maybe I was finally in the club. But I wasn't going to Mexico with a bunch of people I already spend too much of my life with. Besides, who wants to go to Mexico on spring break along with all the other college students in the country?

"Oh, I wish you'd told me sooner," I said, trying to fake remorse. "But I've already made other plans." Spring break was a month away. That was enough time to come up with alternate plans. But Lashelle would not be rebuffed that easily.

Her penciled-in brows went up. "Oh, really? Where are you going?"

I had to think fast. St. Tropez? No one would believe that.

"Dominica," I said quickly. Oh, I'm an idiot.

"The Dominican Republic?" She looked incredulous.

"No, it's another . . . a small island in the West Indies. Former British colony . . ." I was beginning to sound like I'd memorized the data from the CIA World Factbook.

She sniffed. "Oh, I see. What's down there?"

"Um . . . well . . . a friend of mine. We're gonna do some hiking and . . ."

She got up from the chair. "That sounds like fun." She patted me on the shoulder and walked away. I was 100 percent sure she was off to spread the gossip.

Oh, well. All I'd have to do was hunker down in my room during spring break so I wouldn't run the risk of running into anyone who might spill my little secret. Hiking? Was I losing my mind?

Chapter 8

There were times when I felt totally beautiful, smart, content with all the decisions I'd ever made, and generally at peace with my life. Those times were very rare. For Whitney, however, the issue was when didn't she feel that way? She wore optimism like her skin. I just didn't get it. She didn't have the right because her stuff was just messed up. Messed up!

We waited forty frigid minutes before we were seated at an okay table at Stephanie's. The place was very popular, on Newbury Street, and thus jumping on this Saturday night. Fine by me because the crackling excitement in the room was charging up my sputtering mood.

Whitney was positively glowing and happy. The sex was that good, she said.

Hmmm . . . Good sex. I'd stopped talking about sex with Whitney once things got out of control with bête noire. By out of control I mean once I'd started sleeping with him. I hadn't planned it. But that's what all adulterers and their co-conspirators say, right? He was a stay-at-home dad who picked up and dropped off his boys every day at the school. He'd left the corporate rat race to stay home with his kids and pursue his dream of becoming a writer. He was living my dream. Although, I've never really written anything and I probably never will. But I like to think that if I ever got myself together that I could maybe someday write a great novel.

We chatted about his son Trevor at first. Trevor was highly intelligent and belligerent, so there was much to talk about. Before I knew it, we started to talk about more personal things. Then every extramarital affair cliché one could ever dream up happened to me. I felt like I was living in a Danielle Steel novel. I let him lie to me, stand me up, make a fool out of me for a year and a half. Then his novel was published. The school, the surrounding neighborhood, everyone began to gossip about who the "temptress teacher" character could possibly be. It didn't take long for them to figure it out; I was the only black female on the staff. The school asked me to leave because they were cutting back on costs, but I knew it was because the scandal was just too embarrassing. His wife left him temporarily and then came back once she threatened to beat the hell out of me and I apologized to her and vowed that I'd never go near him again. That had been my last brush with good sex. I really don't miss it that much.

"What are you going to have?" Whitney asked, frowning at the menu. She once had a slight weight problem. In her typical single-minded and focused way, she decided that she was going to lose weight and just up and did it. Six months later, she'd gone from a size 12 to a 4. I don't think I ever heard her complain about being hungry or being sore from exercise.

"I don't know." I looked around the restaurant. Everything was shimmering gold against black or deep brown. I loved the décor. People were laughing, eating. The food smelled delicious. I love Stephanie's. I think I once saw Woody Allen in here, though I wasn't sure.

"So, anyway, he's just so passionate about human rights. It's a huge turn-on," Whitney said.

I sipped my virgin frosty drink. I got it that Max, the Tunisian, was passionate about human rights. What I didn't get was the part that she'd quickly glossed over while we were sitting at the bar waiting for a table: The part about him personally protesting the PATRIOT Act by not reporting to Immigration as our paranoid government requires all Arab men to. To Whitney, this added to Max's allure; it made him so brave, and "passionate." To me, that was a bit too out there. And I would know. My roommates have not missed a hell-raising protest since I've known them. They burned Bill Gates in effigy in Seattle, slashed tires on a Ford Denali in Detroit, laid in coffins in Times Square before the Iraq invasion. I was quite familiar with civil disobedience in the name of political passions, but Kelly and James were U.S. citizens; this Max guy was on a student visa. For crying out loud, he was a frigging scientist at MIT. From Tunisia! Profile, anyone? I'm sorry, I told Whitney, he fit the terrorist stereotype to a T. She glared at me.

"He is not a terrorist! Just because he won't surrender his civil rights to Bush's authoritarian regime . . ."

I decided to mess with her. "They're gonna come looking for him some day. You don't want Alberto Gonzales kicking down the door to your crib. Know what I'm saying?"

She rolled her eyes. "They're not going to come after him. And even if they do, so what? The research he's doing . . . He's working on a cure for diabetes . . . He knows a lot of powerful people. . . ."

This was the problem. I cannot say again how smart Whitney is. Matter of fact, if I asked her now she could tell me where St. Tropez is and probably its off-season population and GDP without even stopping to consider the question. But there was something that happened to her brain whenever a penis became involved. The same brain that could master a regression analysis would turn to mush and pretty soon she'd be spouting nonsense as in the above.

"Whitney, seriously, I'd be careful with this guy."

"Oh, come on. You think he's in Al Qaeda or something?"

I couldn't help but giggle at that. "If he were that devout, he wouldn't be having sex with you, getting drunk with you . . . I'm just saying be careful of those passionate men. They always seem to get you in trouble."

She brightened up at this statement. "Oh, so it's not him you're worried about. You're worried that I'll fall too hard for him and then go off the deep end when things don't work out?"

Bingo, I wanted to say, but I just sipped my frosty drink.

"I'm not that person anymore, Amelia. I mean, I worked out all my issues at McLean. That thing with Tosin . . . I was just lashing out at him because I was taking his rejection as an extension of those feelings of rejection I had as a foster kid." She was reciting a therapy session, obviously. "I'm all over that. Max is just what I need now, just fun, sex, no strings. Besides, he's only here for another six months; then he's going to France to continue his research."

What a relief. How much damage could they do in six months?

"But what about Duncan? Big D?" I asked. We ordered from a friendly waitress who looked like she could be a model. I tried not to stare at her skinny legs, but they inspired me to get grilled salmon with vegetables instead of something slathered in cheese or cream sauce.

Whitney shrugged. "I think he wanted something serious. He kept wanting to have these deep conversations." She made a face.

"Like, what's the meaning of it all?"

She ignored the crack. "Did I tell you Max went to Palestine when Yasser Arafat died?"

It was my turn to sigh. "So, what does he think of you being this independent, sassy woman about town if he's such a traditional Muslim?"

She was on her third glass of wine. Max loved wine, and of course, he'd introduced her to so many new ones since they'd been hanging out, she'd said.

"That doesn't really come up. We both know we're just in it for the sex. Unless it turns into something more."

"Something more like what? Are you ready to convert?"

"Calm down, okay. He finds me sexy and intellectually challenging," she said, making quotes with her fingers. "It could turn into something."

"Right. But you didn't answer me. Would you convert to Islam if it did?"

"You mean like start wearing a burka and stuff?"

"Whitney, I can't stand it when you start talking like an airhead."

"What?" She brushed a dreadlock off her shoulder.

"Why are you putting this guy on such a pedestal? You said he's just in it for the sex. . . ."

She looked up at the ceiling as if seriously pondering my question. "Wellllll . . . He's so angry and he wants to change the world . . . kinda like your Caribbean guy."

Can't really compare the two, I thought. My so-called Caribbean guy did not wear a kaffiyeh and call America the Great Satan.

"You mean, angry like Bakari?" Bakari was another of Whitney's mistakes. He was an African-American studies major who was trying to revive the Black Panthers to its former prominence. Whitney had fallen hard for him. Unfortunately, his revolutionary leanings straightened out when he was accepted into Yale Law School. Whitney dumped him shortly thereafter, but not before she cursed him out in broad daylight at Downtown Crossing. I was there when she called him a "bitch-ass, spineless, corporate sellout." This is the same Whitney who works for Microsoft. But in her defense, she at least didn't pretend to be a revolutionary. I wondered what would happen if her little Muslim revolutionary came up with the cure for diabetes and sold out to Merck or Pfizer.

"So when are you gonna go see him?" Whitney asked.

I shook my head as I took a bite of my grilled salmon steak. I really wanted fries and a huge burger, but I'm doing so well. Even my spin class instructor had noticed the difference. "Wow," she'd chirped, sidling up to me in her barely-there little workout outfit. "You're looking great these days." That had made my day. Big-time!

"I don't know. We've been e-mailing every day back and forth for the last two weeks, and it's starting to feel so . . . so weird."

"You've talked, right?"

"Yes, three or four times."

Did we talk? If only she knew. I didn't tell her that my phone bill would probably be a week's salary and that it had gotten to the point where I had to hear his voice every day else I'd get all crabby and depressed. I know that's not a good thing, but addictive behavior is in my genes.

Last night I'd barely gotten any sleep. The memory of the conversation still made me feel like I was living inside a kind of mocha frapuccino heaven, with swirly whipped cream on top.

He'd called me late and immediately said, "This is getting out of control. We spoke this morning but I feel like it's been days."

"It has," I'd replied. "It's been like eons." If I'd heard anyone else speak those words I would've wanted to stab him or her repeatedly. This was me—unromantic Amelia, saying ooey gooey stuff to a guy. But it felt good.

"I'll have to mortgage my house to pay your phone bill."

"Oh, please. How was your day?"

"I worked out, then I worked, and tried not think of you. Didn't work."

"Same here. We're so pathetic."

"I liked your new pictures," he'd said. I tensed up. I'd let Kelly take some new pictures of me since I'd lost these last couple of pounds, just so he could see that I was on the way to being less, um, less ample.

"Thank you." At least he didn't mention my weight.

"Ever think of traveling to the tropics to get some sun on that beautiful skin?"

"Are you saying that I look pale?"

He laughed. "I'm not walking into that one. I'm just saying you'd have a good time down here. There's lots to do. Great food, great people."

"You're sounding like the tourism board chief."

"I do my part to help the economy."

"So this is not about you. It's your patriotism doing the talking?"

"Yeah, that and my other selfish interests."

"I see. I'm considering it. I'd like to do my part to help the Dominican economy."

"I admire your generosity."

"Awww, thank you."

"I'm serious, though. I want you to be a part of my life."

"I . . . okay. Yes, I feel the same way."

And so it went. We talked about everything and nothing, and four hours later I was yawning but still unwilling to say good night. This was big trouble, indeed.

"So, why not go visit? Go down on spring break."

Huh? Whitney interrupted my thoughts.

"Please stay here with me on earth while I talk to you."

"Oh, sorry." I rolled my eyes back at her. "I can't go there alone." I had never left the country in my entire life. Heck, I'd only been out of the state of Massachusetts about five times.

"You wouldn't be alone. You'd be going to meet him! What are you afraid of? Live a little."

It wasn't that I hadn't thought of it. And we, Drew and I, had talked about it, but I was, as Whitney said, afraid. What if I hated it there? What if he hated me on sight and I was stuck in a foreign country for a whole week, miserable and alone?

"I'd offer to come with you, but I don't want to be away from Max. . . ."

"The sex is that good, huh?"

"Ooooh, girl, yeah, it is. Usually I have to be with a brother to get that kind of action, but this man is smoking . . ."

I tuned her out. I couldn't help but be a little envious. I wondered if I would describe Drew as smoking if we were to ever, um, find ourselves in that situation.

"Wouldn't it be cool if you went down and you guys just hit it off and you move down there and live happily ever after?"

"Thanks, Whitney. I never once thought of that the whole time I've been talking to him."

"It could happen," she said. "Well, no. You'd find some way to screw it up."

"Thanks for the vote of confidence."

"Seriously, though, Amelia, if I were you I'd go down there and lay out on the beach, go diving, know what I mean? It's not just about going to meet him. It's about getting away from this place for a week."

"Yeah, you have a point. I'll think about it."

Later that night in bed I did think about it. So much that I could feel sand trickling between my toes as I fell asleep. I could smell the salty ocean in my dreams. Hear calypso music swirling and thumping like my heartbeat. See a ferociously beautiful sun high up in a clear blue sky. I didn't want to wake up.

Chapter 9

My life was changing. I was becoming even more of a recluse; shut in by an irrational infatuation. Drew was making it so hard for me to live my life in peace without thinking about him constantly, craving warm weather, hot days under the sun, smoking nights under the sheets.

James and Kelly commented on the amount of time I spent on the phone and the computer, and Kelly one day actually bought me a phone card. "For your own good," she said. The thought had never occurred to me, but it turned out to be a huge money saver.

I'd become so overwhelmed by this online/phone relationship that I'd forgotten to buy Ma's groceries one week. She'd called me wailing, saying that I was intentionally trying to starve her to death. "Is that what it's going to take?" I asked her. She hung up the phone. She doesn't get my humor sometimes. I'd run out to the Stop & Shop early Sunday morning, dropped off the bags in her living room, and rushed back home to read Drew's latest e-mail.

Hi, Amelia. It's about 4:30 A.M. and it's pitch-black outside. I'm up in the country, where I spend most of my time. I like it out here because it's quiet, cool, and very beautiful. I think you would like it up here, too. I have a huge jacaranda tree in the back with a hammock under it. It's great for reading or whatever else one might want to do on a cool afternoon. I came up with the idea for building schools while sitting here one day. I had started to feel restless again and worried that I would never accomplish anything that would change anyone's life. It's kind of like what you told me the other day about teaching. That you know you could be doing something else that's more lucrative or even less stressful, but that you liked the idea that you were doing something that was truly important. I can identify with that. With you. Will you come down on spring break, Amelia? I know you have reservations, but with every day that goes by I become more and more consumed by thoughts of you. I look at your picture and I know that there is so much more I could know if I could just look into your eyes—in real life. I want to touch your hair, smell your skin, hear your voice without the static. I know you're afraid of what may happen or what may not happen, but I don't think you need to be. If nothing else, this would be a sunny vacation for you in a great place and you would have made a new friend. I'm awaiting your response.

Drew: I'm up early, too. I couldn't sleep. I was really wrestling with a lot of things. On the one hand, I could use the vacation. I need to be away from my family and roommates right now. Sometimes I feel that there is absolutely no one in my life who gets where I'm coming from. That was a tangent, by the way. On the other hand, I feel strange flying two thousand miles to meet a man I've never met. I feel

> the same way you do. These days I can't take a breath without thinking about you. And even with all of that, it still somehow doesn't feel real. I don't think it would until I could meet you in person. And that's so exciting to me. Sometimes I think that it would be the best thing that could ever happen to me, and then other times I worry. What if we don't hit it off? What if we hate each other? I know. You've already answered that question—I would have a great spring break on warm, sunny Dominica. But this life I'm living now, the one with you in the starring role, is so much fun. I almost don't want to give it up. Do you get what I mean? It's like the unrealness (Is that a word?) is much more fun than the possibility of real life. But I am thinking about it. Seriously.

Later, as I worked on my lesson plans for the week, began to picture myself a brave heroine, willing to do any thing for love. It had been done before. I tried to find prece dent in the literary canon. People who had risked it all fo love, or the possibility of love: Romeo, Juliet, Jane Eyre Madame Bovary, even the tragic Antoinette Cosway from *Wid Sargasso Sea*. . . . The results did not look promising. Wha if I ended up like Antoinette? Crazy, locked in a room some where, while Drew went off with some other Jane Eyre. . . Was I crazy? If I told my mother any of this she would laug at me. "You're going where to meet who?"

Actually, that made the concept a bit more appealing Maybe then she would finally see that I just may not be her forever, and that it was time for her to start getting her lif straight. If I did this, it would be the craziest and braves thing I'd ever done. Was it worth it? He could be an ax mur derer. A kidnapper. Or worse. On the other hand, he could b exactly what he said he was. Remember: Expect great thing to happen and they will. Maybe I should ask him to com ere, then. Whitney had suggested that. But I wanted to go here—at least to see what it was like in another country. I ad no clue what I should do.

Treyon was back in school the next day. He seemed subdued, although he glared at me each time our eyes met. The acation week was only two weeks away, and the students vere restless. They owed me a paper on *The Grapes of Wrath* and I didn't want to incite any more hostility. So we alked about Tom Joad and how he would compare with omeone they knew in real life. Few hands went up when I sked the question, but then once Tina started talking the vhole class got going. Yes, I told her, the Joadses' struggle an be paralleled to the struggle for racial justice in America, but not just racial, but for all poor people, poor blacks, mmigrants, laborers. . . . I told her that she might want to vrite her paper on the topic. Her eyes lit up and my heart nelted. I'd give her an A just for tackling the topic. Three ther kids asked if they could write their three-page paper n the same topic and I told them yes, of course. I felt so . . . o vindicated. See, I wanted to tell Tina, a book does not ave to be by a black author in order for it to relate to your xperience. But I decided to just bask in the glow of my ids actually showing that the text had provoked some hought.

I told this to the principal, Mr. Bell, and he seemed impressed. "See, I told you that you wouldn't regret your decision to come here. Those private schools may be less of a hallenge but the rewards are bigger here. You're doing God's vork now," he said. I laughed because I thought he was being acetious. But he was dead serious. I cleared my throat. God's vork. Oh, boy. I really needed to take my job more seriously.

"So you all ready for your trip?" Lashelle asked as Mr. Bell valked away.

"Yeah, gonna do some shopping this weekend." I would ave gone shopping anyway.

"Oh, Filene's Basement is having a big sale on swimsuits You're going to the Caribbean, right?"

How do I get away from her?

"Which country again?"

I told her and I felt as if she were quizzing me. As if she suspected that I might be lying and she was retesting to see whether I'd be able to keep my facts straight. She was really getting on my nerves, and her butt seemed even bigger than usual in that tight gray skirt. Didn't she own a mirror? Or a sense of decency?

"Gotta head home," I said, and grabbed my bag. I left her standing there.

As I drove home, the temperature dropped. Gosh, it was late March and the weather still would not break! But it had been a good day; I'd gotten my kids to talk, and it seemed that several of them had even read the text. I turned up the heat in the car. Now if this weather would just warm up.

Chapter 10

Our apartment is large but you couldn't tell that from the clutter. Mountain bikes, skis, sneakers, posters, canvas paintings, frames, books are everywhere. I don't mind the mess; most of the books belong to me. Kelly describes our décor as creative chaos. But whenever we have visitors they look around and say with awe or disgust: "Wow, you guys have a lot of stuff."

Kelly, God bless her, thought it would be a good idea to have Whitney and her Tunisian over for dinner. She loves everyone who she thinks may share her hatred for capitalism, the G8, and status symbols. When I told her about Max, she pooh-poohed my worries. She thought it was quite admirable that Max was refusing to register with the USCIS. She thought the PATRIOT Act was unconstitutional on many levels, and thus it was okay for Max to ignore it. And put us all at risk for a raid, Elián González style.

But when Max entered the apartment I could see how Whitney had temporarily lost her mind. He was something to look at. Tall, dark olive skin, and light green eyes. My goodness, did all Tunisians look like that? And how long was the flight? Turned out, he was some kind of racial mutt; his dad was Tunisian and his mother was something else. Thank goodness for race mixing.

"Can I smoke?" he asked with a French accent. Whitney couldn't take her eyes off him. I liked to watch her go all goo-goo over him; it made me want to laugh.

Whitney pulled out a lighter and I wondered when she'd started carrying one; she sure didn't smoke. Kelly blanched and Max began losing points immediately.

"Sorry, dude. We don't allow smoking in here," James said, his mouth full of tortilla chips.

Max nodded, expansively, as if to say: You sissy Americans and your silly hang-ups about secondhand smoke and lung cancer. You are such cowards, I say!

What I was wondering was how could a Ph.D. student so "passionate" about finding a cure for a deadly disease like diabetes be a heavy smoker. I asked Whitney later and she said that his work was very stressful. Uh, okay, that explains everything.

His work, Max told us, as we sat in the living room eating the hors d'oevres that Kelly had made—chips, salsa, and a rather sad imitation of those avocado egg rolls that the Cheesecake Factory makes—involved putting proteins under certain extreme conditions and then leaving them overnight in the lab. He apparently sometimes has to wake up at two or three in the morning to go to the lab to see how the proteins were doing. My eyes were glazing over. I mean, I was glad there were people like him who were willing to spend their lives studying molecules and babysitting proteins so the rest of us could live long, healthy lives. But why did I have to listen to all the gory details? The only person not pretending to be interested in Max's oratory was Whitney. And I was 100 percent sure she'd heard all of it before. Is that what good sex does to people?

I only grew more and more annoyed at dinner. The conversation turned to politics and James and Kelly were on fire.

"Oh, it's total treason what the Bush administration has done. . . ."

I had to tune out. What was Drew doing? Was he thinking about me? Would it be rude if I excused myself to go sneak a peek at my e-mail?

"I don't care if they deport me!" Max exclaimed, his fine nostrils flaring and his green eyes darkening. "The work I am doing here will benefit Americans more than any other people in the world. I will not report to their immigration bureau! How dare they?"

Yeah, I thought, but you'd better be careful. You'll be chilling in Guantánamo Bay in a hot minute if they ever catch you.

"You're quiet tonight," Whitney said. And my mind jerked back to faking interest in the present.

"Oh, just a little tired, that's all."

"Have you decided on spring break yet?"

Kelly and James looked on eagerly.

"I'm leaning toward going. We'll see."

"What is going on with the spring break?" Max asked.

Whitney and Kelly filled him in and I sat there feeling a bit pathetic. I wasn't sure that I wanted this guy knowing all the particulars of my relationship, er friendship, with Drew. Whom I'd never met.

Max's eyebrows kept going up and down and he kept smiling at me slyly.

"You should go," he said finally, slapping one hand on the table. "It sounds like an adventure. He might be your soul mate."

I could only laugh. I really hated that guy, I decided. It's like he was just saying those things to move the conversation forward. Or backward, any which way that led to him. What in the world was Whitney doing with him? Oh, yeah. Green eyes. Good sex.

"Let me tell you about the last time I was in the Caribbean . . ."

Aha!!! He always had a story to tell.

Later, after Max and Whitney had left and James had gone off to sit at his laptop, Kelly and I cleaned up the kitchen.

"What do you think of him?"

"Of Max?"

She was stalling, so I elbowed her in the ribs.

"Okay, Okay. He's kinda . . . kinda stuck on himself. And phony. But he seems really smart. And sexy. And I know that's a big thing for Whitney. They're both eggheads. But . . ."

"He's an ass."

"Um . . . Yeah, definitely."

We laughed so hard James asked us what was so funny.

"Think he's gonna hang around long enough for Whitney to see through him?" Kelly giggled.

"I don't know," I said, really wondering. "I'm hoping she'll drop him in a couple of weeks. I think all it might take is one more conversation about the proteins."

We burst out laughing again. "Oh my God, Ames. I was like, what in the world is he talking about?"

"Me, too! It was like I was in biology all over again. I was trying so hard not to yawn!"

We laughed long and hard as Kelly mimicked Max's accent. I'd miss her when I went away on spring break, I thought. What? What did my mind just say? Oh, my goodness. I was going. My mind had made itself up. I was going! I couldn't wait to tell Drew.

"Ames, you got mail!" James sang as I limped into the house, sore from spin class. They were sitting in the living room, both with laptops on their laps. The picture caused envy to boil up to my throat. I really needed to get out of this house if only just to give them their space. People who were so in love needed their own home. Besides, I just didn't think I could make it another year being surrounded by all this love that didn't belong to me.

"You got a package today," Kelly teased.

Atop the pile of mail on the foyer table was a twenty-inch padded envelope. "Who's it from?" I asked, knowing full well that it had to be from Drew since they'd made note of it.

I looked at the thing, held it in my hands, and turned it over a couple of times.

"Open it!" Kelly said impatiently.

"Geez, give her a break, dude," James admonished. I thought it was cute the way he called her dude sometimes. She hated that. She told him that it makes him sound like a teenage boy.

Anyway, I didn't want to open it with the two of them sitting there, but I did anyway. It was corny. Candy of some sort, guava something or the other. And a letter. I showed them and they did the requisite "awwws."

In my room, I sat on the bed and read the letter away from James's and Kelly's inquiring eyes.

He's a romantic, that Drew. His handwriting seemed as earnest as his words. A flash of doubt ran through me again and I worried that all of this seemed too easy. I needed to hold back a bit. He also sent me a book. An old hardback copy of *Wide Sargasso Sea*. It was old and dusty, a 1971 edition. Where did he find this? I hadn't even been born yet when this was published. A note on it said he borrowed it from the Roseau Public Library: *"Read it again and we'll return it together when you get here."*

I was melting. It was that easy.

As I was near molten rereading Drew's letter, the phone rang.

"Hi, Ma." I hoped the disappointment in my voice did not poison the conversation because I didn't want to spoil my mood.

"Amelia, you need to come over here right now."

"What's wrong?" I assumed the worst. Gerard had been in an accident?

"Just get over here now." And she hung up.

I dropped the letter and put my coat back on.

"What's up?" Kelly asked as I ran out the door, but I didn't even stop to answer. I was afraid. What if something had happened to my baby brother? What if he was in the hospital? Lying smashed up somewhere? I drove through a red light on Columbia Road and a few horns blared. But I didn't even look back to see what damage I might have caused.

I pulled up in front of our house, my mother's house, and a wave of depression weighed me down. I hated that house. I used to love it when my dad was around, but now every time I look at it I feel weary and sad. It's a beautiful nineteenth-century Georgian house, like many others on the street. Except that ours had not been expensively renovated and sliced into condos. I'd suggested selling it, but Grace Wilson would not hear of it. The house belonged to her Jewish grandmother. And she was very proud of that fact. I'm not even sure she did have a Jewish grandmother. But Grace Wilson holds on to what she can when she wants to. She was standing at the door in a flannel robe.

"Ma, what's wrong?"

"Look at this." She shoved a sheet of paper into my hand.

Inside, the house was steaming hot. She liked to turn the heat all the way up to eighty during the winter. My dad fought with her over this all the time when I was a kid. He'd turn it down to sixty-seven, and then she'd turn it right back up to eighty when he left for work. Then they would fight again when the bill came.

I read the paper twice, three times. It was an order to appear in court. Apparently, my mother's car had been involved in an accident. She had fled the scene of an accident. I looked at her.

"You had an accident?"

"No! Look at the date, Amelia."

I did and it meant nothing to me.

"It's the day I let Gerard use the car; the day he said he had a job interview!"

Gerard had a job interview?

"He told me he'd run into a wall. One of his friends fixed the car the next day. What am I going to do, Amelia?"

I sank into the tattered couch. I had to take off my coat, it was too hot!

"Have you talked to him?"

"No, but I left him a message on his cell phone. He's avoiding me."

She looked defeated and what could I say. They enabled each other's behavior. This was not the first time she'd gotten in trouble because of my brother's problems. He'd wrecked one car before. Had junkie friends come over and steal from her. Even had the police come to the house once looking for some friend of his who was wanted in a homicide.

"What should I do?" she asked helplessly. There was a glass on the table and a bottle of Tanqueray, my father's favorite drink, next to it.

"You have to go to the police and tell them you weren't driving the car." I couldn't believe Gerard had done this to her.

"But . . ." She hesitated. "I'd have to tell them he did it."

"Yes, Ma. What? Did you want to take the blame for it?"

"He's still on parole . . ."

"Yeah, and you don't want to go to jail."

She sat down heavily. Was she crying? I couldn't stand

that. I didn't want to see that today. I wanted to go back to my room. To Drew's letter. To my sixty-seven-degree apartment with my anarchist roommates.

"What am I going to do?"

"Ma, you have to call the police and tell them what happened. Hopefully, this accident wasn't too serious. And it couldn't have been, else they would have been outside with guns waiting to pick you up. Just call the cops and get it straight. Your insurance is gonna go up and Gerard's gonna get in trouble again. That's all there is to it."

I was so angry with Gerard that I didn't even want to think of how sad the idea of him going back to jail made me. How many times was he going to screw up?

"I can't do that to my son, Amelia. I can't do that to him. He's doing so well with his new job."

I sighed. "Fine, then. Take the blame. But you're gonna have to go to court."

I truly didn't know what would happen to her if she took the blame for Gerard's screwup. What I did know was that she would do it. She loved him like that. Me, she could verbally abuse all the day long. But Gerard was her little man. She would coddle him till the day he died.

I hugged her and told her that everything would be okay. Then I went into the kitchen to make sure she had enough food. There was one other bottle of liquor in the cabinet. I stuck it in my bag. She'd finish the Tanqueray, then she'd have no more unless she went to the store, and she certainly wouldn't go out in this cold weather.

"Bye, Ma. Call me and let me know what you want to do. I'll come to the police station with you if you want."

She waved as I pulled away. Aaargh! Gerard, just grow up already, I thought. I tried calling his cell but he would not pick up. Fine, little brother, have it your way. I was so tired of my family!

Chapter 11

For some reason, I picked up the phone and dialed his number. His machine came on but he picked up halfway through the recording.

"I knew it would be you," he said, and my heart immediately warmed over like I'd just eaten a bowl of cream of wheat on a cold, cold morning.

"I got your package. Now I'll be up all night rereading *Wide Sargasso Sea.*"

"That's a really sexy book," he said. "I read it in about a day and a half. I think Antoinette Cosway was kinda hot. Crazy, but still hot."

"I see. You like the crazy type."

"Not really. I like bookish types, with steamy chapters."

The minutes disappeared in a stream of revelations I had not planned. I told him about Ma and Gerard, their problems, my responsibilities in all of it. I never thought I could ever talk to anyone else about those things, except Whitney. Not even James and Kelly were aware of the extent of my family's baggage. It was something that so shamed me that I engaged in my mother's lies to my colleagues and casual friends. When Gerard had been locked away, I told everyone, along with my mother, that he was studying computer science at UNH.

Lying was easy. It had started when my father began to drink heavily. I would call his work sometimes to tell them he wouldn't be in because he was sick. Then when he really got sick, we told everyone that it was diabetes that was killing him and not drunk's diseases or a busted-up liver. Lies, lies, lies. Then I started covering for my mother when she would screw up at her job, and then for Gerard when he'd done something to some neighbor's property or some kid's bike. I was always lying for my family. But here I was spilling embarrassing truths to Drew. Maybe it was easy to be honest because I'd never seen him before. Maybe that fact made him somehow less real to me. Maybe I was still lying in some sense.

"Sometimes I wish I could just trade them in for a new family. Divorce them, you know?"

"You don't have to be so close to them if you don't want to be," he said. "You're a big girl. You can move away. You cannot let their problems take over your life."

"I can't do that, Drew. I've tried. But I always worry. It's like the drama keeps pulling me back."

"Well, there's your answer. You're a loving, caring person and you don't want to see your mother or your brother get hurt. What's so bad about that?"

"I don't want to always have to be the one to save them."

"Then don't be. Let them fall sometimes. They'll learn to pick themselves up eventually."

"Yeah, you're right. I'm sure your family is perfect," I said, wishing that he would have some major gripe that I could latch on to and feel somewhat better about my situation.

"Not really. My dad was kind of a tyrant. I miss him now that he's gone, but while he was alive we didn't always get along."

"You mean he was a bad man? I thought he was loved and respected by everyone in your country."

"That was just for show. He had a public persona that he used to get votes and then there was the other side of him that only my mother and I got to see. It wasn't pretty."

"What was it like?"

He paused. "He did his best. He was just conflicted for the most part . . . You know, trying to be a good leader, a good father and husband. It was a lot for him to handle."

I sensed that he didn't want to talk about it. "What about your mom, then?"

"She's great. She's always been my champion. I think she spoiled me a bit. She's my best friend, really."

"She sounds like a great person." If she'd raised him to be what he is, then she must be a phenomenal sister!

"I just wish things between my mom and me would just be normal. I'm tired of this up and down."

"You have a choice," he said.

Later, I looked out the window before settling into bed. It was snowing again and the windowpane was freezing. Drew's voice was still echoing in my head. I so wanted to be where he was. And not here. I didn't want to have to think about going to court with Ma and about what would happen to Gerard if the cops found out he'd violated parole. Whitney had told me on numerous occasions: "Just let them screw their lives the hell up. Let Gerard go back to jail. Let your mom drink her nights and her days away in that old, dark house. Stop trying so hard."

But I couldn't do that. It wasn't as if things weren't bad enough, despite my efforts. It would be worse for them if I weren't here. But would it be worse for me? I wanted to find out. I picked up the phone, cringing as an image of my last phone bill flashed across my mental screen.

"Drew, I've made up my mind," I said. "I'm coming."

I thought I heard him gasp. "You won't regret it, Amelia."

I'd better not, I thought after I'd hung up. I'm doing this just to get a taste of independence. Just a taste.

Chapter 12

"Ma, I'm going away." We were on our way back from her court hearing about Gerard's accident. Luckily, the damage to the other car was very minor. The "victim" was an older woman, as mean as an old dog. The lawyer I'd gotten for Ma tried to persuade the old lady to let us pay for the damage and to end it there, but the old coot wouldn't hear of it. We had to go back to court. Ugh! I hated the thought of more of my mother's savings being used for something Gerard was responsible for, so I'd offered to pay for it. I didn't know why. I guess it was guilt. I'd treat myself once I got to Dominica and that would be my reward.

"Where you going?" She sounded worried.

"I'm going to the Caribbean for spring break."

She paused and shifted in the passenger seat. She always asked me each time I drove her somewhere: "Why do you drive this little car? All the young people these days are driving those big trucks and you driving this little car."

"Which one? Which island?"

"Dominica."

"But you don't speak Spanish, Amelia," she wailed.

I clenched my teeth. I patiently explained to her that it's not that Dominica. She didn't sound impressed.

"Since when you have the money to go on fancy vacations? What about saving up for a house?"

How did I know she was going to try to find some way to make me feel bad about this? And it's funny that she didn't mention that I was about to spend a sizable chunk of money to pay for the result of her and Gerard's drunken shenanigans.

"Ma, when was the last time I ever went anywhere? Did something nice for myself?"

"You go shopping all the time."

Yes, I did. But what the heck? My life was none of her business. And it was me who made sure that all her basic needs were taken care of.

"Anyway, I'm leaving in a few days. I'll stop by before I leave."

She sighed dramatically. "Could you bring me some groceries before you go?"

"I will."

Of course, she had to squeeze something out of me before I went off and had a good time. But I didn't mind. I'd call Gerard and do the same thing and he would be more impressed. He would ask if he could come with me and I'd actually wish that he could. Gerard and I could have fun together if he wouldn't drink. I would have even considered asking him if he hadn't banged up Ma's car and not told her about it. Not that it was my place to punish him, but I couldn't allow him to think that I condoned that kind of behavior.

I read an article once about families like ours. Where there was one person who had "made it out"; however, the family members who were still struggling continued to be a drain on the escapee's success. That bothered me. I shouldn't have been seeing myself in that article. For one thing, Gerard is smarter than I am. Better at everything, math especially. He'd kill the A's in algebra while I flailed and flagged with the most basic calculations. Gerard's weakness was partying; he did too much of it, and Ma never was as hard on him as she was on me. If he'd spent his teenage years under lockdown as I did, he'd be a doctor or a lawyer or on his way to becoming a U.S. senator today. Ma always indulged him, especially after my dad died. It's sad that her version of love hurt him more than it helped.

From day one, he was the little overachiever in elementary school, a star at Pop Warner games, the best swimmer at the public pool, and every teacher's great hope.

Gerard was the one who helped me study for the test to get into Boston Latin. He himself had gotten a perfect score, but he refused to go. He said that it was a sissy school; all his friends were going to the other publics like Dorchester High, Jeremiah Burke, and Madison Park. He didn't want to feel left out. And Ma, true to character, told him, "Go where you'll be happy." But even at Madison Park he excelled without even trying. Even after Dad died Gerard never needed motivation to do well in school. He performed well despite his laissez-faire attitude.

He'd flirted with light rebellion since he was old enough to talk, but Dad had always set him straight. Dad was a god to him, even though they fought a lot. Sometimes I think that Gerard did so well at everything not because he wanted to but because he wanted our father to be proud of him.

But eventually he just stopped trying. He began to run the streets like the other boys who had one parent, no parents, or two parents and zero hope. I passed him almost every day on my way home from school hanging out on the corner with his friends, all of them trying to affect menacing looks. He hardly ever came home for dinner as I was forced to; he slept out of the house most nights, something I'd never have gotten away with. My mother soon gave up on trying to set him straight and turned to the bottle.

I resented him most of my teenage years mostly because I felt helpless. I was in denial about my dad's death, and Gerard's problems were an added annoyance to me. I'd ignore him sometimes, lecture him at others, but he just laughed at me. "You need to stay in school and study 'cause ain't no man gonna wanna marry your nagging ass." In retrospect, I realized that I was no better than Ma. I'd given up on him, too, and sometimes I felt guilty about it.

We were all hurting after Dad died. Our family never emerged from crisis mode. My mother buried my father, then enveloped me in her prison of depression and alcoholism. She created random rules that stifled me most of my teenage years into a life of schoolwork, housework, and not much else. She let Gerard run free, hoping that the freedom would somehow ease his pain. It didn't. Instead, she limited his options by throwing him into the hungry maw of the streets. Now there seemed to be little hope for my brother.

I'd read so many books about alcoholism and addiction that I had my family's problems all figured out. I knew all about enabling and tough love and all the jargon. That's why I tried to take a firm line with Ma and Gerard, but sometimes it was hard to turn away.

This trip would be a break from all of this. I planned not to think about them at all. And maybe I would just run away and never come back.

Chapter 13

When the tiny, fourteen-seater plane landed, passengers cheered loudly, whistling and clapping. I looked around dazed. What was all the fuss about? Then the flight attendant announced that Dominica presents one of the most challenging landings in the world for even the most experienced pilots—because of the mountains. The CIA World Factbook seemed to have omitted this pertinent fact from its otherwise comprehensive overview.

Fortunately, I'd been oblivious because I'd closed my eyes when I looked out the window and saw that a mountain peak was within touching distance of my window. That sight had convinced me that I didn't need to see anything else until the plane was safely on terra firma. Challenging landing? Ignorance sure is bliss.

A curtain of heat overwhelmed me as soon as I stepped out of the plane, but I didn't dwell on it because I was in jaw-dropping awe. Everything around me was so wildly green. Not spring green after a snowy winter or deep autumn green about to turn red, orange, or yellow. But emerald-green-green, like the way you imagined God had truly intended when He said, "Let there be green." There were also wildflowers everywhere in the brightest pinks, purples, and reds I'd ever seen, and we were surrounded by mountains, formidable peaks that seemed to be peering down at me in disapproval.

The airport terminal could have been an outdoor shed in some rich person's backyard. It looked like a garage, with its one-story, concrete building painted pink with white design cement blocks. What looked like a 1979 fire engine idled nearby. A group of uniformed men smoked and gazed at the passengers alighting. They seemed unimpressed by us. I had only one bag and I'd carried it under my seat the whole way. Drew had warned me not to bring too much luggage. Where was he, by the way?

I walked into the airport building, feeling sweat prickle the skin of my back, and joined the line for customs. I'm in the Third World, I thought, and tried not to stare at the black people all around me whom I couldn't recognize or identify with. They spoke quickly and harshly in English I didn't quite understand. They obviously knew what they were doing as they pulled out documents and signaled to what looked like drivers on the other side of the counter. They acted as if they were right at home. Well, of course, they were. It was me who was out of place. When it was my turn in the front of the line, I showed the stocky, stern-looking officer with the bad perm my passport.

"Tourist?"

"Um . . . yes?"

She stamped my passport and looked past me. Next in line! Wow. Weren't all Caribbean people supposed to be warm and friendly?

I lugged my travel bag and followed the signs through the packed terminal toward the exit. Where was he? What if he didn't show? What if I was stuck in this tiny airport, which closed at sunset, for a whole week? All I saw beyond the walls of the airport were trees and mountains. There were some men, cabdrivers I presumed, looking at me with a question in their eyes. I averted mine. I had a ride. I hoped.

Then a black Range Rover pulled up to where I was standing. My heart lurched, then my stomach tightened. He was taller than I thought he would be. Darker than in his picture. He had cut his hair. He looked neat and handsome. Crisp white T-shirt, blue shorts. Tevas. Oh. My. God. I don't care anymore.

I don't know when or how I ended up kissing this guy I'd never met before, but that was just how it went down. I guess I was that kind of girl, after all. When I finally came up for air, he looked at me and laughed. "How was the flight?"

"Long," I said, embarrassed.

Then he kissed me again, this time harder.

I heard a few whistles in the background.

"Let's get out of here," he said.

Once we pulled away from the airport he drove with one hand and held my hand with the other. I couldn't stop talking. About the delays in Puerto Rico. The fact that I could see the pilot from my seat on the small Cessna that brought us here. That I had to close my eyes when I noticed how low we were flying, but that the water looked absolutely gorgeous. The fact that the airport terminal seemed to be about the size of my mother's house. He laughed and brought my hand to his mouth a couple times.

"See, I told you we'd hit it off," he said.

And I agreed, wanting to burst with happiness. I needn't have worried. I didn't feel weird or afraid. I felt that I belonged with this man in this truck on this narrow, bumpy road with all these mountains surrounding us, azure sky and big sun just beaming down and digging the two of us together.

The drive to the capital was long and I had to disengage from Drew's hand several times so I could snap pictures. Dominica reminded me of documentary film shots of central African countries. It was lush, wet, wild, and colorful. There were fruit trees and flowers everywhere. My eyes drank in the sights greedily. I'd never been in a place where nature's beauty just seemed to overflow in such ridiculous, obscene abundance. I saw tiny, neat houses off the road with small gardens on the side. A man was riding a donkey just ahead of us to the side of the narrow road. I had to snap that. Two minutes later, a late-model Mercedes flew past us in the opposite direction.

As if reading my mind, Drew explained. The country had always operated with a vast inequality of wealth. If you were part of the one percent who had money, or among the Arab, Chinese, and Taiwanese businessmen who often came here to hide, or a high-level government worker or professional, then you would be fine. You could send your children abroad to be educated. You could build yourself a huge mansion with an amazing view of the ocean. You could make enough money to live a life insulated from the poverty that struck the other ninety-nine percent of the population. That ninety-nine percent was well educated enough thanks to a decent British-based school system, but jobs were scarce, so most of the young were underemployed and frustrated, hence the high emigration rate.

I saw further evidence of the disparity in the huge mansions atop mini-mountains that looked down on tiny villages filled with rows of corrugated iron shacks. I took pictures of all of it; I would think about the injustice later. Drew seemed content to provide commentary as we drove, but I was so taken in by the sights I don't think I was paying close attention.

Two hours later, we pulled into a long, circular driveway that led up to a white house, or maybe estate would be a more appropriate word. A big, ornate one that I think I wouldn't dare dream of living in even in my wildest dreams.

"This is your place?"

He laughed. "I wish." It was his family's place, and I guess for a former prime minister's residence it wasn't too bad.

A tall woman who looked a lot like Drew ran out of the heavy oak front door, laughing. She looked young enough to be his older sister. She wore her hair in long, tiny black braids; a colorful dress came down almost to her toes. She was barefoot and her toenails were painted coral. Scads of bracelets jingled on her arms. She was Diana Ross, in an earth-mother kind of way.

"Amelia! It's so nice to meet you." Her accent was singsongy and pleasant. I think I liked her on the spot.

I walked into her arms and smiled. Wow. A hugger.

"How was the flight?"

Before I could answer, more people came streaming out of the door, I was meeting the whole Anderson clan: Drew's mom, Vanessa, the hugger, his sisters Sophie and Stella, their husbands, their kids, a few aunts and uncles.

"I'm well. It's great to meet you, too," I said, hoping I sounded as open and friendly as his family.

"Come on in, let's eat," Vanessa said, putting her arm around my shoulder.

I was overwhelmed and a little bit uneasy as I answered questions from strange, smiling people. Where was Drew? I noticed him teasing somebody's baby.

"Yes, I had a great flight. Your home is magnificent," I complimented Vanessa.

She beamed at me. "My husband and I built it once we outgrew the prime minister's mansion."

Vanessa continued to refer to Drew's father as her husband although he'd been dead for several years. It was almost as if she expected him to come walking in the door at any moment.

"You sit right next to me," she said, guiding me to a chair near the head of a large, long table.

"Mom, don't scare her away just yet," Drew's sister said.

"Don't mind my daughters," Vanessa said. "They get jealous whenever another woman competes with them for my attention."

"Oh, get over yourself, woman," Sophie scoffed and everyone laughed.

As we sat down to eat, a trio of uniformed waiters appeared out of nowhere and began to pour us drinks.

"Some wine, ma'am?" one of them asked me.

I politely asked for sparkling water.

"She doesn't drink," Drew said, taking the chair next to me, leaving me flanked between him and Vanessa.

"Oh," Vanessa raised an eyebrow. "That's admirable."

The conversation flowed around the table. I noticed that they were a big, happy family. Drew joked around with his sisters, their husbands, his nieces and nephews. He teased Vanessa mercilessly, and she obviously enjoyed every minute of it. They were indeed best friends. I racked my brain to recall a time I'd sat down at a table with Ma and Gerard and just laughed and laughed. Ugh. I had come straight from the airport to a family gathering that only made me see how short my family fell.

The doorbell rang and soon more people walked into the dining room, pulling up chairs. It was a bit off-putting. Here I thought that Drew and I would be all alone this week getting to know each other, and it seemed that I'd just walked into a huge welcome dinner. And I was the guest of honor! I began to feel uncomfortable.

I smiled as aunts, uncles, and close friends of the family greeted me and asked about my flight, my job as a teacher, life in America. Drew was so busy introducing me to everyone that we never even got a chance to talk. What was going on? I wasn't ready for all this attention.

"So, Amelia, tell me all about you. What do you like to do? Besides work, of course," Vanessa said this as the staff took away our appetizer dishes. There were about thirty people at the never-ending mahogany table. I noticed a few impressive-looking paintings on the wall. My knowledge of art left a lot to be desired, but I think I recognized a Basquiat.

I shrugged off any talk about my lowly profession and tried to steer the conversation to Vanessa. But she wanted to talk about me. Was I getting the old overprotective mom shakedown?

"You're such a pretty girl. I'm surprised you're not married yet. Or at least have been married."

"Well, women in America get married much later in life these days."

"I think a woman should start building a family by at least age twenty-five. But I'm old-fashioned . . ."

"Mom, tell her about the time you spent in Boston," Drew said as the three waiters began to serve us. I wondered if these people worked for Vanessa permanently or were hired just for the day. The food smelled delicious.

"Oh, that was a long time ago," Vanessa said. "I was a model . . . I did some print work for Filene's and Macy's."

"Oh, how interesting," I said. Great, she just had to be a former model! She must think I'm a cow.

"It was very boring," Vanessa said. "I was glad when my husband rescued me from it all." Then her expression changed from sunlight to gathering storm. "Excuse me, Amelia." She turned to the waiter, a burly middle-aged man. "Charles, you're going to have to move a little bit faster," Vanessa hissed.

"Yes, ma'am," Charles replied, his eyes falling.

Drew rolled his eyes. "Sorry," he patted my hand. "She gets a little crazy . . ."

Vanessa sniffed. "Andrew, you don't have to apologize for me. I'm not being unreasonable."

Drew's sister Sophie leaned over in my direction. "Amelia, your hair is just gorgeous. But you're going to have a hard time keeping it looking like this in this weather."

"Thanks," I told her. "I'm thinking of going natural anyway."

"Oh, really?" Vanessa said. "You could pull off a look like that very nicely."

Ha! Take that, Grace Wilson, I thought.

An hour later, the table was cleared and I hadn't embarrassed myself by eating too much. I noticed that Vanessa and both her daughters refused dessert, so I did, too. But I felt absolutely sick with desire as I watched Drew and the other men and a few women devour chocolate raspberry rum cake. I wanted a slice so bad I could have snatched it off his plate. Oh my God. I'm such a pig. I sipped sparkling water and tried to imagine that I was swallowing chocolate raspberry rum cake. All I tasted was fizzy nothing.

Soon after dinner some of the aunts and uncles said their good-byes. It was a Monday evening, an early night, they explained. While Vanessa was off hobnobbing, Drew grabbed my hand and led me out through the huge kitchen to the back of the house, where there was an Olympic-size swimming pool in the back.

"This place is unbelievable!" I exclaimed. It was cut into the side of a mountain, so from one side there's a view of the Atlantic and a range of mountains from the other. "You must have had a lot of fun living here," I told him as I stared off into a shimmering blue ocean miles and miles away.

"I never really lived here. I lived in the prime minister's mansion while I was growing up. My folks got this place after I went off to Morehouse. I think they were trying to tell me something."

"If I were you I'd be living here now."

"I prefer my privacy. You don't know what it's like living with my mother."

I could imagine. The way she doted on him told me a lot.

"So when do we go to your place?" I wanted to be alone with him, away from all these people. Even away from this magnificent house.

"Tomorrow, maybe."

I was disappointed. I wanted to go now. Before I could complain, Vanessa fluttered in out of nowhere.

"Amelia, I want to show you where you'll be staying. Drew, can you go make sure Gerda got Amelia's room ready?"

Drew walked off obediently.

"Well?" She looked at me and smiled expectantly. I thought she was asking about the view.

"It's gorgeous out here," I said, returning her perky smile.

"No, I meant, how's everything so far?"

Oh! "Everything's great, Vanessa. Just wonderful."

"I'm glad you're happy. The food wasn't too much, was it?"

"Not at all."

"Good. Some Americans think West Indian food is over-seasoned but . . ."

"Not me, I eat a lot of West Indian food back home in Boston. I love it." Was I laying it on too thick?

"Great. I'm sure you'll enjoy staying here. It's so much better than that little shack Drew lives in. I don't know why he won't let me help him find a better place. You know, he's going to be prime minister of this country someday, Amelia. I told him he needs to start acting like it."

I cleared my throat.

"That's why I think someone like you would be so good for him. You have great manners. Style. And plus you're American. The people here, they love Americans. You'd fit in quite well."

"Well, Drew and I are just getting to know each other, Vanessa."

"Of course," she said quickly as if checking herself. "I just meant that your friendship will be valuable to him no matter what."

Valuable? Was I an asset in the campaign war chest? I put

the thought out of my mind. It was starting to get dark and the sun was starting to go down.

Drew came up behind me and put his arm around my waist. "Can you leave us alone now, Mom?"

Vanessa smiled and walked away. "I'll see you in the morning, Amelia."

We sat on a low chaise near the pool and faced the sunset.

"This is amazing," I said as the sky erupted into a carnival of color. Layers and layers of purple, pink, blue, orange, and yellow blended together and formed a tent over the ocean. I reached for my camera and realized that my bag was with Gerda, whoever she was.

"It is," Drew said. "But I've seen better." He kissed me on the neck.

I turned to face him. "Your mother seems to think that you'll be running for president . . . er . . . prime minister pretty soon and . . ."

"Don't listen to her. That's what she's hoping; I'm not ready for that yet. Okay?"

"Okay," I said. And I believed him. Not that it would be a bad thing if he were. But still . . .

Later, in a big, comfortable bed in a room that seemed to be quite far away from anyone else's, I closed my eyes and replayed the day. I was exhausted but unable to sleep. I wanted to talk to Drew, but I also wanted to absorb everything that had happened. He didn't warn me about all of this. This big, cozy, happy family of his . . . . How could some people be so lucky? So happy?

There was a knock on the door.

"Did I wake you?"

"No." It was only eight P.M. but I was exhausted.

He sat on the bed next to me and took my hand. "My mother thinks I've sprung too much on you too fast. She said you looked uncomfortable."

"I didn't know I was walking into all of this." I gestured

at the room, meaning the house, the family, him, my overwhelming urge to rip his shirt off, all of it.

"Sorry. I really wanted everyone to meet you."

"No need to apologize. I just wish I'd been warned."

He was sheepish. "Can I make it up to you?"

"You don't need to."

"I have to go home," he said, kissing me again.

"Why? I thought you were staying here with me."

"That probably wouldn't work; besides, I have work waiting for me at home. You'll see the place tomorrow."

I wished I had been brave enough to say that I'd stay with him at his place. We'd argued over it in a string of e-mails. At first I'd insisted on staying in a hotel, but then he said his mother lived in a large, empty house and she'd love to have the company. I'd agreed to that. But now, I didn't want him to go. Me and my reservations.

"Well, maybe I can bring my stuff over tomorrow, then?" I said this hoping he'd get my meaning.

"It's not as fancy as this house," he said.

"Is it like the Unabomber's cabin?" That would certainly change things.

"It's a little better than that. I have indoor plumbing."

He was funny. "What would your mother say about that, though? If I went to stay with you."

"She probably wouldn't like it."

"Okay, I guess I'm staying here then. At Knots Landing."

"Knots Landing? You're silly."

We kissed good-bye. For about ten minutes.

Chapter 14

Vanessa woke me early. It was only 6:03, and although I'd slept like a well-fed baby all through the night, it still felt too early to be wide awake.

"I like to have breakfast when the sun is coming up," she said, her head sticking halfway into my room. I noticed that she was already fully made up, bejeweled, and be-Chaneled.

"Okay," I mumbled groggily. Who was so bright, cheery, and perfumed this early? I ran to the bathroom and dressed quickly. I hoped that if I missed a few minutes of the sunrise that it wouldn't permanently tarnish me in her eyes. Despite her diva-like quirks, she seemed sweet and open, like one of those hip slim black mothers you see in optimistic TV commercials.

I went out onto the porch where she sat at a white table with two wicker chairs around it. It was casual and beautiful; her furnishings suited her so well that they could have been accessories, like one of her many bracelets. I couldn't compliment her on her taste again without sounding like a hick. From the moment I'd walked in the house I'd been awed by its grandeur. She was very proud of it; who wouldn't be? I certainly would be if I had a mansion way up on a mountain with a view of the ocean on one end and the mountains at the other.

"Beautiful morning," I said. I could see little hints of orange nudging against the dark green of the mountaintops. It was breathtaking. I watched for a while, a croissant in my hand and my mouth probably hanging open.

"See," she said. "If I don't do this every day, then I'm just undone. Just undone." She sipped coffee from a maroon demitasse.

"It's gorgeous," was all I could say. I just didn't have the words. The scene was Steinbeck perfect. There were unidentifiable birds and insects chirping in the background, the air was cool, the smell of wildflowers plus the ones in the potted plants along the porch perfumed the air. It was a slice of heaven. I didn't dare imagine what it would be like to live life so serenely every day. If I did, though, I'd be a very different person. Nicer, more laid-back, more goddess-like. I'd probably have to start reading Iyanla Vanzant and start wearing lots of bracelets, too. And probably dreadlocks. I'd have to change my name to something African and start writing poetry.

We sat, eating croissants and sipping coffee and not saying anything. Amid all the beauty, I got the feeling that she wanted me to be silent. I obliged. Minutes later, when the sun had risen halfway over the mountain, she spoke.

"So, Amelia, I was thinking about our conversation last evening and I just have one question. What should I expect from you and my son?"

Gulp. I hadn't anticipated that. I didn't even know what I was expecting from this, and I was a principal player.

"Well, we're just friends at this stage. We're still getting to know each other." How was that, I wanted to ask her? Is that okay? Can I go to my room now?

She smiled at me benignly and I wanted to look away, back at the sun that asked no prying questions.

"Don't look so nervous," she laughed. "I'm just being

nosy. But you should know that Drew can be a little driven. He tends to go for what he wants with a lot of gusto and sometimes without really thinking things through."

So I should what? Be careful?

I nodded. She didn't say anything else and so I felt compelled to fill the silence. "You don't have to worry."

Her eyebrows went up quickly. "Oh, I'm not worried about Drew."

Okaaaaay.

"So, how do your people feel about you coming all the way down here to meet my son?"

"Actually, I saw this as more of a vacation. Meeting Drew was just icing on the cake. I was all set to stay at the Fort Young Hotel; he insisted I stay here." In other words, I can be out of here in a minute if need be.

She beamed her friendly whites again. "I hope I didn't sound judgmental. I guess it's just the mother in me." She sipped her coffee daintily. "A lot of the young ladies down here are so bold. They know his worth, but they're not worthy of him. Thankfully, he hasn't shown any real interest in any of them. I keep telling him if he likes American women so much he shouldn't have moved back here."

The coffee was too strong; I was already beginning to feel jumpy.

"That's interesting," I said, wondering exactly what I meant by that. At least it filled the silence. What else could I say? Drew and I had talked about this, and obviously she wasn't being totally honest. Vanessa had tried to set him up with all of her friends' children. She'd wanted him to marry a local, a native, whatever you call it. He'd tried many and hadn't found the right one. I believed him more than I believed her when she said that no one was worthy of him. He was special, but he wasn't God. I just hoped she didn't think that I was some evil, calculating American on the make; some Stella trying to get my groove on with her Worthy Son.

"Well, everybody seems to like you, so I wouldn't worry about anything," she said suddenly. Did she read minds?

"I had a great time last night," I said, thinking back to how overwhelmed I was by the whole family. "And I'm having a good time now," I said.

"Me too," she said, raising her coffee cup.

Thankfully, Drew showed up at 7:30 on the dot. By then I'd had enough of playing nice and making small talk with Vanessa. I'd figured her out. She was a lot like my mother in that she thought her son was the best thing ever to happen to manhood.

She fussed over Drew. "Have you had breakfast? Should I have Charles make you something?"

"No, Mom. We have to get going."

Drew took my hand and pulled me toward the front door.

"See you later, Vanessa," I said. She winked at me. What did that mean?

"Have a good time. And drive safely, Drew," she waved.

"Did you two talk?" Drew asked as I put on my seat belt.

"Umm . . . yeah. We had a nice chat."

He started up the engine. "Did she threaten you? Tell you not to break my heart or else."

"Not in so many words. Why? Is that her M.O.?"

"Nah. Actually, she had the same talk with me before you came. She's just being herself. She likes to worry. But we're both adults, right?"

"I hope so." Boy, he was in a good mood today. "Where are we going?"

"We're going to go see my place. Then I'm going to drive you to the other end of the island. It's the type of drive that would probably take an hour on an American highway, but with these roads it will probably take three."

I tensed. "Is it safe, though?"

"If you're asking whether they're bandits lying in wait for us, then, yes, it's safe. But the roads are narrow, winding, and carved into mountains. I hope you have a steady stomach."

Oh, cripes!

"It's beautiful, though. You'll love it." He patted my leg and I tried to feel less apprehensive.

"So when do I get to see the new school? The one you're building."

"Probably tomorrow. I could take you to the high school in the capital, too."

"What's it like teaching high school here? Are the kids well behaved?"

"Depends on the teacher, I think. I taught for a year and I never had any problems with discipline, but I know a lot of teachers who do. Sometimes it's the teacher who's the problem, not the kids."

I didn't want to get into an argument with him but his comment just hit too close to home. "Well, some of my kids are pretty awful. It's hard . . ."

"Amelia, relax. I wasn't referring to you. I'm sure you're a great teacher. You're also fine as hell with those soft lips and gorgeous brown eyes."

"Nice way to back out of an argument."

"It's one of my many talents."

We laughed and he took my hand, steering with the other.

We drove down a steep, narrow, barely paved road that seemed to descend straight down into the earth from the sky. A tiny car, a Nissan maybe, with a young woman at the wheel and two toddlers looking out the window, groaned up the incline.

"They're not in car seats!" I gasped, looking back as the tiny car crawled up the hill.

"You're not going to see a lot of that here," Drew said. "People get along fine without that."

"But aren't there a lot of accidents? These roads look pretty treacherous."

"Not as many as you'd think. The people who tend to get into car accidents are mostly tourists and people who've moved back here after living abroad for a few years. We're used to these roads."

I held onto my seat as we hit flat road and he hit the accelerator. I looked out the window so it wouldn't feel that I was flying through space in a funnel. Gosh, this place was so beautiful. We roared along the coast, and the same ocean that I saw from Vanessa's porch a thousand feet up in the hills was within a few steps now. The water was blue and calm, bordered by a rocky coastline and an occasional stretch of black sand. I noticed a few small kayaks on the water, being rowed by fishermen. I felt like Hemingway in Cuba!

As we neared Canefield, I saw a small plane coming in for landing at Dominica's second airport. It was so small it looked like a model plane a child would fly against a blue sky on a clear day. We crossed a bridge with an arc over it and what looked like the remains of some type of colonial-era structure. And a cannon! A real live cannon! I wanted to ask him the story behind it but someone driving in the other direction had stopped—in the middle of the road—to say hello.

It was another young brother about Drew's age also driving a huge SUV. I could see two toddlers in the back, but they were in car seats. They chatted for a couple of minutes before the brother went on his way, waving to me.

"He moved back here from New York two years ago," Drew said. "Was a lawyer in Manhattan for a long time."

"What's he doing down here?" I asked. As much as I loved this beautiful little country, I still didn't see what would cause a person to leave America behind for good.

"He's practicing law and is involved in politics. He'll probably become a judge in a couple of years."

"Wow. That's impressive for a guy who's barely thirty."

"Our prime minister was only thirty-one when he took office."

That was true: another American-educated brother who came back to be the big fish in a little pond.

"It's easier to be here if you have big dreams than in America. Your education, ambition goes much further," Drew said.

I could definitely see that.

"So you'd never move back to the States?"

He paused for a minute and slowed down as the traffic thickened. We had reached an industrial area. There was a huge car dealership, a few gas stations, and what looked like a factory. The smell of diesel coated the air and the sun was beginning to shine brightly. I could see the sweat on the brows of people who stood on the roadside, waiting for a bus, I imagined.

"That's hard to say. I miss certain things about the U.S. The conveniences. The feeling that you're not completely isolated from the rest of the world. But I have a responsibility to this place. I mean, these people, they're poor and they don't have a whole lot of hope except for people like me and Freddie, whom I was just talking to. I don't know if I could ever turn my back on that forever."

Oh, he was making my heart melt.

He turned on the radio and the deejay spoke in a rapid-fire patois of Dominican slang, English, mixed in with a little Ebonics. Then a hip-hop song came on and I laughed.

"Yep, it's everywhere you go. Can't escape the ghetto's influence," Drew said. "Is that okay?" He gestured to the radio.

"It's fine. Reminds me of home."

"You're not homesick, are you?"

"No! I'm having a great time." Though I did feel a pang when that song came on. I wondered how Ma was doing, whether Gerard had shown up yet and owned up to what he did, whether Whitney was still dating Max. It suddenly occurred to me that I did have a life. When I was back home I often thought that I had nothing and no one. But now that I was in this little country, I felt a bit naked and unsure. And what was the word that Drew used? Isolated. Everything was so unfamiliar. I didn't quite miss home yet, but I was sure that I would soon.

We had to drive through the capital to get to Drew's house, and I pulled out my digital camera expectantly. Roseau was not spectacular, but it sure was bustling. Traffic clogged the tiny, crumbling streets. There were little, colorful wooden houses along the main thoroughfares with a few shops spliced in. We drove past a KFC and simultaneously burst out laughing. The colonel just looked so out of place in this quaint little city. The people seemed unhurried as they ran errands or walked to work in the hot morning sun. Street vendors sold bags, slippers, bras, and snacks on the sidewalk.

More than twice, Drew stopped to talk to people he knew.

"So, what's this about you becoming the Minister of Education?"

He shrugged. "That's just gossip," he said. "One person said it and now it's going around. I'm not ready for politics."

But I wasn't convinced. It sounded serious when yet another person stopped us and asked him whether he was going to accept the position.

"Vanessa has you on track to be the prime minister someday, and everybody else thinks you're going to be education minister. Am I missing something?"

He only looked at me and laughed.

What would that mean for us? For me? Could this ever go anywhere? This guy was so tied to this place, and I didn't see how in the world I could live here. I had yet to see a sin gle Gap, Banana Republic, or Ann Taylor. How would I survive? Did the stores here carry Häagen-Dazs? Since there was no winter, did that mean I'd never get to wear my knee-high leather boots ever again?

His hand went to my leg as we drove away from Roseau. "What are you thinking about?"

"I guess, just that you seem so much a part of this place. Everyone knows you."

"That can happen when there are barely thirty thousand people in an entire metropolitan area. And they know my father—not me. They miss him; we haven't had a truly great leader since he died." Drew paused. "They think I'm their great hope."

We drove past the high school, Dominica Grammar School, where Drew attended high school. "Maybe we'll go in tomorrow," he said.

It was a huge school, and I could see a few students playing basketball on a court in the front. They were wearing uniforms, the girls as well as the boys. They looked so well behaved. I had already built an image of these Dominican students in my mind, based solely on my Harry Potter knowledge of English schools. I expected the kids would be witty, well disciplined, and formal. I couldn't wait to meet them.

We drove through Bath Estate, a community of small and midsize houses bordered by a huge mountain. I snapped a few pictures.

"This used to be a huge lime plantation," Drew said. "Way, way back when my parents were kids."

I snapped more pics as I saw a barefoot girl walking two goats down the street.

"God, you live really far away!" I said after we had passed Bath Estate.

"We're almost there," he said.

I just wanted us to get out of the truck and really be with

each other. Ten minutes later, we were in the country again. I could hear a river flowing nearby over the engine of the truck. Tall, majestic trees leaned over the road on one side and a rocky cliff bounded it on the other. The sun was somewhere high in the sky, but I couldn't see it through the trees; the air felt pleasantly cool. We had to be nearing his place. This was exactly how he had described it. We turned up a dirt road, passed one other house high up with its own private road, and then stopped outside a white house.

"This is it," he said as he put the car into park.

He grabbed my bag and I followed him up the stairs onto the tiled porch. A huge German shepherd bounded out from nowhere. That was Sonny. I'd heard of him but didn't expect him to be so big. His nose went straight to my crotch. I yelped.

"Sonny!" Drew grabbed the dog by its collar. "Sorry, he's one of those negroes who just doesn't believe in small talk first."

I had to laugh. I patted the dog on its head and it licked my hands enthusiastically. I wasn't a big dog fan, but Sonny seemed friendly. As long as he kept his nose out of my business, then we should get along fine.

The house was cozy, very much Drew. There were hundreds of books on bookshelves, on the floor, and on the coffee table. The furniture was simple and tasteful. It looked to me a scaled-down version of Vanessa's style. The furniture was upholstered in blue chambray; mahogany bookshelves lined the living room. There was a huge stereo system and a plasma television system. He had satellite. "For sports," he'd said.

He looked a bit sheepish as I surveyed the place. When he'd said the place was small, peaceful, and in an isolated area, I'd truly expected some little log cabin out in the middle of nowhere. Instead, this was a nice house with every comfort. He took me out to the back where I could see a mountain looming in the distance, a thicket of trees a few dozen feet away, and the roar of some river in the background.

"Is the river near here?" I asked.

"Kind of. But that's not what you hear. That's a waterfall."

My eyes opened wide. "Really? There's a waterfall near here?"

"Just a short walk away."

"Can we go see it?"

"Can we eat first? I'm starving."

I realized, too, that I was hungry. It seemed like forever since I'd had that croissant and coffee on Vanessa's porch. All I'd had since was about half a gallon of water.

"I made us something earlier, but I'm going to have to warm it up."

Whatever it was, it smelled good. It was some kind of fish and vegetable dish and I was growing hungrier by the second.

I tried not to shove the food into my mouth once we sat down to eat, but I was ravenous, and the food was delicious.

"Wow. You are a great cook!"

"Thanks. I can't wait to see what you can do."

I'd show him all right, though it probably wouldn't be as healthy as this.

We ate on the back patio, looking out at the forest of trees in his backyard. A hammock swung from a beautiful jacaranda, the one he'd described in his e-mails. I could hear all kinds of birds chirping. I saw a few blue jays mucking about and grabbed my camera.

"You don't have to do that so often," he said.

I was embarrassed. "Why? Does it bother you?"

"Not really. When you take all these pictures it looks as if you don't ever plan to be here again."

I thought this over as I sipped passion fruit juice, which would be my new favorite drink.

"I want to have memories. And I promised my friends I'd bring back a lot of pictures."

"I see," he said.

"Do you mind if I take a shower after we're finished eating? I'm really hot and sticky." I'd brought a change of clothes in my canvas tote. Just in case.

He nodded, then we began to clean up the dishes. "You don't have a dishwasher?"

"Nah, don't need one. The electricity up here can be really sporadic, so it's just not worth it."

"So the lights go out all the time?" I didn't like the idea of being out here in the woods in the dark. On the way here I'd only seen one house that could be described as belonging to a neighbor.

"I have a generator, but I hardly ever use it. I'm used to the unpredictability."

"Are you thinking that I'm incredibly spoiled?"

"Not at all. I think it's kinda cute," he said as we stood over the sink.

I looked at him and smiled. And then I kissed him. He pulled back a bit. "Hey, I wanted that to be my move."

"Sorry, I beat you to it." I kissed him again; I didn't even feel self-conscious about it. Everything just felt so right; me being here with him, kissing him.

He put his arm around me and I felt so, so held. I mean, he was a big guy and that was a good thing for me; I felt truly enveloped in him. We kissed deeply, passionately, and he ground his body against mine. I swooned as his hands traveled the length of my body. Before I knew it I was following him to what I guessed was the bedroom.

Oh my God! I don't think that my mother would approve of what I was doing. Vanessa probably wouldn't either. But he was peeling off my dress and soon I was under him on the big, king-size bed in the middle of the room. I opened my eyes just a bit to look around me. My eyes made contact with a white fan, circling. It was too late to suddenly become a good girl.

I moaned as his mouth went around one of my nipples. His hands traveled downward. Who was I? What was my name again? I felt so inexperienced as he undressed himself. I guess I should have done that? But I wasn't too sure. Maybe it wasn't too late to warn him that I didn't know what in the heck I was doing because it had been so long. But his mouth was on my nipple again and I went off to la-la land.

It didn't last long. I heard a noise. A loud bang. I think I must have screamed.

"You okay?" he asked, concerned.

"What was that?" I pulled away from him, looking around the room.

"That's the housekeeper's car. Her engine backfires sometimes."

"Housekeeper?"

"Uh-huh."

"She's here now?"

He nodded and kissed my forehead, my lips. "We were just getting to the good part, Amelia."

I was a little distressed by the inelegance of the housekeeper's entrance. "So, there's someone else in the house now?"

"Is that a problem?"

"It's . . . I don't know if I can . . ."

"She's not going to come in here," he said.

"You didn't tell me you had a housekeeper."

"She only comes a few times a month. I forgot to tell her not to come this week."

I sat up in the bed. The mood was gone. It had backfired with the housekeeper's car engine.

He sighed.

"I'm sorry. I just can't do it with her out there."

Drew seemed largely unfazed. He lay next to me, playing with my hair. "It's okay. We have all week."

I lay back on the bed and tried to relax. The air conditioner was really kicking in and I felt chilly. I snuggled up to him. His body felt hard and warm against my softness. I realized then that not once in the last half hour or so had I thought of being fat. I did not even remember to feel self-conscious about my stomach or my thighs or my butt. And that had felt good. I wanted to stay in this nonfat mental place forever.

We did not see the rest of the island that afternoon. Instead, I begged him to take me to see the waterfall.

"You realize that you might have to actually see the housekeeper once you leave this room," he joked.

The woman was pleasant, but cool. She shook my hand limply when Drew introduced us.

"She works for my mother," Drew said apologetically. "Her son does landscaping up at the house."

Of course, I thought. All things lead back to Vanessa.

We trudged through thick grass and prickly bushes, and I could hear the waterfall crashing down closer and closer with each step. I so wanted to see it. Then his cell phone rang.

I didn't like the expression on his face. "Mom, why didn't you tell me this earlier?"

He looked at me, an apology already in his eyes. What was Vanessa up to now?

"What's wrong?" I asked when he switched off the phone.

"Nothing," he shrugged. "Looks like Mom's got more people for you to meet."

"Drew!" I couldn't stop myself from groaning. "I thought we were going to be together this week."

"We are," he said. "We will be. We're just going to have

to go to her party tonight. That's all. We don't have to stay long."

"So do we have to leave now?"

"We probably should. We'll need to get ready . . ."

So, no waterfall. I was so disappointed. Grrrrr! Vanessa!

"Can't we just ditch her party?" I laughed, but I was only half kidding.

"We could. But she tends to hold grudges over that sort of thing. We don't have to stay long," he said again.

Fine. Fine. Fine. I'll go off to another party and be the charming American.

As I showered in Drew's bathroom I thought of how close we had come to doing the deed. There had been enough electricity in that room to light up Texas. Yeah, chemistry would definitely not be a problem. Yes! I thought. This trip was not a wash. Now if only I could get Vanessa to just leave us alone for the rest of the week.

"You might end up having a great time," Drew said as we climbed back into the Range Rover a few minutes later.

"I'm sure I will," I lied as I looked back at the housekeeper peering at us from the front window.

Chapter 15

Sweating was something I was only lately getting accustomed to. And here I was doing it in front of the man I was trying so hard to impress. But I couldn't help it. On Dominica, the heat was constant and relentless. Once outside, there was no escaping it.

Thank God for spin class, at least I'd developed a passable level of fitness. Six months ago, I would have keeled over after a half hour of walking up this steep mountain.

"You all right?" Drew looked concerned. "If you want we can stop to rest."

I nodded. Yeah. I needed to just catch my breath and have some water.

I felt the warm, tawny earth on my behind, not caring that my khaki shorts would probably be stained. I was so wiped out. Drew hadn't even broken a sweat yet. He was up before dawn every day for long, punishing runs on hilly trails behind the house. I felt horribly out of shape next to him and I worried that he might think I was some kind of slug. Well, I was a slug, but I was working on not being one! He sat next to me and leaned back on his elbows, his knees up to the sky.

"Maybe we should head back down if the climb's too

much for you." I thought I caught a sliver of disappointment on his face.

"I'll be fine," I said. I took a deep breath and I was beginning to feel better. My heart had stopped pounding and my vision had cleared. Wow, I thought. Had I been on the verge of a heart attack? "I'm sorry I'm not very athletic."

He shrugged. "You're fine. Stop apologizing."

I scrutinized his face. Was the fact that I was always apologizing irritating? Would it irritate him further if I even asked that question?

"I think you're sexy when you're all tired and helpless like this." He turned to me on one elbow.

I grinned. "At this point you can go ahead and have your way with me because there's no way I could fight you off."

"Is that right?" He leaned in to me and kissed me hard on the lips.

I grabbed the waistband of his shorts and pulled him closer, and we began to go at it again under the bright, blue sky in front of God and nature. I hoped there were no other hikers in the vicinity else they'd certainly get an eyeful, and judging from the way I was finding that I couldn't control myself, an earful, too.

Then we heard voices. Children laughing. "Oh my God!" I pulled up my shorts and searched for my bra in the grass.

Drew swore.

The voices drew nearer and I struggled to put my clothes back on.

I stood up quickly, the same moment that a kid, about 12, came walking up to us.

"Hi," I said, smiling innocently. Drew stood up, cool as a cucumber, taking a swig of water from a bottle.

"Hello, Mr. Anderson," the kid said.

The kid knew him?

"How are you, Marcus?" Drew gave the kid his I'm-future-prime minister smile.

"I'm well," the kid said. And soon an army of 12-year-olds were on us, led by an attractive young sister.

"Drew! Long time no see!" she squealed.

They embraced and he turned to introduce me. Her name was Daphne, Miss Daphne he called her, because I guess that's what everyone, including the kids, called her.

"We're doing our nature hike today," she said in her sing-songy accent. "We don't have time to stop and chat, though, Amelia. Come on, children!" She clapped her hands and a dozen boys came running.

"Maybe we'll see you at the top of the mountain?" She gathered the kids and trudged off, not looking tired at all. I felt like a fat slug.

"That was close," Drew said.

"That would have been really embarrassing," I said.

This was the third time we'd been rudely interrupted this way. First it was the housekeeper. Then the night before at Vanessa's party, we'd tried to escape to my room. Vanessa came knocking on the door two minutes later. She had yet another friend who wanted to meet me. I was beginning to think that we were under some kind of forced abstinence curse. It was highly frustrating.

I followed Drew up to the top of the mountain and I felt my lungs heaving and straining. Would I die? Would Grace Wilson have to come down to this little island to claim my body? I could just imagine her reaction: Amelia went hiking and then she died? Amelia went hiking? Hiking?

"We're almost there," Drew said, grabbing my hand as I stumbled over a rock. Sweat was pouring down my back and between my legs. It wasn't even very hot this high up, but the effort made me feel like this was spin class on steroids. "You'll get used to the climbing after a while," he said. Then he stopped. "That is, if you decide to come back."

"Oh, I'll definitely be back," I said. Though probably not to this mountain.

"Here we are," Drew said fifteen arduous minutes later.

I looked around, and yes, we were at the top of Morne Trois Pitons. I could see the two other peaks in the near distance. I was up three thousand, three hundred and forty-two feet into the sky. I could see Daphne and her students eating lunch a few hundred feet away. The area was otherwise deserted except for some mournful-sounding birds. It was almost two P.M. Where had the day gone?

"This is spectacular," I said, snapping pictures of the marvelous view from atop the mountains. I could see green, plenty of green. We'd passed waterfalls and hot springs on the way up and all kinds of strange-looking plants and trees, some of which I thought were alive.

"Actually, we'd have to climb about another thousand feet to truly get to the top, but it's a rough climb. I think you've had enough." He took the camera from my hand. We sat at the base of a big, shady tree and ate our unglamorous lunch of trail mix, water, and peanut butter and jelly sandwiches.

"I still want to see the boiling lake," I said, knowing that I was way too tired to even attempt that.

"Maybe when you come back," Drew said. "That's an even rougher hike. A lot of climbing and crawling involved."

Climbing and crawling? "I'll cook dinner for us tonight," I said. That was something that I could do without fearing for life and limb.

Daphne and her students had begun to climb again. "They're going to the very top?"

"Looks like it," Drew said. "Daphne does this all the time, though. She's an athlete."

Wow, I thought, enviously. She didn't even look tired. The kids followed after, laughing and joking and she played right along with them. I really needed to get myself in shape; a bunch of 12-year-olds had just kicked my behind!

* * *

Later that evening I was making tarragon chicken, when Drew asked whether I would mind Vanessa coming over for dinner. "Here?" I asked. No! No way! I was just about to light some candles! No way!

He'd just come in from taking the dog for its run, and he was all sweaty. How did he have the energy to run after all the hiking we'd done today? I wanted to rip off his sweaty T-shirt. "Yeah, she's probably lonely up there all by herself," he said.

This was maddening! Tonight was supposed to be The Night. On the long drive home from Morne Trois Pitons, or the mountain with three peaks, I'd devised a plan. Cook him a nice dinner and then let nature take its course. So far, it had worked out well. I'd showered and put on my flowery, flirty Tracy Reese dress. I was chopping vegetables and letting my imagination run wild, getting used to the idea of just the two of us in this house, in the world really, and he wanted to bring his mother here? Tonight? I wanted to scream No! Instead, I said, "Sure, that would be nice." Aaaargh!

She was there within the hour, riding in on a cloud of Chanel No. 5. "Oh, that smells marvelous," she said. "You must really know your way around a kitchen, Amelia."

Grrrrr . . .

I sat across from Drew, and she sat next to him. She talked a lot, mostly about island politics. Apparently, the prospect of Drew joining the prime minister's cabinet was not as far-fetched as he'd made it sound. Matter of fact, Vanessa sounded as if it were a done deal. "So, you see, Amelia, he's going to do really important things for his country. It's too bad more young people like him don't come back home instead of making America and England even richer than they already are."

I nodded. I liked Vanessa, I kept telling myself. She was a hip, pretty, loving mom. One I'd wish for myself. But she needed to leave us alone!

She continued her speech about responsibility and giving

back to the community. I dug at the chicken, which was pretty good if I did say so myself. I wanted to be alone with Drew. I had cooked this meal, wanting him to compliment me on it. Hoping we'd wash dishes together after we were finished and then go straight to bed and have roof-raising sex. The waiting was killing me and it looked like it wasn't over. She was spoiling it. *Go away, Vanessa. Go back home to your lovely Barbie mansion and play with your makeup or something.*

The night seemed to drag on as Vanessa made endless small talk. I told her about hiking, leaving out the parts where I was panting for breath and near death, and running into the grammar school students. She gushed about all she'd done to make the school what it is today. At that point I stretched my foot under the table hoping to play footsie with Drew but what I felt was the pointy end of a pump that was promptly pulled back. Her eyes registered surprise.

"Oh, sorry," I said. "I was just stretching my legs."

She didn't look convinced. She cleared her throat and stood up. "Let me help you put those away," she said of the dishes.

"Oh, no, that's fine. Drew and I will do it." I couldn't imagine her ruining her delicate French manicure by doing dishes. I'm sure she didn't expect him to take her up on the offer, however.

When I said Drew and I, her left eyebrow rose and her eyes clouded over with some sort of veiled warning. I made a mental note: Never refer to yourself and Drew as if you were a couple. Vanessa obviously was not ready for that.

"Yeah, we'll do it, Mom," he said. "Besides, you should get going before it gets too dark."

She looked at me and laughed. "He's always worrying about me, Amelia." Then to him: "Drew, I can take care of myself. Sam is a perfectly good driver."

"Mom, he's ninety years old."

Vanessa giggled. "See how he worries about me?"

Oh, give me a break, I thought, as I rolled my eyes on the inside but smiled at her dutifully.

"So, you're staying here tonight?" she asked.

"Yes, I am," I said, trying my best to sound confident though my insides were churning. I could just see the wheels turning in her head and I waited for the lecture. Instead, she said, "Well, I'll see you tomorrow then."

I breathed a sigh of relief as I watched her get into her car with her octogenarian driver. When she left, we stood at the sink, our favorite place in the whole house, I was starting to think.

"You and your mom are really close." I was trying to be tactful.

He shrugged. "I'm the youngest, the only one who doesn't have his own family and kids, so she still treats me like a baby."

"And you like it," I said, only half teasing him.

"Sometimes," he said.

I looked at him to see if he was joking, but he didn't seem to be.

"What about you and your mom? Talked to her lately?"

"Not really. I want this week to be a real vacation . . . no contact with the civilized world."

He furrowed his eyebrows. "Civilized world?"

Oh, shoot. I'd said something wrong. "You know what I mean, Drew." I elbowed his side to make sure he knew that it was just a slip of the tongue.

"It wouldn't be a good idea to keep making jokes like that."

"I didn't mean anything by it."

"I know that. But think before you say something like that next time. It's really offensive to people here when Americans think of our country as uncivilized."

I felt like an idiot. How did I let that slip out? "I'm sorry. I feel, like, terrible."

He shrugged. "Don't worry about it."

I opened my mouth to say something but then the doorbell rang. It was almost ten P.M. "Who could that be?"

He went to the door, and I heard voices negotiating. I tried to get as close to the conversation as I could; all I could hear was some woman profusely thanking him and a child's voice laughing. What was going on? I backtracked into the kitchen as I heard him close the front door. He walked into the kitchen carrying a toddler, a boy, of about 7 on his back.

"Amelia, this is Jimmy, my favorite neighbor."

"Hi, Jimmy," I said in my friendliest voice. The kid eyed me suspiciously and didn't say hi back. How does one interact with a 7-year-old? I wasn't too sure. I like babies, tiny ones, but once they got to the toddler stage it was a different story.

"May I have something to drink?" Jimmy asked, looking at me.

"Say please, Jimmy," Drew said, and Jimmy obeyed. I hopped to the fridge to get Jimmy some juice.

"Trudy got called into the hospital and Darren's gone to St. Lucia for the whole week so they're strapped. His sitter's sick."

Trudy and Darren were Drew's neighbors; they lived about a half mile down the road. I'd never met them, though I'd heard a lot about them. They were both medical doctors, who seemed to be gone a lot.

"So, he's staying here tonight?" I asked, proffering my best I'm-accommodating smile.

"He sure is," Drew said, setting Jimmy down on the floor. He held out a hand in my direction. Oh, right. The juice.

"You don't mind, do you?"

"Me? No, of course I don't mind. I love kids." I do. I really do.

"Good, he should be asleep within the hour."

But Jimmy seemed to develop a raging case of insomnia, and he kept us up until three A.M. After the 300th game of hide-and-seek I surrendered. "I'm going to bed," I yawned.

Drew yawned, too. "I'll be there in a second. He's about to nod off."

I looked at little Jimmy as he watched cartoons wide-eyed and attentively. It was a minute past three in the morning. This kid was diabolical! Why couldn't we have just been firm and told him that it was way past his bedtime and that he needed to go to sleep so we could have sex?

"Night, Jimmy," I said. He didn't look away from the television, nor did he acknowledge that I'd just spoken. Stuck-up little brat!

I kissed Drew on the forehead.

"I'll be there in a few minutes," he said.

A few minutes later I was out cold.

Chapter 16

He was already a star politician; it was in the way he talked and that genial familiarity he had with everyone. He loved people and they loved him. All the tourist guides knew him. They came up to shake his hand as if he were some kind of celebrity. Like he was their great hope. Their Bill Clinton. I felt as if I were intruding. Everywhere we went, they called out to him and he waved to them from his truck as if he were royalty. When I commented on it, he shrugged it off. "People here are just like that."

Yeah, whatever. *They're in love with you,* I thought. The people always gave me a sideways look and then smiled dismissively, like I didn't matter. Like I might as well disappear standing next to him.

"Drew! Drew!" A middle-aged man called out from the sidewalk. He was among four older men sitting at a rickety table outside a storefront, playing dominoes and smoking cigars. I wished I knew how to paint. That scene was just so quaint.

"Ninian, man, what you up to, fella?" Drew broke into his deepest Dominican accent, the one he used when he talked to "his people," the one that made me feel left out and out of place. Why can't I be less selfish? Why does this even bother me?

"Man, I waitin' for you to make your move. Bring some jobs down here for us, man!"

"I hear you, man," Drew laughed.

"These guys are crazy," he said as he accelerated.

I paged through a brochure that identified all the marine life we would be seeing on this diving trip. Actually, Drew would be diving; I would be snorkeling. I was really excited because, of course, I'd never done anything like this. I'd slept late into the morning, missing a chance to say good-bye to sleepless Jimmy. "He said you were pretty," Drew said as we ate breakfast together. Somehow I didn't believe that sleepless Jimmy would have said that about me. I hoped I'd never have to see that kid again.

"Seems like people are pinning their hopes on you."

"You think so?"

"Hell, yeah. It's great. I think you'd make a great leader. Plus, you don't really have a choice; Vanessa would kill you if you didn't take the job."

He laughed. "My mother likes you, you know."

"She does?"

"She really does."

Then why won't she leave us alone? "Okay. I like her too."

"She's used to me always being there for her. I think she's a little jealous you're taking up some of my time."

"I'm only here for a week. She'll have you back and all to herself in two days."

"Are you being sarcastic?"

"No." Was I?

"Okay. You're going to love Castle Comfort," he said. "I've been diving up here for years, and each time I go down I see something new. I just wish you could come down with me."

"Maybe some day I'll get certified . . ." I really didn't mean that. There was no way I was going deep down into the ocean to see some fish. What if I got swallowed by a whale? Like Jonah. Or bit by a shark? I could just imagine my mother's reaction: Who do you think you are going scuba diving? You deserve to get your butt bit by a shark.

Ten minutes later, we'd gone our separate ways, though we were in the same body of water. But I didn't dwell too long on the fact that Drew had left me. I was so entranced by what I saw. I was being timid as usual, preferring to stay only about seven feet down. Soon I began to recognize the marine life from the slide brochure and I forgot all about Drew. I identified two types of crab: rough box crab and ocellate swimming crab. Then there were the scary Southern stingray and Viper Moray, the ominous and gray-spotted sharptail eel, and an orange octopus. When I saw the beautiful angel fish with a blue halo around its yellow body I thought I was hallucinating. The blue light reflected around the fish's body was so spectacularly unreal, like brushstrokes in a modern art painting.

A huge school of soldier fish swam by, making me jump. I didn't want to come up. I forgot how uncomfortable, how fat I'd felt, as I'd stood next to that European tourist in the bikini, who was now only a couple of inches from me snapping pictures. Oh, shoot! I'd left my camera in the car. No one would believe that I'd gone snorkeling. No one! But there I was. Doing it all by myself. This was too much fun.

Drew was waiting for me when I came up. "You finally decided to come up?"

"I saw all these fish!" I told him all the ones I could identify and remember.

"You're not going to remember all those names two hours from now."

"I will! I wish I'd done this sooner. I wanna go down again!"

"You could always come back. Dominica's not going anywhere."

"What are we doing next?"

"Lunch? I know a really cool place. It's not fancy, though."

As long as Vanessa's not there, then it's perfect, I thought.

Gravel and sand crunched under our feet as we walked over to a small shack with a blue wooden sign that said CLARA'S. There was smoke pouring out the back, and I could smell barbecue something or the other. I was ravenous.

"Miss Clara!" Drew made a loud entrance into the tiny place, which was basically four rickety tables under a corrugated iron roof with a door leading to what I guessed was a kitchen in the back. The only other person in the restaurant was a young, bored-looking pregnant girl. She couldn't have been more than 16.

"How are you, Melody?" Drew asked her. Did he know everyone?

"I'm fine, Mr. Anderson," she said, sounding weary.

"You're almost there," he said, looking at her belly.

She touched her bump. "Two more weeks. I can't wait."

"Then you're going back to school next term, right?"

"Yes, Mr. Anderson. I'm going back," she said.

A massive woman came in from the back room, with a wide smile on her pretty face. She had to be Melody's mother.

"Eh!" she exclaimed. "Boy, where you been? So long I waitin' to meet your friend!"

She looked at me and I couldn't help but mirror her smile. "Hello," I said.

"Hello, Amelia." She came up to me and took my hand in both of hers. "I heard a lot about you. This boy here trying to keep you all to hisself."

I didn't know what to say.

"What you got to eat?" Drew asked.

"That's all he cares about," Miss Clara said. "Food. I don't know where it all goes, though." She shrugged and disappeared into the kitchen.

"Are you all related?" I asked him.

"Nah, she used to cook for my folks back when my dad was alive."

A few minutes later, we sat at one of those rickety tables with huge plates of steaming barbecue chicken, fried plantains, and rice and beans. Oh, it was so delicious!

"Eat up. Eat up," Clara said, patting me on the shoulder. "You American women are so crazy with your diets and whatnot."

If only she knew. But I ate until I couldn't eat any more, which surprisingly, was less than the usual amount. I was actually leaving food on my plate. Had my stomach shrunk in the last few days? I watched Drew enviously as he dug into his food. I was too full for dessert.

"So you're leaving us already?" Miss Clara brought out two slices of black cake.

"Yes, I go back to school next week," I said.

"My daughter wants to be a teacher, too," Clara said, gesturing to Melody who was talking on a cell phone, watching a small black-and-white television, and rubbing her belly at the same time. "I don't know how she's going to do it in her situation. But God is good."

"She can do it. She will do it," Drew said quickly. "Melody is smart. One mistake is not going to change that."

Miss Clara smiled. "See, that's why I like to keep this boy around me. If it wasn't for him I would have killed that girl when she came home with that belly. . . ."

Drew looked at me apologetically. But it was okay. I was enjoying this: Great food, an optimistic mother who still believed in her pregnant teenage daughter.

An hour later, we piled into the Range Rover, and I waved good-bye to Miss Clara. "Make sure you come back, Amelia!"

"I will!" I yelled back. "Thanks for lunch!"

The house was sparkling clean when we got back that evening. Even Sonny, who preferred to spend his days rolling in dirt and chasing any stinky creature he could find, looked clean and happy. My clothes, which I had left askew in Drew's room that morning, were hung up neatly in his closet.

"The housekeeper was here," I said.

"Uh-huh," he said, turning on the TV. There was a huge soccer match that he'd warned me he would be watching.

"I thought you said she only came a couple times a month."

"She does. She's probably just curious about you."

"So she came back an extra day?"

He shrugged. "It happens. She'll have something to gossip about. What's the big deal?"

What's the big deal? Would she be gossiping about the fact that I leave my stuff lying around? That my panty size is L7?

"Drew, you're so laid back about this."

"Okay. How should I react? Fire her for doing her job?"

"She's . . . she's intruding . . ." I realized that I was starting to sound like a whining witch. So I stopped. "You're right. It's just that I'm not used to all this attention. Everywhere we go people stop to say hello. They know about me even before I've met them."

He stretched out his arms across the top of the couch, and I sat next to him. "I told you, Amelia. This is a small place. You can't really hide much here."

"So much for my little fantasy of us being marooned all alone on a tiny deserted island."

"I can arrange that," he said, pulling me closer to him. "There's another island not too far away from this one. It's completely deserted . . . but I hear there are really big snakes there."

I elbowed him. "You can have that one all to yourself."

"I can't believe tomorrow's my last day here," I complained. It had all gone by so fast, yet I felt that I'd been in this safe, comfortable place with Drew forever. I could even allow myself not to care that he was ignoring me for Australia vs. Nigeria. I lay against him, exhausted but happy. So much had happened over the week. I'd climbed mountains, swam in the ocean, snorkeled, met so many interesting people, and been lulled to sleep by the sounds of a waterfall. This had been probably the most magical week of my entire life.

I woke up at four A.M. My head was in Drew's lap, he was snoring, and the TV was on. I looked around for a few moments, confused. I could already hear at least one bird chirping. The sun would start peeking from the mountaintops pretty soon. I'd make him a big breakfast, and hopefully we could go bathe under the waterfall after he took the dog out for its run. I'd just nap for a few more minutes.

I woke up again to the phone ringing; the sun was shining brightly through the windows. What time was it?

"Hey, Mom," Drew mumbled sleepily into the phone. It was seven-thirty.

Drew handed me the phone and closed his eyes. "Hello?"

Vanessa sounded perky. "Hi, Amelia. Since it's your last day here, I wanted to do something special. A friend of mine, an American expat, has a great place out in Portsmouth. I was thinking we could all go out there for the day. The beaches there are just marvelous."

Drew was barely awake; his eyes were closed. But I could tell that he knew what Vanessa had asked me. Did I have permission to say no? I poked him in the ribs. "Drew, do we have to go to this place?" I whispered, my hand over the receiver.

He shrugged and opened his eyes. "Do you want to go?"

A more appropriate question would have been did I want to say no to Vanessa. I didn't.

"Wonderful!" she sang. "Why don't you and Drew meet us here in a couple of hours?"

I poked him again. "We're going to Portsmouth."

He groaned and pulled me toward him, but I pulled back.

"Why didn't you tell her that we wanted the day to ourselves?"

"I didn't know if you'd want to go," he said.

It sounded like a lame excuse to me. I disengaged from him and reluctantly went to get ready for another day with Vanessa.

Her friend turned out to be another version of her, only male. He was a professor at Ross University Medical School with a flamboyant manner that made me wonder whether he was gay. I didn't dare ask anyone. His home was far from humble; it was almost as large as Vanessa's and very overdone. But I liked him; he reminded me of my dentist, a beautiful man who loved to tell stories and be the center of attention. Drew was very formal with him, dropping his easygoing manner, and that made me suspect even more that Guy was gay.

Vanessa had filled the two-hour drive to Portsmouth with oodles of inane conversation that I'd tuned out after a while. Stella, her daughter, would meet us for dinner, and that turned out to be a fun thing. Stella was hugely funny when her kids were not around. "I warned you your hair would just frizz up in this weather," she laughed when she met us that evening at Guy's house. "I don't even try with mine," she said. "I just let it go wild, like a burning bush." She ran her hand through her massive head of hair that she wore in two-strand twists.

I have to get rid of my perm!

I chatted with her as Drew talked with another older man at the dinner table, who seemed to be giving him political advice. We'd had hardly a minute alone the whole day and I missed him desperately. Once we'd gotten to Guy's place, it was lunchtime. He then took us on a tour of Portsmouth and the medical school, which attracted students from all over the world it seemed. Then it was back to Guy's place for dinner. Before I knew it, I was packing in my room at Vanessa's house.

Drew knocked, then walked in smiling sheepishly. "You're mad, aren't you?"

"Nope," I said. I was disappointed that we didn't spend the day alone, but I was not angry about it. Portsmouth had been interesting; it was nothing like Roseau. The university gave the city an even more laid-back feel, and the international students made it as cosmopolitan a city as could exist on Dominica.

He sat on the bed. "I can't believe you're leaving already."

"The week did fly by."

"We'll have to do it again soon."

"That could get expensive."

"You don't have to worry about that."

I wanted to find the right words to say, but they would not come. What had happened this week between us? We'd made a connection, but could it go anywhere with all those miles between us?

"I wish you could stay here tonight," I said.

"My mother wouldn't . . ."

"I know."

"I'll see you in the morning," he said, holding me tightly.

I couldn't sleep that night; I only felt relieved when traces of sunlight peeked into my room. Vanessa was aflutter as usual, making sure that I did not forget anything.

"Amelia, I hope we see you again very soon," she said as Drew piled my stuff into his truck. I thanked her for her lovely hospitality and allowed her to squeeze me to her. "Make sure you come back," she said again.

"I will," I told her.

On the way to the airport we did not say much. "I wish we'd slept together last night," he said and took my hand.

"Me too."

"I think I'll miss that most," he said. "Being next to you."

The main road to the Melville Hall airport was deserted this early in the morning, and several times we stopped to let some goats cross or we had to drive around a recalcitrant cow who'd decided to park itself in the middle of the road. I'd miss this place. And, yes, I'd miss being next to Drew, too.

"I'll come visit you," he said after a long silence. "That'll make us even."

Was he afraid as I was that this was doomed?

The last thing he said to me before I boarded the plane was, "We'll find a way to make it work. I promise."

I wanted to believe him.

I believed him.

I did.

Chapter 17

On the flight back, I tried to look forward to my life as I'd known it: I'd return to school the next day and face Treyon and his friends, who were probably thinking up new ways to torment me. I wondered what trouble Ma and Gerard had stirred up. Had Whitney joined Al Qaeda or the Taliban without me around to keep her in check?

My vacation glow began to dissipate in the immigration line at Logan Airport as I waited behind a couple of girls who had boarded the plane with me in Puerto Rico. They were teenyboppers, with freshly braided blond hair. They were snapping gum and gossiping about their spring break and who had been with whom. Ugh! How could I possibly face my students tomorrow? I needed another week just to reacclimate to being in America.

It was cold. Freezing. We must have had a snowstorm while I was gone because there were huge piles of snow plowed off to the sides of the road. The cab driver was in a foul mood, and I was relieved because I did not feel like talking.

Thankfully, James and Kelly's VW was not outside the house. My mood had dipped so low that I wasn't sure that I wouldn't snap at them. I missed Drew. I missed being in his house. The sound of the waterfall. The green of the trees and the brightness of the flowers. Even Vanessa, with her dignified, meddling kindness. When could I go back to Dominica?

The house was dark and I went straight to my room, ignoring the pile of mail in the foyer. Before I could pick it up to dial, the phone rang.

"Amelia." It was him.

"Hey, I just walked in."

"I figured. I timed you. I miss you already."

I sat on the bed and pressed the phone to my ear.

"I wish I had stayed." I didn't care how impractical it sounded; it was the truth. So sue me. I was an emotional blathering idiot. But the last place I wanted to be was in this old, cold house.

"Sonny wishes you'd stayed, too. He misses sniffing you."

That made me laugh. We talked for a bit, mostly about my flight and Vanessa's over-the-top good-bye. I had gained something quickly only to lose it as quickly. And Drew could sense it.

"I'll see you soon, okay," he said.

"Soon?" We hadn't made any concrete plans, and that had plagued my thoughts during the seven-hour flight. He'd said we didn't have to make any promises until we'd both had a chance to "digest" what had happened. Things had obviously changed on his end.

"This morning I booked a flight. I'm coming to Boston in a month."

"You are?"

"Yup. I figured I could take care of some business and spend some time with you. Kill two birds with one stone."

I was tired, emotional, and badly in need of a hug or a Snickers bar, so I said, "Oh, God, Drew, I love you." The words hung in the air like a hawk waiting before it swooped to devour its prey.

There was silence on the other end. "I can't wait to see you," he said.

I bit my lip and clenched my fists. *Oh, Amelia, you've done it now.*

I made a quick excuse to hang up. Then I screamed loudly at the room.

Then a key turned in the door. Oh, no. They were home, and I was not in the mood to face anyone.

"Ames! Ames!" Kelly called out.

She knocked on my door and ran into my room, not waiting for me to even answer.

"Oh, look at you! You look all tan and slim. My goodness, what did you all do down there all week? How was it?"

I couldn't help laughing as I hugged her. I guess I did miss Kelly. James stood by the door smiling. "Did you guys hit it off?" he asked.

"Yeah, we did. I had a really great time."

"A great time? Tell me all about it," Kelly said, sitting on my bed and giving James a look that told him to get lost so us girls could talk.

I forgot about how tired I was and told Kelly about how Drew and I basically spent the whole week doing everything but having sex. Her eyes popped when I told her I'd climbed Morne Trois Pitons and that I'd gone snorkeling. It occurred to me that I'd stepped out of my usual boring repertoire and it felt good to talk about it, even about Vanessa. "Sounds like James's mom," Kelly said.

"She's a trip. But I miss her, too. Isn't that weird?"

"So what's gonna happen now, girlie?"

I shrugged. "He's coming to visit in a month, I think." I didn't tell her about my passionate outburst. I would take that to the grave with me.

"Wow. This could be serious, huh?"

"I think so. Is that bad?"

"No! Not at all. It's a good thing . . . If you move there, James and I will have someplace warm to visit every year."

"Right," I laughed. "We'll have to find some way to make it work or we're just going to have to end it when it becomes too big of a pain."

She looked at me, thinking. "Well, how did you like the people? The culture?"

I told her that it felt strange to be in a country full of black people but to still feel that I was an outsider. That I'd loved the people's politeness and kindness but was a bit put off by their assumptions that I was a rich American.

"So, would you move there if he asked you to?"

I knew that question was coming. And I had pondered it all week long, but I still didn't know the answer. "I don't know, Kelly. I had fun down there and it's all so perfect. Drew's perfect. His family is perfect, except for Vanessa. I could just see us having this perfectly happy life down there. But I don't know if I could leave my life behind. You know? My mom, Gerard, Whitney. Whitney! I need to call Whitney."

"You could always come and visit your family and friends anytime you want, Ames."

"I don't know. I have strong feelings for him, but I don't even know if they're real. Or if I'm just infatuated . . ."

"You'll find out in a couple weeks when the glow wears off."

"I guess I will."

"Oh, not to steal your moment in the sun, so to speak, but we have big news," she said, her face lighting up. "I'm pregnant!"

My hand went to my mouth. "Oh my God, Kelly. Congratulations! When, how far along?"

I immediately thought: What would happen to me? They would have to get their own place. We couldn't all live in this apartment, with a baby. So I'd have to find new roommates or get my own place. Oh, why now? Why did they have to go and get pregnant now?

"Kelly, that's so great," I said as she told me that she was only nine weeks along.

"And we're starting to house hunt," she said, searching my face.

"That's great," I said. "It'll be great to have this place all to myself," I joked.

But we both knew that I couldn't afford the rent on my own. Darn. This could have been great news. For someone else. Now I had huge decisions to make. The glow was fading quickly.

I fell asleep exhausted, feeling bad that I did not call Whitney, but I just did not have the energy. Luckily, I had prepared my lesson plan on the plane. My eyes closed as soon as I hit the pillow.

The next day, the sky looked ominous and it began to rain as soon as I pulled into the school's parking lot. I hadn't even brought an umbrella. Sheesh! What a nice welcome back, I thought as I raced from my car to the building. I could feel my hair flatten with each raindrop that landed on my head. I would look a mess. An absolute mess!

My first period was boisterous and I sat back and let the students go crazy for a good fifteen minutes. I just sat there and looked at them, screaming at one another, throwing things, dozing, eating, bopping their heads to some inaudible hip-hop beat. It didn't really bother me. They'd settle down sooner or later; I wasn't going to hurry them along. I was hanging on to my glow for dear life; I wouldn't let them spoil it. But then the door to the classroom opened and Mr. Bell walked in with two official-looking people.

I straightened up immediately and tried to get the attention of the students who were oblivious that the principal had just walked in. The bedlam continued and I tried to smile at Mr. Bell. Sure, I'm in control here.

"Ms. Wilson," was all he said, reproachfully.

He said something to the two middle-aged white women, who were wearing suits and unflattering black pumps, and they walked out of the class but not before he looked back at me with a look of such sheer and utter disappointment that I almost cried. My vacation glow began to flicker again.

The day only got worse as Lashelle showed everyone her engagement ring. For someone who drove such a monstrous SUV, her boyfriend sure gave small diamonds. Someone told her that she was all "blinged up now." I thought, Ugh! But I congratulated her. I couldn't focus on Lashelle and her good news. I'd just been admonished by the principal for not taking control of my classroom. "This is not Meadow Academy," he reprimanded me. Yeah, no need to remind me of that, sir. But thanks.

The rain came down hard and heavy and splashed into my shoes as I walked to my Beetle at the end of the day. I had missed my car and I'd wanted to take it out for a long drive the day I returned home. My plan had been to drive down to Providence to Nordstrom after school, but the rain had ruined my plans.

I called Whitney as I waited for the engine to warm up and for the parking lot to clear up. She sounded down.

"What's wrong, babe?"

"Nothing. Tell me all about the trip. How was the sex?"

"That's the punch line, girl. There was none!" I told her about the week, not sparing any detail, but her response was cool. I was expecting screams and squeals. Whitney always said she would "go crazy" when I finally found a decent guy. But I was getting none of that from her.

"Okay, Whitney, tell me what's going on."

She sighed. "He's gone."

"Who's gone?"

"Max."

The terrorist? Well, I wasn't surprised. God help us all, though.

"What do you mean gone?"

"I mean, he's vanished. He's left school, his job at the lab. He's just gone." Poor Whitney, she was a magnet for the freaks who loved to hit and run, and this Max dude was no different.

"Maybe he's just out of town."

"No," she sounded exasperated. "I spoke with his boss at the lab. They think he's gone back to Tunisia. But they don't know why."

That was strange, but then again this was a guy who could talk about proteins for hours on end. "Maybe he had a family emergency. . . ."

"I don't think so, Amelia. He hates his parents. He's not close to any of his brothers or sisters."

I didn't have any ideas. "So what are you going to do?"

"I don't know. I guess I could try to get over it or try to find him."

"I think you should just forget it. Find someone new. He'll probably resurface in a month. He probably just needed a break or something."

"I don't think that's what it was. I have an idea, but I know you'll think I'm crazy."

Oh, no. "No, I'm not going to think you're crazy."

"Remember when I first met him you were worried that he could get in trouble for not reporting himself to Immigration?"

Surely, she did not think . . .

"I think the FBI or the CIA could have picked him up."

"What?"

"I'm serious, Amelia. I went to his place and all his clothes are still there. The only things missing are his laptop and his wallet."

"How did you get into his place? Never mind." I really didn't want to know.

"I think I'm going to make some calls."

"Some calls? To whom?"

"To the FBI!" Whitney said this as if I should have known. Well, silly me.

"Can you just call them up and say . . . And say what? What would you ask them?"

"I'll think of something," Whitney said, determination in her voice. I'd heard that tone before. And I was scared.

Chapter 18

I checked my e-mail in the teacher's lounge, relieved that I'd made it through yet another school day without killing nyone. I had one message from Vanessa, thanking me for ianking her for her hospitality, and another from Melody, Aiss Clara's pregnant daughter. Oh, how sweet, I thought, 'd actually made a lasting impression. She asked me for a coots CD. Oh, well. Kids are kids wherever you go, I guess.

I read Drew's e-mail, realizing that Whitney would kill ne if she knew I was discussing her private life with some-ne she'd never even met. But he gave such good advice! I iust be turning into one of those women. Those women /ho lost all loyalty to their girlfriends once they fell in love. light then, I promised myself to hold back a little. I didn't ave to tell him everything. Especially when it included ther people's business. But he did give really good advice!

Next was an opus from Whitney that made about as much ense as the original text of the Magna Carta. She'd obvi-usly gone on a fact-finding mission and was operating in ull paranoia mode.

"I KNOW that something is up because this has hap-ened before." She cited a case in which a Canadian citizen

was seized and shipped off to the Middle East to be ques
tioned by the authorities there and was jailed there "for
whole year, Amelia!!!!!" It was pages and pages of rantin
about the reasons, the clues, and the rationale behind th
government's plan to seize Max. After reading about half o
it, I was almost convinced. That's when I chose to stop read
ing. This girl needed some help.

I called her as soon as I got in the car. She did not pick u
her cell phone, but I left her a message to call me bac
ASAP.

She called an hour later, sounding out of breath.

"I was at Max's place," she said.

"Doing what?"

"Just checking things out. There were a couple of officia
looking cars parked outside his building."

"Whitney, I think you're taking this a little too far."
hoped I sounded serious enough to get through to her.

"Listen, Amelia. You don't know what's going on, okay?

"Then, tell me! Tell me what's going on. Because you jus
sound crazy to me."

"I sound crazy? I sound crazy?" Then she paused. "H
told me," she lowered her voice, "that he knows some peop
who have done some things."

"So?" I immediately thought, *I know you and you'v
done and are doing some "things."*

"I don't expect you to care. You're all hung up on thi
Drew guy."

"Whitney, I care. About you. This is not funny anymore
You need to just stop. Even if he's Osama bin Laden's god
son, just let it go. Move on. Let his family worry about him.

"His family's not going to care. And I know what tha
feels like, Amelia."

I sighed. I couldn't take this anymore.

"Whitney, I'm going to hang up now. But just don't g
over there again, okay? Please."

She didn't answer at first. "You'll see when I expose—"

"Whitney, stop it already!" I yelled.

She hung up on me.

The last time I'd been in a courtroom was with Whitney. She'd poured purple paint all over some guy's car, slashed his tires, and threatened to kill him. He filed charges. The judge ordered her to pay for the damage and issued a restraining order. They got back together a month later, but broke up two weeks later after she found him cheating again. Another guy had gotten a restraining order against her while she was in grad school. She laughed those things off; I took them way more seriously than she did. I'd say, "Whitney, you have a criminal record!" And she'd shrug and reply, "Yeah, guess I can't run for president after all."

Now I was sitting in Roxbury District Court, which should have been one of Dante's nine circles of hell, with a nervous Grace Wilson. I'd gotten her a lawyer who was somewhere in the back of the room, chatting on his cell phone. He'd said, "Not to worry. This is gonna go by quickly." But she looked worried anyway.

I had taken the day off from school to do this, and I wasn't happy to be there. I hated being in a room full of criminals and people who existed solely to put away or defend such criminals. We didn't talk. I was so angry with her for taking the blame for something she did not do just to protect Gerard. And dragging me into it.

Hours later, I was positively burning with anger and impatience. I'd spent an entire morning in a courthouse full of brothers wearing throwbacks, Timberlands, and bad attitudes; and long-suffering mothers and girlfriends who just had to bring their crying babies along. It was purgatory!

They finally called her name and I waited in the wings. Her accuser, an elderly woman who'd lost a fence and some shrubs in the incident, could barely speak when asked. I couldn't help but roll my eyes. This was like the *Judge Judy* show. But the lawyer was all right. He told some crazy story about my mother not being aware of the extent of the damage because it was dark, blah blah blah. Judge Judy, however, must have been in a bad mood because she still fined Ma $500 and suspended her license for six months. The fine would be a hassle; the suspension wouldn't matter because she hardly ever drove. And we were done. I thanked the lawyer, who before we'd even left the courtroom was already on his cell phone.

She was quiet in the car.

"I'm glad that's over with," I said.

Silence.

"At least you won't have to go to jail."

No laughter, not even a smile.

"Are you all right, Ma?"

"I'm fine."

Okaaaay.

"Amelia, I worry about what's gonna happen to me sometimes."

"How?"

"Well, I don't have nobody, except for you and Gerard."

"Ma, you'll be fine."

"I know you get sick of me sometimes."

I wouldn't argue with that.

Silence ensued again the rest of the way home. I didn't want to get into a big, heavy conversation with her. I felt filthy and angry from being in that courtroom all day.

I slowed down as we neared the house and she asked about my trip again. I'd told her about it before on the phone.

"So, this was all about some man?"

"Not really. I wanted to see a new place. I've never been anywhere."

"Don't go running after any man who smiles at you just 'cause you wanna get away from me."

"Thanks, Grace," I said dryly.

Then she thanked me. Thanked me for getting her the lawyer and for taking her to court. A cold day in the seventh circle of hell, maybe?

"You're welcome, Ma."

"You coming in?"

"No, I gotta go plan my lessons."

She kissed me on the cheek. I got the urge to laugh and I did because I couldn't hold it back. She laughed, too. "That judge was an ugly, mean old woman," she said.

"She was. And I'm so glad that's over."

I watched her disappear inside the house. I'd done my duty as the good daughter. Now if only I could get Gerard to take my calls so I could give him a piece of my mind. . . .

As soon as I got home I called Whitney. I'd had this sinking feeling that something wasn't right. I was afraid of what she'd do and what she'd already done that she hadn't told me.

But she sounded upbeat.

"I think I'm making some progress. I spoke with someone at the FBI who might be able to help me."

"What? Whitney, I thought you were going to leave this alone!" My head ached.

"I can't leave it alone, Amelia! I think they're holding him against his will, without a lawyer. His rights are being violated. I have to do something!"

"Whitney, please. For all you know the guy could be down in Miami with some other chick. Don't go crazy over this." I'd said the wrong thing.

"Go crazy?" She laughed bitterly. "That's what you think? That I'm going crazy because Max dumped me?"

That about summed it up.

"You don't know what we had. It was too perfect for him to just walk away."

"Whitney, I don't . . . I just don't think he's in any kind of trouble. That's all."

"You don't know what I know."

"What do you mean?"

"I mean, there are things that I can't tell you. All I know is that I have to find a way to see him and get him some help."

"When you said that there are things you can't tell me, what exactly are you talking about?"

"I can't talk about it, okay? Just trust me on this, Amelia. I am not losing my mind."

What the heck was I supposed to do now? The worst-case scenario I could imagine was that this guy was indeed some shady character and Whitney was right, he had been seized by the authorities and was probably being tortured as of this very moment. But I just couldn't fall for that. I'd seen Max, heard him talk about himself and his proteins. He loved himself too much to care about what the infidels were up to. My hunch was that he was off somewhere sweeping some other girl off her feet. But I knew that there was no way I could convince Whitney of that. When she fell in love she lost touch with reality. I just didn't know how far she would go with this and in how much trouble she could get into.

Why did I have to deal with this? Why couldn't I be in the backyard of Drew's house in the hammock, listening to the waterfall, reading a romance novel?

"Do you believe these bastards?" Whitney was hysterical, screaming through the phone.

"Who?"

"They're trying to get me fired. They actually sent a cease-

and-desist order to my house and to my freaking job. They said I'm harassing people in their offices."

My jaw almost hit the ground.

"Whitney," I tried to remain calm. "When did all of this happen?"

"Last week. My boss called me today telling me that some FBI goon came to his office. In freaking Redmond, Washington!"

She kept on jabbering and I could not get a word in. "They can't intimidate me!"

The last time she scared me like this, I had called her foster mom, who arranged for her to go to McLean Hospital. But she hadn't spoken to the woman in years. Whitney literally had no family except for me. And I had no idea what to do. I couldn't just call a doctor and say, hey, I think my girlfriend's crazy, can you come and take her away? But I also couldn't encourage this fantasy of hers. Either way, it seemed that I would be the one making the decision. I decided to wait it out some more. Maybe the threat of losing her job would straighten her out.

"So what did your boss say?"

"Told me to take some time off. They forced me to take a three-month leave. Screw 'em. I haven't done any real work in a year anyway."

"What are you going to do? Is this leave without pay?" I wondered if she'd thought this all the way through. She had a mortgage, car payments, and a designer-clothing and spa habit.

"They're paying me. What are you worried about? I'm not worried. They'd better not screw with me else I'm suing them, too."

Too?

"What do you mean, too?"

"I got a lawyer. He's really good. He's suing the FBI, the

Department of Homeland Security, and the CIA on my behalf. Hopefully, we can force them to release any information they have about Max and tell us where he is."

"Whitney, you can't be serious!"

I couldn't believe that any ethical lawyer would take a case like that. How much of this was in her head and how much was real?

"What's the lawyer's name?"

"I can't tell you that, Amelia." She said this as if I should know. "I shouldn't even be talking to you about this on the phone. They probably have my phones tapped."

I was speechless.

"Whitney, I'm gonna come over now, okay?"

"Why?" She sounded genuinely surprised.

"So we can talk about this in person. Without worrying about anything," I added to make her feel better.

"Okay," she sighed. "But I can't tell you everything. I don't want you getting involved in this."

Chapter 19

I was doing the unthinkable and Whitney would never forgive me if she knew. But I had no choice. This had been Drew's idea, and I had to admit it was a bit crazy, but I had to know whether all of this was real or just a figment of her imagination.

After school, I put myself through the hell of downtown traffic to get to the Mass. General lab. I was fuming because this little truth-seeking excursion would cost me seven dollars an hour in parking. I hadn't called ahead or anything, I just decided to do a surprise drop-in. And once the security guard told me where to go, I began to get nervous. I had no right to be doing this. . . .

I went down one floor on the elevator, down a freezing hallway, and followed a white-coated guy into a little office that led to another room in the back. I didn't see anyone, so I called out, "Hello?" The white-coated guy had disappeared in the back, so I decided to follow. There were more rooms leading to other rooms, and then I finally hit a wall. I needed a keycard to get access beyond that point. This must be where I needed to be! There were scary-looking signs on the door about nonauthorized persons not entering and biohazards and whatnot. I stood there and pondered my next move. If Whitney were here she'd know what to do. But then again, Whitney was the reason I was here.

Then I heard footsteps and the door opened. I looked up and there he was. God had literally made him appear.

"Max!"

He jumped. His face turned red then white, and he looked around as if searching for a place to run or hide.

"What are you doing here?" His surprise turned to anger.

"I . . . I . . ." What was I doing there? "I wasn't expecting to see you," was all I could manage. I was so shocked to see him so alive and well. So, he wasn't being tortured in a prison on Guantánamo Bay or in Kuwait?

"Is she here?" He looked around the room warily.

"Who? Whitney? No, she's not."

He looked at me as if he didn't believe me. "What do you want?" he scowled.

"I just wanted to know what was going on. She thinks you've disappeared off the face of the earth." I folded my arms and stood in front of him. There was no way I'd let him get away without answering my questions.

"Listen, because of your friend I've had to leave my apartment; force my coworkers to lie about my whereabouts. She's ruining my life. You tell her to stay away from me else I'll get a restraining order."

He knew all this time that she'd been trying to reach him? And he'd been hiding from her! What a jerk.

"She's been worried about you, Max. She thinks the government is holding you hostage or something."

He laughed crazily. "She knows what's going on. I told her I didn't want to see her anymore and she went nuts. She was showing up at my apartment at all hours. She even came here and made a huge scene. I gave hospital security her picture."

I leaned against a wall. I didn't understand. So where did Whitney get this idea that Max had disappeared? He was right here, saying that he'd broken things off. Where had those ideas of hers come from?

But I hated that guy. I turned to leave. "Okay, Max. I'm sure she won't bother you anymore."

"Hey, how did things go with your Caribbean trip?" he asked.

"Go to hell," I said, not even looking back. That bastard. I just knew he'd dump her eventually, and he had the nerve to think that I'd hang back and make chitchat with him? After the way he'd treated Whitney?

I drove straight to Whitney's. I had to see how she took this latest development.

About thirty minutes later, I was flustered enough from driving through rush hour traffic that I considered just going home and talking to Drew, but I couldn't. I had to get this straightened out with Whitney. She had to face reality, and I would give her the tough love she needed to get her there.

I knocked on her door for five minutes, but she did not answer. Her car was outside, so I called her from my cell phone. She answered the phone in a low whisper.

"Whitney, babe, I'm outside. Why aren't you answering the door?"

She hung up and a few seconds later I could see her peering through the front window. Then the door opened just a crack.

"Come in! Come in!" she hissed.

I walked in the house and she quickly locked the door behind me. It was a mess. Books were strewn all over the floor. Clothes lay across the furniture, and there were dirty dishes and half-full coffee cups on the coffee table. This was so unlike Whitney. Her house was her pride and joy, and she kept it in immaculate condition.

"What happened in here?" I took a good look at her and noticed that she had lost at least fifteen pounds since I'd last seen her.

"Whitney, what's happened to you?" I went closer. Her hair was a tangled mess she'd pulled back in a scrunchy. There was crust around her eyes, and her breath was atrocious. If I didn't know better I'd think she was on the bottle. I'd seen my mother like this on her worst days.

"They're after me now, Amelia." She looked scared, genuinely afraid.

"Who's after you?"

"The FBI. They think I'm helping him." She started to cry. "It's just so crazy how they think they can just ruin my life. They're taking everything from me. My job. My man. They're gonna want my house next."

"Whitney, what are you talking about? The FBI is not after you." I guided her to the one clear spot on the couch.

"Don't tell me they're not," she cried. "I know. They've called my job. They watch my house at night. I see them driving by. And it's all because of Max. They're holding him and they don't want me to find out what they did with him, Amelia."

I sighed. "Whitney, I saw Max this afternoon." I said this firmly and flatly.

She stopped crying and looked at me. Then it was as if she hadn't heard what I said. She went back to crying and talking about the FBI staking out her house. I held her and let her cry and jabber on. I had to make sense of this.

"When did they start driving by your house, Whitney?"

"A couple weeks ago. Right after Max disappeared. At first I didn't make the connection, but then after they got to my job I started to notice things."

I nodded and kept on holding her. "And this all started after you started calling them and asking about Max, right?"

She nodded in my shoulder.

"What about your lawyer, Whitney? What's he saying about this?"

She pulled her head away from my shoulder. "He's working for them, too. He said he couldn't keep the case. That I should get some help. I think they got to him, too." She started crying again. "I'm not giving up, Amelia. I'm going to find out what they did to Max."

"Okay," I said, holding her. Then I noticed the prescription bottle on the coffee table. I knew that over the years that she'd been on Prozac, then Zoloft, then some other new drug.

"Have you been taking your medicine, Whitney?"

She nodded again into my shoulder. "It's not working, though. I can't sleep at nights, and I get these headaches."

She sniffed and stopped crying. "Do you think they got to my doctor and they're drugging me?" Her eyes opened wide.

I was no doctor, but I'd read enough to know that these drugs had all manner of side effects. It looked to me that Whitney could be hallucinating or suffering from some kind of paranoia. I made a mental note to remember the name of the doctor on the prescription bottle. I'd give the woman a call once I got home. In the meantime, though, I'd have to get Whitney as close to the land of living as I possibly could.

"Okay, girlie. I'm gonna get this place cleaned up and we're gonna go out to dinner."

Her eyes opened wide. "No! I can't go out!"

I stood there in shock at her reaction.

"All right, Whitney. Then we'll stay here. I'll order us a pizza."

"Don't have them deliver it, go to the restaurant to pick it up."

I sighed. "Maybe I'll cook us something to eat."

I began to clean up the living room, putting books back on bookshelves and gathering the clothes she had strewn about into one pile. Whitney was sick, and it was tearing me up inside. I recognized it. She was this way when she'd gone away to McLean the first time. This time I hoped it wasn't that serious, but I had to talk to her doctor and find out what I should do next.

"You wanna take a shower and wash your hair, babe?" I asked her lightly. "I'll give you a roller set."

She ran her hand over her hair and nodded.

"Go ahead. I'll make us pasta."

When I heard the water flowing upstairs, I called her doctor's office. Luckily, the doctor was in the office and came to the phone quickly.

I told her who I was and what was going on with Whitney. She listened without interrupting. "Is there any way you can bring her in to see me?" the doctor asked.

"I don't know," I said. "She's terrified to go outside."

"I need to be able to see her soon. I think it might be the medication, but it could also be the trauma of the breakup. I need to be able to talk to her."

"Is there any way you can come here? To her house?"

The doctor was silent for a few minutes.

"That's not really something that's encouraged. I mean, this is an HMO. . . ."

"Doctor, I don't think I can get her out of the house. Please . . ."

"Okay, I'll stop by this evening. How about in an hour or so?"

I thanked the woman as if she were saving my own life.

As Whitney and I sat down to dinner, I told her that the doctor was on her way over.

"Why?"

"She thinks something might be wrong with your prescription. She just wants to take a look at you."

Whitney looked down at her plate, but then continued eating. She ate ravenously like she hadn't eaten in days.

I guessed that she'd been living on coffee and grapes. That was all I'd seen in the dirty dishes and cups that she'd left about the house.

"I'm not going back to that hospital," she said.

"I'm sure you won't have to. They just have to change your pills. That's all."

She sniffed and took another forkful of spaghetti into her mouth. "They'll admit me again. This is what they want."

I couldn't bear to ask her who "they" were.

The doctor came earlier than I expected.

"Do you mind?" she asked as she sat at the table with Whitney.

I went into the living room and turned the TV up loud so she would know that I wasn't eavesdropping.

It was almost eight P.M. and I hadn't gone home yet. I was exhausted. I pulled my cell phone out and dialed Drew's number. This call would cost me more than I wanted to think about, but I was so emotionally beaten up I needed to hear his voice.

He was sympathetic when I told him about Whitney.

"I'm sorry," he said. "Wish I was there for you."

"I wish you were here, too."

Then I heard footsteps behind me. The doctor and Whitney came out of the dining room, both with grave expressions on their faces. I said a quick good-bye to Drew.

"Amelia," the doctor said, pronouncing my name with a question mark at the end. "Whitney and I decided it'd be best if we checked her into the hospital for observation. Just for tonight."

I looked at Whitney and all I saw in her face was defeat.

"Is that necessary?" I stood up. How did she get Whitney to agree to this?

"For now? Yes, I think she shouldn't be by herself."

"But I'm here with her. I'll stay with her!"

"I meant she should be under medical supervision."

I looked at Whitney again, and she was saying nothing. Not defending herself. Not resisting. I didn't get it. Whitney didn't belong in a hospital. She was just going through breakup hell. She'd be fine.

"Whitney, are you sure you want to go?"

She nodded.

"Do you want to drive her there? Or . . ."

"Yes, I'll drive her," I said.

She didn't say anything as I drove through the city, following the doctor to the hospital. Twice I asked her if she was sure she wanted to do this and both times she answered yes. She didn't cry. But I did as I watched my best friend get admitted to McLean for the second time since I'd known her. It was so freaking unfair.

Again, I was no psychiatrist, but I thought Whitney has abandonment issues. It not only went back to the fact that she was a foster kid. There was more to it than that. See, Whitney knows her mom. The lady gave her up after her dad left and married some other woman. Her mom left Massachusetts in the early 80s and Whitney actually tracked her down to somewhere in Houston. They'd talked a few times, but the woman had no interest in seeing Whitney or even coming back to Massachusetts for a visit. The bigger problem was Whitney's dad. He was still here. Matter of fact, he lived just fifteen minutes away from Whitney in some mansion in Newton. I helped her track him down when we were in twelfth grade at Latin. We would stake out his house sometimes, watching him from behind a tree across the street. Back then he drove a silver Volvo and his wife, a white woman, drove a black one. He was a tall, good-looking man who works for the governor. But he didn't always do that. He used to be a college professor. Over the years I'd stopped thinking about him and I thought Whitney had, too. But then she contacted him right before she graduated MIT. She told him who she was and that she wanted him to come to her graduation. She said that he was angry. Told her not to call him anymore and that if she needed anything from him it would be best if she found herself a lawyer. When she asked him what he meant by that, he told her that he wasn't sure that he was her father. That her mother was not the woman he thought she was, and that she should stay away from him and his family.

Shortly after that the Korean broke up with her and the stalking began. I hated to be one of those people who traces every adult trauma back to childhood, or worse to parents, but I think in Whitney's case it was warranted. I wondered whether she still stalked her father. She told me that he had a teenage daughter who looked like him and went to Newton North High School, drove his old silver Volvo, and all. That must be hard to take. To have a sister and not be able to talk to her. But she hadn't talked about him and his family in a while. For all I know she could be totally over it. I wondered if her dad's feelings toward her had changed over the years. What a mess this was!

I couldn't go straight home after I'd dropped Whitney off at the hospital. I could at least finish cleaning up her place so it would be nice and clutter-free when she came back home. Ugh. Things had changed so suddenly. So awfully.

How in the world could I be happy when Whitney was falling apart? Drew would be here in a week, yet I felt unsettled and depressed. I literally felt as if my hands were tied. I couldn't help Whitney and I couldn't feel better until she was back to her old self.

I was cleaning up Whitney's study, when I happened upon her computer screen.

I noticed that her Hotmail screen was still open. It was an e-mail from her supervisor, asking her to report to Microsoft's headquarters ASAP. That was a month ago. Oh, shoot! Did Whitney still have her job? I called the supervisor immediately, hoping he would still be in the office.

I told him who I was and he sounded exasperated. "What's going on? What's the deal with Whitney?"

I told him that she'd been very sick, and that she was in the hospital.

"Listen, we need to talk to her, okay? She's got to check in. Just tell her to check in with us when these things happen, okay?"

I hung up the phone, feeling lost again. Whitney was drugged out of her mind. She was in no position to think about work. I decided not to even burden her with this. If she lost her job, so be it. It wasn't worth the stress. God! I hated feeling this helpless. I wanted to do something nice for her. And an idea came to me.

Chapter 20

My spring break vacation had been over for exactly a month and I'd returned to a storm in Boston that did not seem to be ending. The only thing that kept me sane was the fact that Drew would be here soon.

James and Kelly conveniently decided to go visit James's parents in California the week Drew was coming to visit, reminding me that I really loved those two. It didn't negate the fact that I needed to find a place of my own. But with everything on my plate, I felt entitled to being a slacker.

Whitney had been readmitted to McLean, and the doctor's diagnosis was that she'd had another breakdown. I went to see her nearly every day, but nothing much came out of the visits. She said nothing except "hi" and then "bye" right before I left. It was frustrating, but the doctor said that was typical. She'd "come out of it when she was ready."

So I'd gone to the mall to medicate. I'd hit Victoria's Secret first and spent a good $300 on lingerie. All I wanted was for Drew to get here and for us to get busy ASAP. I'd never missed sex after the split with bête noire, and that was over a year ago. But after spending one sexless week with Drew it was all I could think about.

Maybe it had to do with the fact that I had lost a few pounds. Does sex drive have an inverse correlation to body weight? All my size 14 clothes were now a bit baggy, but I still wasn't quite a 12. I needed something sexy to wear. The weather was finally starting to break. I decided to go against my morals and good sense and paid $134.99 for a pair of jeans at Neiman's. I didn't even like to walk by the darned store. It filled me with fury—all the things I wanted yet could never afford. While I cased the store I reevaluated my career choice. Why didn't I have the math gene, like Whitney, who probably made millions and billions of dollars from her egghead job at Microsoft? Okay, she probably didn't get paid millions, but her salary was probably three or four times mine. Why did I have this desire to be a teacher, and why did I not want to do anything else? Something glamorous and lucrative. Oh, well. I guess it all went back to my fear of success. And it probably had something to do with Grace Wilson, too.

These thoughts ran through my mind as I stood in Terminal E at Logan Airport, waiting for Drew's flight. According to the screen, the plane had just landed. I was so impatient to see him I could have run past security into the gates. I did one more pace up and down the terminal just to quell my impatience and relieve my butt from the uncomfortable chair. Those new jeans fit well—they were a tiny 14—but they still needed some breaking in.

"Amelia!" I looked toward the escalator and my heart leapt. I wanted to sprint toward him and jump into his arms, but that would have been so TV. And it's not like I was some 105-pound girl. I collected myself, smiled, and walked quickly toward him.

We embraced for a long time, and I said it again, "I love you." I think I meant it this time. And before I could even feel embarrassed about saying it, he said it back and then kissed me before I could talk. Oh, my gosh. We'd said it. Did that finally mean that I was no longer a relationship arriviste? I was in? I'm in!

We walked hand in hand to the dark parking lot and he laughed at my Beetle. "Wow. Amelia, like, your car's, like, soooo adorable," he mocked.

"Don't be a hater, Drew. I love my car."

"James and Kelly are in California for the whole week, so we have the place all to ourselves," I smiled.

"Cool," he said. "At least you won't have to keep your voice down. . . ."

Thank goodness, he was as horny as I was. Else I would have been ashamed of myself.

"Oh, man. This is beautiful," he said, gazing at the lit-up Boston skyline. "You don't appreciate those things until you've been away from it for a while."

"I felt the same way when I looked up at the sky and saw all these stars that first night on Dominica."

He paused. "You're right. There's no skyline that could compete with that."

That night we stayed up all night, talking, making love, talking, making love. It was beautiful, and I was exhausted by the time the sun came up on a gorgeous spring Saturday morning. I was so happy! My man was here.

As a teacher one cannot just take a week off from work. It's just not done. You have all summer, and all those breaks during the year. So my week with Drew was no vacation. I went to work; he found ways to amuse himself during the day; then I came home. We'd hang out, make love, and then go to sleep. On the surface it seemed pedestrian and a bit boring, but it felt romantic and luxuriously comfortable. It felt like we were a real couple.

He said he spent the days exploring the city. He bought

me artifacts from the MFA and the Freedom Trail. Those are things, despite living in Boston my entire life, I had never even done. Well, I did go to the MFA once, but it wasn't to look at art. It was for First Fridays. I hadn't gotten lucky, so that had been my first and last Friday there.

We drove out to Carlisle to Kimball Farms for ice cream one day after school. I wanted to turn him on to my favorite flavor, Khalua Crunch.

"I wouldn't mind living out here," he said as he glanced at the old Colonials along Route 225 in Lexington and Bedford, and the sprawling farms in Carlisle. It was chilly but the sun was shining so we sat on a bench in the tiny flower garden at the back of the ice-cream stand.

"It's so peaceful," he said. "Kind of reminds me of home—minus the sub-fifty-degree temperature."

"Then why don't you move back to the U.S., then?" It wasn't that I hadn't been thinking about this from the get-go. Why did I have to be the one to move? Was it because I was the woman?

"It could be nice, but this is still America. Not the best place for an ambitious brother like myself."

"Ah, I see. The man will keep you down."

He laughed. "Not really. I did all right while I was here. I'd just much rather be in a place where I'm the man."

"How come your father chose to send you here for school?"

"He loved the idea of reckless capitalism and thought I'd learn a lot more here than I would back there."

"Do you think he'd want you to run for office?"

"I don't think he'd want me to run right now. He'd probably think that I wasn't ready yet."

"Why is that?"

"My father was from the old school. He believed in rules, process, taking all the appropriate steps in the right order, that kind of thing. He'd probably want me to start small, probably village council."

"Did you have a good relationship with him?"

"It was all right. He was busy."

"Really?" I wanted him to say more but I didn't want to make him feel as if he was in a therapy session.

"Amelia, it's not like your relationship with your mother. It was all good. We just didn't have a lot to say to each other."

"But he invested so much in you. . . . He must have loved you a lot. Don't you miss him?"

"Of course, I miss him. Sometimes. We really weren't that close."

"Everyone down there wants you to be him."

"I know."

"Isn't that a huge responsibility?"

"I don't want to be him so I don't see it that way."

"Why not? I thought you said he was a great leader."

"He was a great leader for his time. A lot of people got left behind during his administration."

"And you think you can help those people better than he could?"

"Maybe. Can we talk about something else? I feel like I've just been interviewed by Dan Rather."

"Dan Rather retired."

"Oh, right. Peter Jennings?"

"He's gone, too."

"I really need to watch more American TV."

"No, you don't."

As we drove back into town, my cell phone rang. I didn't recognize the number nor the male voice on the other end. It was for Drew. I handed him the phone, confused.

"I'm great," he said. "Got here fine. Everything worked out well. I'll call you if I need to."

"Who was that?" I asked as he handed the phone back to me.

"My lawyer."

"Your lawyer?"

"Yep, we're working on a financing deal for another project; he just wanted to make sure he could find me. In case something comes up."

"Oh."

"You don't mind, right?"

"No. No, of course not."

That night we had dinner at Stephanie's, and he just had to go and do it.

"I'd like to meet Grace," he said. "If you don't mind."

"You would?" Stalling. "Why?"

"Because she's your mother. And you've met my mother."

"If I'd known that we were engaging in some kind of quid pro quo . . ."

He looked at me. "Are you ashamed of me?"

I snorted, loudly enough that a trio of girls at the table next to us looked on in distaste and then whispered to each other. I was positive that they were saying: "That's how she conducts herself on a date? Bet he won't ask her out again." I know because that's what I would have said.

"Why would I be ashamed of you?"

"Okay. Then why can't I meet her?"

"I didn't say you couldn't."

"Fine. Good. We'll go tomorrow then."

"I'll have to check with her."

He looked at me squarely as if to say that he was not backing down. "Sure."

The next day I worried from first period to last. This could be a disaster waiting to happen. Grace Wilson wasn't the kind of person to oooh and aaah over some strange person in her house. She wouldn't offer to have anyone over for dinner or anything like that. She liked her solace, except for the occasional "male friend," and that was that. When I told her about Drew the next day, she was skeptical.

"Why he want to meet me?"

"He's just curious."

"About me?"

"Can you just be there, Ma? I'll bring takeout, and we can all eat together."

I picked up some Thai food from Bangkok Basil in Brookline. I got her some shrimp fried rice—I knew she'd eat that.

I was nervous as we drove the ten minutes from the apartment to her house.

"You gonna be all right?" Drew asked for the third time.

"I'm fine."

"I'm not going to judge you or her, so relax. Besides, you know my mother is not perfect."

But did Vanessa know that? Of course, I said nothing.

Grace let us in graciously. She was wearing a white sweater and jeans and she'd let her hair down about her face. She looked beautiful. I noticed that he appraised her the way guys look at women they think are attractive. It was a quick yet appreciative once-over that made me want to smack him really hard. I bet he thought that I didn't notice. Now, I had one other reason to resent Grace Wilson.

I got busy setting up the food in the dining room while they talked in the living room. She'd smiled at him shyly and shook his hand all ladylike when I introduced them. That pissed me off! All of a sudden she was being cute?

When we sat down to eat it got worse, she talked about herself nonstop.

"I wish I still could work, but my asthma . . ." She clutched her chest dramatically.

He nodded. "That's understandable, Ms. Wilson."

"Oh, you are too much! Call me Grace, honey."

Oh, gag me with a rusty spoon!

"You know, I wanted to cook dinner tonight but my daughter doesn't think I'm sophisticated enough. . . ."

"Ma!"

"This is fine. You didn't need to go to any trouble. . . ."

Why was he falling for her little act after all I'd told him about her?

"I'd love to go to the Caribbean someday," she said wistfully.

She didn't even want to go to the grocery store!

"You should come down and visit. You'd have a good time."

"Are all the men down there as good-looking as you?"

He laughed. I cringed.

After dinner, we sat in the living room. She had to show him pictures of me from infancy, childhood, adolescence and on up. I didn't mind. I'd been a cute kid. It's when I got older that it all went downhill.

"This is my husband," she pointed to a picture of my dad—tall, brown, and smiling in a gray suit on our front porch. "He was a very handsome man," she said proudly.

Before it could get more uncomfortable the doorbell rang. I silently hoped it wasn't one of her boyfriends come calling.

I went to go get the door because she gave me that expectant look.

It was Gerard. "Who invited you?"

He brushed past me into the living room. He didn't smell as if he'd been drinking, thank goodness.

"Gerry, I didn't think you'd show," Ma said, standing up so she could hug and kiss her favorite child. It so irritated me the way they fawned over each other. He held out a hand to Drew, who stood up and introduced himself.

"Nice to meet you, man," Gerard said. "Ma, ya'll got any food left?"

And just like that he stalked out of the living room and into the kitchen, rubbing his belly.

She shrugged. "I have to apologize for my son. . . ."

"It's all right," Drew said.

I followed Gerard into the kitchen.

"Can you be any ruder?"

He was foraging through the refrigerator and did not answer at first. Then he looked at me, a carton of leftover Thai in his hand.

"All I can say is, at least he ain't white."

"What!"

"I'm just sayin' he ain't the realest cat in the world. But I always expected you to bring home a white boy." He shoved some noodles into his mouth.

"You're an idiot, Gerard."

"Yeah? 'Cause I don't talk like Colin Powell out there?"

"Whatever," I said. "And we're just friends. I didn't *bring him home*."

"Yeah, right! Since when you bringing your friends to meet Ma and me?"

"For your information, I didn't bring him to meet you, Gerard. You're only here for the food."

"And? Your point is?"

My brother got on my nerves sometimes. I left him stuffing his face and went back to the living room. They were laughing at something. I noticed that she had her hand on his arm.

"What's so funny?" I sat close to Drew and put my hand on his leg. My brain didn't have to tell me how pathetic my behavior was, but where did she get off acting like she'd known him all her life?

"I was just telling him about how you used to walk in your sleep when you were young and how we found you in the middle of the street one night. . . ."

"Ma!"

Drew laughed. "You never told me that."

"I think that's actually a disease. Not a laughing matter." I think I'd read that somewhere. Or saw it on *Oprah*.

But she had more jokes. She told him about when I lost a citywide spelling bee and wouldn't leave the house for days until my father promised to pay me twenty dollars to go back to school. And the time I got bit in the ankle by a squirrel and had to get rabies shots. I just sat there and endured it, keeping one eye on the clock. Mercifully, ten o' clock landed quickly. I had to be up early for school the next day.

"Ma, we need to get going."

Gerard came out of the kitchen, looking thoroughly satisfied. I was pretty sure that there was probably not a trace of food left.

"I gotta bounce, ya'll," he said.

"You gotta what? Gerard, why do you talk like that?" Ma looked at Drew apologetically.

"See you later, Ma." Gerard kissed her on the cheek.

Drew stood up and held out his hand. Gerard gave him the black handshake.

"Good to meet you, bro," Drew said.

"Aiiiight," Gerard said.

I walked him to the door.

"At least he knew the handshake," Gerard half whispered.

"You like him. You know you do."

"I don't like nobody," Gerard said, then closed the door.

But he did. I could tell that he did. If Ma liked Drew, then Gerard would like him, too. They were two of the same.

Later in bed, relief and pure happiness flooded my body from head to toe. The night had gone well. Drew had gotten along well with Grace—better than I did. And he'd passed Gerard's test, whatever that was. Now there was only one more hurdle. I wanted him to meet Whitney. But who knows how she would be these days? I still would go by there tomorrow.

If tonight had been any indication, maybe it would go well. Maybe she'd say more than two words. Maybe it might cheer her up to see someone new, besides me. Maybe seeing me so happy would boost her mood. But then what if it didn't? I wouldn't worry. If I'd made it through tonight, then everything else would turn out just fine.

I held on to Drew as he slept. I wanted this to last forever. But we only had a couple more days before we went back to the e-mails and telephone calls. How was this going to work, Amelia? I liked this so much better than the long-distance shenanigans. *Someone's going to have to move.*

Chapter 21

"You've been running out of here all week. What's going on?" Lashelle asked as I packed up my stuff.

"Oh, I've got a friend in town."

"Oh, yeah? Male friend?"

I stopped shoving papers into my bag. "Yes."

"Your friend from spring break?"

Boy, she had a lot of deductive powers, didn't she?

"Yes."

"You go, girl." Lashelle poked me in the arm. "A sister finally getting some."

Finally? Had it been that obvious? Or was she just conjecturing that I hadn't gotten laid in . . . in . . . forever? What business was it of hers anyway?

"You gonna have to show me a picture sometime."

I started packing up my stuff again. Yeah right, Lashelle.

"See you later."

"Don't do anything I wouldn't do."

What the heck was that supposed to mean?

"You're too much, Lashelle," I said. Too nosy was what I meant.

As I drove home, I realized that I hadn't been to spin class all week. But it was just one week! Damn. And I'd been eating like a hog, too. I'd been cooking these elaborate meals for Drew, complete with dessert. And that was when we didn't go out. I could feel the weight on my stomach. Ugh. Man, it was going to take another whole month to lose the three or four pounds I was sure I'd gained.

He was watching television when I walked in. "You ready?" I asked.

"Someone called from the hospital," he said.

"What? Did something happen?"

"No, they said Whitney wouldn't be taking any visitors today."

"Are you serious?"

I wanted to hear it myself. I called McLean, and sure enough one of the nurses said that Whitney was having a "bad day."

What in the world? I'd go up there right away, I decided. I had to find out what was going on with Whitney.

"Do you think that's a good idea?" Drew asked.

"Yes! I've never heard of her having a bad day before." I grabbed my pocketbook.

"I was hoping we could go see a movie or something."

"Drew, she could be having some kind of crisis."

"Don't you think they would have told you if she was?"

"You don't have to come."

"I wasn't saying that at all. I just thought if she didn't want to have visitors, why throw yourself on her?"

"I'm not throwing myself on her. I just want to make sure everything's okay." I was surprised and a little bit angry that he would be so insensitive, that he wouldn't understand.

"I think I'll stay here," he said. "Maybe you two need to be alone. And I need to make some calls."

I looked at him for a second. He seemed unperturbed, certainly not as angry as I felt. "Fine. I'll see you when I get back."

"Yeah, maybe we can go to a movie."

What was it with him and the movie? Couldn't he see I was worried about Whitney?

Once I had slogged through the traffic and gotten to the hospital, I walked quickly to Whitney's room, expecting the worst. But all I saw was Whitney laying on her bed reading.

"What up, chica?"

She didn't even look up. "I thought I told them no visitors today."

At least she was talking.

"I was worried about you."

"Why?"

"They said you were having a bad day. I thought something was wrong."

I sat at the foot of the bed.

"I wanted you to meet Drew."

"Maybe some other time."

"He's leaving in two days."

"Oh, well."

"Whitney, did I do something wrong?"

"Sure, Amelia. It's always about you."

"Not really. I just really wanted . . ."

"Exactly what I mean, Amelia. It's always about you."

"Do you want me to leave?"

"I didn't want you to come here today. I don't feel like seeing anyone today," she said, still not looking up from her book. I noticed it was some scientific thing on intelligent design.

"Is that book any good?"

"Yes."

"I'll go now then, Whitney."

"Okay."

"Bye."

"Bye."

But I sat there for a couple more minutes.

"I'm leaving here in a week," she said.

"You are! Whitney . . . Good. I'm so happy. . . ."

She put the book down. "Amelia, what made you think that I'd want your man to see me in this place?"

"I didn't . . . I hadn't thought of it that way."

"See what I mean? You never even thought that I might be embarrassed. That I might not even want him to know that I'm in this place? He's a total stranger to me!"

"I'm sorry. I'm so sorry. I just didn't think . . ."

"Yeah," she said, still not looking at me. "You never think."

"I'm sorry."

She shook her head and went back to shielding her face with the book.

"I'll leave you alone." I walked out of there feeling lower than dirt. I was such an idiot. If it had been me, would I want her bringing Max to see me in a place like that? God, Amelia. Can you be any more selfish? I'd gotten so caught up in wanting to show off Drew that I didn't even think of her and what she was going through.

I got home feeling dejected. Drew was on the phone with Vanessa. I could tell from the submissive tone in his voice. That woman sure had a hold on him. I waved at him. He put his hand over the receiver. "Mom says hi," he mouthed.

"Right back at her," I said.

He got off the phone, probably sensing my mood.

"What's up with Whitney?"

"She's okay. Listen, I shouldn't have told you about her situation."

"What do you mean?"

"I mean, it was private."

"What's the big deal? It's not like I'm going to tell anyone."

"Yeah, but she doesn't feel comfortable about that . . . that you know all this stuff about her and she doesn't even know you."

Drew sighed. "Why do I feel like I'm in the middle of a soap opera?"

"Drew!"

"Okay, fine. I won't . . . We won't talk about Whitney and her problems anymore."

I fumbled around in the kitchen, still feeling guilty about Whitney. What kind of a friend was I?

"So what are we doing tonight?" He came up behind me. "Going out or staying in?" He rubbed himself against me.

"I don't know." I tried to wiggle away. "I'm kind of upset about Whitney."

"Amelia, I'm only here for two more days. . . ."

I turned to face him. I let him kiss me and tried to respond, but I was faking it. It was the first time I'd faked it with him. But I just wasn't into it.

Saturday came screeching toward us. Kelly and James would be back on Sunday, and I'd be back to planning my lessons and trying not to overeat. Blech! Drew hadn't left yet, but I hated my life already.

"I wish you didn't have to go back," I whined as I drove him to the airport.

"But I'll see you in a few weeks, won't I?" he said.

"You will?"

"Yep, you're spending the summer with me."

What???

"When did we decide this?" I asked, immediately warming to the idea.

"Somewhere between me knowing that we need to be together."

"Oh. But . . ."

"But nothing, Amelia," Drew said. "You have six or seven weeks to prepare yourself."

"I've never been away from home that long."

"Now's a good time to start. Besides, you like new experiences, right?"

"I do. I'm just . . . I'm sure it will be fun."

I slowed down as we neared the airport exit. The traffic sure was busy for a Saturday midmorning. That was the only thing that could ruin an otherwise perfect spring day. Everybody and their mother came out of the woodwork, to joyride, shop, or whatever, just to get out of the house because the sun was shining. Before you knew it, a gorgeous day would turn into a horn-blowing, finger-giving mess, and every other driver would show his or her Masshole colors.

"The whole summer in Dominica?" I was beginning to picture it, smell it even.

Matter of fact, I wished I could get on the plane with Drew that very moment and never again be stuck in another traffic jam.

"So what do you do during the summer?"

"Work . . . I told you about the new school we're starting in that village up north. Plus, one of my boys and me might be working on this resort in Barbados if the seller takes our offer."

I hadn't known about that. I thought now would be a good time to ask one question that had been bugging me for quite a while. I mean, I knew he had been successful while he was in the States. But just how successful had he been? And where was all this money coming from? A part of me was afraid that he was some charismatic yet brutal drug dealer, and that sooner or later I'd end up his hostage while the DEA trained guns on his house. But those kinds of thoughts made me have flashbacks of Whitney's breakdown. I had to stop.

"Where do you get all the cash to do these things?" I said this lightly so as not to sound like Christiane Amanpour.

He didn't miss a beat. "I sell young children into slavery."

Um . . .

"I'm kidding, Amelia. Geez. I have a lot of investments. I'm not rich, but I'm not too bad with money. Does that satisfy you, or will you be needing bank statements and tax forms?"

"I was just wondering. I mean, you work, but what you do doesn't seem to have any obvious lucrative value."

"Building a school doesn't?"

"It's a public school."

"The government does pay me for the work I do."

"I see."

"I bet you're probably thinking I'm some kind of criminal."

"I am not! What do you take me for, Drew?"

"A girl with a wild imagination."

"Whatever." I felt stupid. He actually could read my mind. That sucked.

When we said good-bye at the terminal it wasn't sad. I knew I'd see him again soon. I was already packing in my mind. "Love you," he said as he walked into the gate. I stood there and watched him walk away. I liked this feeling. I wasn't wasting my love on some undeserving bastard. This was a good guy. Even my brother liked him! I stood in the airport and let the happiness really sink in for a good ten minutes before going home.

Chapter 22

I called Whitney's room at McLean, eager to make things right with her and to tell her my news, that I was going to spend the whole summer in Dominica. But a nurse said she wasn't there.

"What do you mean she's not there?"

"She checked herself out this morning."

"You let her do that?"

"Ma'am, she's here of her own free will."

I immediately called Whitney at her home. She answered sounding cheery.

"You scared me, chica," I said. "I called up there looking for you and they said you were gone."

"I felt better so I left. I woke up this morning and it was so gorgeous out, I decided that I wanted to be outside. Then I went outside and I wanted to go home. You know, at the beginning of this year I said I was going to start doing my own gardening."

"Uh-huh," She was so chatty and random that I almost wanted to laugh. Was the old Whitney back?

"So, I left that place, took a cab to Home Depot, and

bought a whole bunch of stuff. Now I'm outside in the front, planting tulips."

"Tulips?"

"Yup. And azaleas and some other purple little flowers I don't know the name of. My yard is gonna be the bomb."

"Okay. I'm coming over then. I'll help you."

"Where's your Caribbean man?"

"I just dropped him off at the airport."

"Oh, so now you wanna hang out with a sister?"

"Please, Whitney."

"I'm just playing. . . . Yeah, come over. We'll garden and then we'll go shopping."

That sounded like a fine plan for a Saturday to me.

Hours later, we sat at the California Pizza Kitchen in the Back Bay. Whitney ate pizza and I ate a salad grudgingly. There was dirt under my fingernails.

"See what you made happen? You and your gardening . . ."

I looked in my bag for a nail file.

"Dirt is good for you. It's cleansing."

"Whatever, Whitney."

"So, you're really gonna be gone all summer?"

"Yeah." I looked at her, searching for signs of approval or disapproval. "Is that bad? You think it's too much too soon?"

"You're asking *me* if it's too much too soon?" We could laugh at that now.

"I don't know. I just feel so comfortable when I'm with him. We argue about little things and laugh and eat and stuff . . ."

"Yup, you're already like an old married couple." She sipped her iced tea, and I prodded my miserable salad.

"I just don't know how this is gonna work, though."

"You mean the distance?"

"Obviously someone's gonna have to move."

"It's gonna have to be you," she said.

"Why me?"

"Sounds like he has a lot more to give up than you."

"And what is that supposed to mean?"

"No offense, but you have this job that you can do anywhere in the world. There's really nothing tying you to Boston. Or America for that matter." Her eyebrows narrowed. "Actually, I have an idea. I think I'll go spend the summer in Rome. I've always wanted to do that and since you won't be here . . ."

"Don't go to Rome for the summer!"

"Why not?"

"Because that's my fantasy!"

"No offense, but you couldn't afford that fantasy, dahling. Anyway, you'll be living my fantasy . . . getting laid every day on some Caribbean island."

"Maybe we could switch up halfway through the summer then."

"You'll have to find me a man down there. I'm not taking your seconds."

"I'm so ready to get out of here," I said. I was going. The plan was now set. I'd spend the summer with Drew in Dominica and Whitney would jaunt off to Rome.

"Maybe you could come spend a weekend with me," she said.

"Unlikely. I just don't have the funds," I said.

"Well, ask your sugar daddy."

I rolled my eyes. "I don't think so."

"Or maybe I'll come down there."

"You should!" I said. "You'd like it. Drew's got a lot of good-looking friends."

"Hmmm . . . Sounds like a plan then."

We didn't talk about her illness. I could tell that she was not in the mood to relive the past few weeks. But she seemed fine. She did say that she was on new meds and that had made her sleep better the last couple of nights. That was probably why her mood had improved so much. But with Whitney, one never knew. I just hoped that this version of her would last. I didn't want to see my girl losing it again.

The weeks flew by as the temperature rose in the city. It seemed that I was always running somewhere. I had increased my exercise time to five days a week because I'd gotten so addicted to the rush I felt when I was on that bike. I was now down to a size 12 proper. But there were still days when I'd go to Godiva and scarf down a handful of raspberry chocolate eggs and two jelly bean cups. I just couldn't help it. That was me. But at least I was exercising.

On the last day of school, my classes were less than half full. The kids were even more cantankerous because they knew summer was at the door. A lot of them I probably wouldn't see next year. That is, if I came back. Even though they were wild and badly behaved I was sad that I was losing another group of kids. Every year it was the same thing; I never got used to it. I was regretful for the ones I hadn't reached and sad to lose the good ones to a higher grade.

"Ms. Wilson, what you doing this summer?" Shanae asked. "You gonna work?"

"Nah, I'm going to the Caribbean to hang out with my friend."

"Ain't it hot down there in the summer?"

"Yes, but it's hot here, too."

"But it's Africa hot down there," one boy, Darryl, said.

"It's a tropical island, so I guess you could compare the two. . . ."

I noticed that Treyon had his hand on a girl's butt, and she was pushing it away only to have him replace it each time.

"Treyon!"

"What?" He glared at me. He took his hand away and the girl scurried away.

I can't lie. I was happy to say good-bye to them at the end of the last period. But then I was so touched when Shawn came up to me and said, "Be careful down there. You don't want to catch Ebola."

"I don't think they have Ebola down there, Shawn."

"They'd never tell you that in the brochures."

"Okay, Shawn. I'll be careful."

Others walked up to the front of the class to hug me. Actual body contact! I'd only seen that happen with Lashelle and her students. Could I possibly be shedding my Mean Ms. Wilson image, or do they get this way just because it's the end of the term? Oh, well. I'd savor the moment. They could be so sweet when they wanted to be, I thought as I watched them running out of the school, raising hell.

In the teacher's lounge, we stood around chatting about the year. I finally felt that I was in the clique.

"So you gonna be with your man all summer?" Lashelle asked.

I nodded.

"That sounds so romantic," Ms. Owens said. She was an older English teacher who was always impeccably dressed, one of those devout, old-time AKAs who continued to live and breathe for her sorority even in her old age. "Make sure that man marries you, girl," she said.

"I'll work on him," I said. But that sounded so devious. It's not that I didn't want it. But it was too soon to think about something like that. At least out loud.

Later I went to see Ma and Gerard. It would be the last time I saw them before I flew down to Dominica.

"Ma?" I called out from downstairs once I'd let myself in. I thought she might be asleep. A few minutes later she came down the stairs in a satin robe, a guilty look on her face.

"What's going on, Ma?"

"I got company."

"Company?" Oh, then it dawned on me. Male company.

"Ma, I thought you were gonna be celibate," I teased.

She glared at me.

"I'm leaving tomorrow."

Her shoulders relaxed. "Amelia, you sure you want to go all the way down there? Is that man worth it?"

"I thought you liked him!"

"Yeah. But why he gotta be so far away? Can't you find someone here?"

"Like you did?"

"Stop minding my business."

"I'll miss you, Grace," I told her, and I smiled. I smiled because she looked uncomfortable standing there in her robe, probably naked underneath, with a man upstairs in her bed. I had her just where I wanted her: vulnerable and ashamed.

"He's a nice man," she said defensively, glancing up the stairwell. I hated it when she read my mind.

"Be careful."

"I should tell you to be careful."

Then she opened her arms and hugged me. "Make sure you go see your brother before you leave."

"I know. I'm going there now. I love you, Ma."

"Don't say that," she said. "You'll make me think something bad's gonna happen to you."

"Okay. I'll call you when I get there."

"You better, Amelia."

"Be careful!" she yelled from the window as I walked to my car.

Yes, Ma, I will.

Gerard's girlfriend, D'Andrea, lived in one of those noisy buildings that I hated just driving by. Someone was always blasting music out loud, and there was always at least three or four roughneck guys hanging out in front. I don't know how she could stand to live there by herself. I knew that Gerard had other girls so he wasn't with her every night.

I rang the doorbell under the icy stare of two teenage boys.

"Who is it?" she yelled through the intercom.

She buzzed me up, and I walked into her and Gerard having a fight in her second-floor apartment.

She was holding his cell phone in her hand and he was trying to snatch it.

"Who's this bitch, this 763 number?" she was yelling.

"Hello?" I stood at the door.

She turned around. "Oh, hey, Amelia. This fool think he's gonna lie to me."

"Shut up, D'Andrea!" Gerard said.

He smiled at me. "So you leaving, huh?" It was as if he'd signaled a time-out from the fight because D'Andrea, on cue, sat docilely on the couch, probably gathering her strength for round two.

The place was neat. D'Andrea worked hard at some insurance agency, and obviously she liked to spend her money on her house. She had a huge flat-screen TV, there were video games neatly stacked in a corner next to a fancy looking stereo. Hundreds of DVDs were in an oak entertainment center to the side of a leather couch, and tons of scented candles were everywhere. Martha Stewart would be proud. No wonder Gerard viewed her as his steady; she was the most stable woman I'd ever seen him with.

"I just came to say bye."

"Aiiight," he said. "Yo, if you see any fine honeys down there, hook a brother up."

D'Andrea was shaking her head and rolling her eyes.

"Gerard, you're silly," I said.

Then I hugged him. "Bye, little brother," I said into his shoulder.

"Take care, sis," he said. "Bring me back some weed."

"You're gonna have to come get that yourself."

"Bye, D'Andrea," I said, hoping her anger at Gerard didn't extend to me.

"Have a good time, Amelia," she said wearily.

As I walked down the hall, I could hear her yelling again. Round two of the fight had begun. One thing I was certain of, I would not miss my family drama.

Chapter 23

I couldn't believe that I was about to be attacked by a herd of goats. Every day I'd walk up in these hills and all I'd ever see was curious little birds, butterflies, caterpillars, and other cute animals. But today I had to run into the goat mafia.

Why did I have to tempt fate and follow that nosy dog all the way up in these hills? And how far had I wandered from the house? Sonny and I had been walking for over two hours and I needed to get back to the house before the sun shone any brighter or hotter. The skin on my bare shoulders and legs was beginning to burn. But from the looks on these goats' faces, they were not letting me go anywhere.

"Sonny, do something!" He did nothing. All 100 German shepherd pounds of him decided to stand right next to me and stare at those mean-looking goats.

"Shoo! Shoo!" I said for the fifth or sixth time. Maybe they didn't understand my American accent?

The biggest one had a formidable pair of horns that I decided could probably kill me. Would anyone find my body? Would Sonny dig up some courage deep down and go find help? Like Lassie.

I looked around for a stick or something. I saw trees, flowers, bushes, the usual sights that made these morning walks so pleasant and peaceful. They were of no help. I'd been on this island exactly two weeks, and with each passing day it was becoming less idyll fantasy and more strange reality.

I hadn't been ready for Drew's ridiculous schedule. He was up at four A.M. every day and then worked out for two hours. Straight. An hour running way up in the hills and then lifting weights. Then he ran the blender at six A.M.—for his protein shake—so that was the time that I woke up. He then read the paper while simultaneously watching CNN International and making phone calls. Then he was gone by seven. He called me throughout the day but I wouldn't see him till after dark. "There's so much to do here," he urged me. "Get out and have fun."

I took Sonny out walking every morning. We ventured high in the hills, bathed in the pool under the waterfall, and I learned not to be afraid of cricks and cracks in the forest-like area around the house. I seldom ever ran into anyone else. Drew's neighbors were workaholics, too. How terrible to live in such a beautiful place but never to be home to enjoy it.

But what was I going to do about these goats? I had the cell phone Drew had given me; I could call him. But what would that solve? How could he make them move? Would I give the phone to the ram with the huge horns and let Drew order him and his crew to get out of my way? I had to figure this one out for myself.

"Sonny, do something!" But the dog just looked at me blankly and then turned to the goats; two of them sat down on the trail. Aw, man!

"Help!" This was pathetic but maybe someone, maybe the goats' owner, would hear me and come running. "Help!"

I waited and waited. No help came. The goats did not move. Neither did Sonny. I'd been standing in the same spot for fifteen minutes. I looked down and saw a rock, a big one. I hated violence. I was a peaceful person, but these goats were not leaving me any choice. I picked up the rock and looked at the goats' leader again. He looked me straight in the eye. He would not be capitulating today. I raised my arm, aimed, ready to throw the rock; he lowered his head and charged toward me. I screamed and dropped the rock.

"Run, Sonny, run!" I yelled and feinted left of the herd and then ran around them as quickly as I could, channeling Flo Jo as best as I could. Sonny ran ahead of me, barking the whole time. *Sure, bark now,* I thought. I looked back after I'd felt that I'd run a good distance. The goats were not in pursuit. We were safe. Whew!

I was soaked in sweat as Sonny and I trudged up the path to the house. Jimmy Wilkes and his sitter, an older woman, were in their garden. She waved to me and I waved back, still out of breath. Jimmy looked at me but didn't even smile. "Hi, Sonny!" he yelled, and Sonny ran over to him.

I couldn't wait to get in the shower. What would I do with myself the rest of the day? I'd brought a huge pile of books and I'd been reading under the jacaranda tree every afternoon. But I didn't want to do that today. I wanted to go out. But where?

I put on a new dress after I'd showered and browsed guide books about all the things I could be doing. Visiting the hot springs and volcano or the boiling lake. Bird watching. Hiking. Swimming. Snorkeling. Diving lessons. Tennis. I turned on the TV.

Then the door opened and I almost jumped out of my skin. It was the housekeeper, Celeste.

"Hi, Celeste," I said. She had company, a woman who looked exactly like her. It was eerie to see the two of them together, so alike, both heavy-set and serious-faced.

"I didn't expect you to be here," she said.

Exactly what I was thinking. I wished I could tell her that she needn't return the rest of the summer. That I didn't mind doing the cleaning.

She disappeared into the kitchen and her sister stood there looking at me expectantly.

"I'm Amelia."

"I'm Celestine," she said, smiling.

We shook hands and I invited her to sit.

"What are you doing today?" she asked.

I shrugged. "I'm not sure. I'll probably hang out here."

"You should come with me to the village," she said. "See a new place."

The village? I remembered a scary movie I'd seen with the same name.

"I can show you where we live."

"Is it far?" I asked her, racking my brain to find a way out of going.

"No, it's a half-hour walk, ten-minute drive."

Celeste came out of the kitchen. "You need a lot of things. Soap and sponges."

I nodded. "I'll let Drew know."

She disappeared into the kitchen again. I looked at Celestine and smiled. Did I dare ask her why her twin was so weird? And why she hated me so much.

"Celeste lost her husband two years ago," she said. "She's still mourning."

I felt like a jerk again. That poor woman. "I'm so sorry to hear that; she never talks much."

"She never talked much anyway," Celestine shrugged.

Fine. I'd have to go to their village, if only to make up for thinking that Celeste was some random weirdo cleaning lady. Celeste told us we could use her car and that she'd stay back at the house to wash the dog. I could have done that! But I had to remember that it was her job. And she'd lost her husband. She needed the work.

Celestine and I sputtered down the hill in the jerky little Datsun. She was right, the village was not too far away, but it was sure hard to get to. We must have gone up and down at least four unpaved roads before we leveled off in a tiny neighborhood of rickety houses with one path running down the middle. It was a path. Not a street.

"Here we are," she said.

I followed her into a tiny house made from cement blocks, painted pink and white on the outside. It was clean and cool inside; the floors were colorful stone tile. The furniture was obviously amateur-made, but it was cute, in an uneven asymmetrical kind of way. It looked like a playhouse.

"You and Celeste live here?"

"Yes," she said, "her husband's family took their house back after he died."

Yikes! That was terrible.

She showed me around; there were several pictures of a white, benevolent Jesus plastered all over the walls in all the rooms. Both she and Celeste had framed Bible verses above their beds in their bedrooms. It was all so . . . so cute.

"Let's go see my brother," she said after the two-minute tour of the tiny house. "He's probably killing something for lunch."

Huh? Maybe I'd heard wrong.

We walked down the dusty path and children were jumping rope and playing hopscotch to the side. "Hi, Ms. Celestine," they sang.

She stopped to talk with them and they crowded around me when she told them that I was visiting from America. "Do you know Ashanti?" one little girl asked me.

I shook my head. Who was Ashanti?

It was several minutes before their questions stopped and we could make our way to Celestine's brother's house. His house was clearly the biggest in the village, and he seemed to have a lot of animals. I could hear them bleating, squawking, mooing, and chirping. We walked around to the back where a large man stood with a huge scythe-looking thing in one hand and a kicking goat in the other. Oh my God! Celestine was not alarmed.

She greeted the man casually. He put the knife down and looked me over. "Who are you?" His voice was loud and rough.

"She's Drew's girlfriend. From America."

The man still eyed me suspiciously. "Hello," he said.

I smiled widely, keeping one eye on the goat that was kicking around in the dirt but not going anywhere because Celestine's brother, George, had a firm grip on its neck.

"What is he doing?" I asked Celestine.

She laughed. "Tell her what you doing, George."

The man eyed me narrowly. "I'm going to make lunch."

Lunch?

He wielded the knife again and the goat bleated. I held my stomach.

"Celestine, is he going to . . . ?"

Before I could say anything else the goat had stopped bleating and there was blood everywhere. My stomach lurched and I leaned against the side of the house weakly. I closed my eyes.

"You all right?!" Celestine grabbed my shoulder.

"I think so," I mustered.

"Let's go inside," she said, leading me into the house from the back door. I think I heard George laughing as I stumbled inside.

"Oh, they die so quickly they don't feel any pain," she said, handing me a glass of ginger ale after she'd sat me down at a large dining table.

I took a deep breath and sipped. "I've never seen anything like that before."

"Sorry, I didn't know."

She looked at me, worry in her eyes as I tried to get my stomach to settle down.

"I saw a bunch of goats this morning up in the hills . . . that could have been one of them," I said.

"Maybe," she said. "But it's too late to worry about that now."

Was it? I had wished those goats were dead when I'd stood there on that path and right in front of me one of them had just been slaughtered. . . . That was just too weird. Too crazy. George walked into the house, a large smile on his face, and blood all over his white apron. I closed my eyes again.

"She staying for lunch?" he asked.

Celestine looked at me and I shook my head. There was no way I would eat that poor goat. No way in hell.

"We're going back," she told George. "Celeste is waiting for the car."

As we walked away from the house I could hear George guffawing. Well, I was glad that I gave someone a good laugh. But still, why did it give him so much pleasure to upset me?

"Sorry," Celestine said again.

"It's all right," I said. I was starting to feel better. "It was an adventure."

"Better than staying inside with a book?"

"Uh-huh." I'd remember this for the rest of my life.

I told Drew about my experience as we ate dinner together. "I don't think I'll ever eat goat meat ever again."

"And you think Frank Perdue hugs his chickens to death?"

"At least I've never seen them get killed."

"George was just trying to screw with you. He likes to get under people's skin."

"He did a good job."

"And you thought Celeste was weird."

"I think their whole family's weird now."

"So are you having a good time? Are you bored?" He asked me this at the end of every day.

"No, I had fun today. First running from the goats, and then watching one go to meet its maker."

"There's more to this place than that, though."

"I'm glad I'm here, Drew." I truly meant it. I wanted to be with him. All the time. It was unfortunate that work had to get in the way and we couldn't spend all day together. I wanted to discover Dominica with him, find little swimming holes, new flowers, strange-looking wildlife. I wanted to do all those things with him.

"We'll do something on the weekend," he said. Then his expression changed.

"What is it?"

"We might have to be a bit more careful. . . . My mother thinks it doesn't look good that we're . . . um . . . living together."

"What?"

"Well, it's just that folks down here are old-fashioned. It doesn't look good for someone in my position."

"We're not living together. I'm just visiting for the summer."

"But you're living here."

"Do you want me to go to a hotel?" Was he losing his mind?

"Of course not." He paused. "Mom thought you could move in with her. You could still spend as much time here as you wanted."

"No way!" It came out as a yelp. I would *not* live with Vanessa. I'd rather spend six months in Siberia wearing a bikini.

He shrugged. "Okay. I don't mind the gossip. It was just an idea."

Ugh! Vanessa! "I don't want to ruin your political reputation."

"You won't," he said. "It's just a matter of keeping up appearances. That's all."

"If it's a huge deal I'll just go to a hotel."

"You hate my mom that much?" He laughed.

"I don't hate her. I just . . . I just don't want to live in that big house. Plus, it's so far away from everything."

"It's not a problem. We'll make it work."

Was I being unfair and selfish? I didn't want to make Drew look bad, but I couldn't imagine a whole summer under Vanessa's roof. Let the people talk, I thought. So, we were shacking up. So what?

Chapter 24

Sonny and I came in from our two-hour walk, and I was ravenous and drenched in sweat. I'd carried a huge stick with me the whole way, watchful for goats or any other critter that dared to get in my way. I was not having it! Thankfully, I didn't run into any.

I looked at the phone, usually I'd call him as soon as I walked in, but I remembered our conversation the night before.

"Are you having fun?" he'd asked again as I began to doze off.

"Yes."

"I don't think you are."

I sat up quickly. "Yes, I am!"

"You don't have to stay the whole summer if you're not having a good time," he said flatly.

"No!" I said, grabbing his shoulder. "I want to stay." I sighed. "I just . . . I'm not used to being in a new place. I don't feel comfortable going to new places by myself."

"Take Sonny with you," Drew said. "Amelia, everybody knows who you are. You'll be fine. I'm not asking you to do anything crazy but go out and enjoy the island. . . . You could even come up to the village with me, to the site. It's nice up there. There's a river where you could go swimming. . . . Just loosen up and have fun." He didn't seem angry, just concerned and a little defeated. As if he were really afraid that I was so bored that I'd get on the next plane to Boston.

"I am," I said defensively. "I'm going out tomorrow."

I had to keep my word. I couldn't call him again. I didn't want to be a naggy girlfriend. I would go out. On my own. By myself. I looked out the window and the day looked positively irresistible. I thought, *"The sun pours down on the earth, on the lovely land that man cannot enjoy. He knows only the fear of his heart." Thanks, Alan Paton. Okay. No fear in my heart; I'm going out to enjoy this lovely land.*

I turned on the TV as I burrowed into a bowl of Raisin Bran. Inflation is so high on Dominica that one box of cereal costs twenty dollars. Twenty dollars for some nasty Raisin Bran! The local news was on and a pretty anchor was mentioning Drew's name. One second later his face appeared, smiling and self-assured. I missed the question he was asked, but he replied, "No, Ms. Wilson is a very good friend of mine and those rumors are untrue. She is staying in my home temporarily, but as anyone who knows me well will tell you I hardly spend any time there. I'm still my mother's son; she can vouch that I spend most of my nights on her estate in Castle Bruce." He smiled, waved away the reporter's microphone from his face, and turned his attention to the construction site behind him.

What the heck? I called him on his cell phone.

"Drew, did you just talk to a reporter?"

"No. What reporter?"

"On the local news?"

"Oh, that. That wasn't live. That happened a couple days ago."

"Why didn't you tell me about it?"

"We talked about it last night. Remember?"

"No, you said Vanessa thought it was a bad idea that we were living together. You didn't tell me the media was on your case about it."

"Calm down. They're not on my case. It's not a big deal."

"Drew!"

"I have to go. We'll talk about it later."

I looked at the phone. It then came to me. He must have gone to Vanessa after the reporter had questioned him, and she must have told him then that we shouldn't be living together. Ugh! Why did he always have to go running to her first?

Screw it! I don't care. I was not living with her no matter what anyone said. Even if we had to sneak around. What was this place anyway?

I had to get outside and get some air. I grabbed the keys to the old red Jeep that looked like it hadn't been driven in a decade. Sonny barked at me as I walked out the door. He hardly ever barked, so I imagined he was saying, "You go, girl!"

The thing heaved and sputtered as the engine warmed up, but I hit the accelerator, hoping it would wake up. *Great. Here we go, little Jeep.*

I drove down the narrow, bumpy road at roughly three miles an hour. The Jeep was noisy and felt plenty stiff. I had never driven any type of four-wheel-drive vehicle so this was a new experience in many scary ways.

"Hey!" I looked to the side and Jimmy was waving to me from his front yard. His sitter was gardening and he was holding some type of garden tool next to her.

I waved back. "Hi, Jimmy."

And that was that. He went back to doing his thing. But the sitter did ask how I was doing and where I was going.

"I have no idea," I told her.

She laughed. "Well, have fun."

This isn't too bad, I thought as I eased out onto the lane that led to the main road. The sun was bright, the sky was clear, with a few cumulus clouds scattered about. Colors splashed from earth to sky; it was another day for Matisse to paint. I had to remind myself to keep my eyes on the road; it was so hard not to stare at the wildflowers and fruit trees to the right and left of me. I was driving too slowly. A small car pulled right up on my bumper, I sped up a bit, hoping he would just pass. But this guy rode my bumper for about a mile, much longer than I'd planned on driving. Before I knew it I was on the main road, the wider road, leading into Roseau, the capital. The rude driver in the small car passed me at the first opportunity, making sure to slow down and glare at me before he sped away.

Well, sorry I wasn't driving fast enough for you, dude!

The road was busy. There were teenagers lining the streets, older people sitting at tables playing sidewalk dominoes in the neighborhood of Citronier. Some kids played barefoot near an exposed drain. This was a seaside area with a crop of teeny, weeny houses crowded together like little boardgame towns. The sea was a rocky walk away and I could see teenage boys walking bare-chested to the shore. They looked bored, but happy. Drew had warned me about some of these boys. Dominica had its own problems with drugs and the related violence. But I had to remind him, I'm from Dorchester. These boys did not scare me. Nor did they even give me a second look.

I continued driving, slowing down to check out the building that housed the one radio station on the island, Dominica Broadcasting Service; the public library that looked like an old plantation house; and the Fort Young Hotel, which I had to say was the closest thing to home with its steady stream of tourists, air conditioning, and the way it seemed to isolate its guests from the real flavor of the island. I never would have experienced the true essence of Dominica if I'd stayed there.

Then it was on to the waterfront. I stopped at a row of street vendors who were selling souvenirs and other useless stuff that looked pretty and exotic. I bought a pair of earrings; I'd mail them to Ma later. A cruise ship had just docked, and throngs of sunburned tourists disembarked, crowding the waterfront. That sight immediately brought a smile to the half-mile-long row of vendors waiting to sell them everything from dolls wearing traditional Dominican dress, coasters carved out of local wood, native jewelry, and other exotic and not-so-exotic fare. It was exciting, like a huge flea market. I walked around for a bit, absorbing the sounds of bargaining, the smells of suntan lotion and sweat, and the general feeling that all was well with the world—at least in this part of it.

Maybe because there were so many tourists around I did not feel as out of place. I heard American accents, British accents, and what I thought was German and Russian being spoken. And everyone was so friendly. Then I felt a tap on my shoulder.

It was Sophie, Drew's sister. "What are you doing out here?" she asked, smiling her big smile. She was tall and thin and very beautiful. She had four kids but it didn't show. I wished I had her genes—and could fit into her jeans.

"Just looking around."

We chatted for a bit; then she asked me to go to lunch. I wavered. "I really hadn't planned on being out for long."

"Oh, come on. I'll introduce you to some people. You need to make friends if you're going to be staying here."

I followed her in the rickety Jeep to a small restaurant in the center of Roseau.

We walked into a flower-filled atrium with about 50 tables covered by huge umbrellas. Soft reggae music played in the background. A couple of tourists ate lunch near the bar, where a bored bartender read a magazine that looked a lot like *The Source*.

"My friend Mona owns this place. She bought it from a British man two years ago."

We walked into the covered part of the restaurant and I sat as Sophie went to fetch her friend Mona. A couple of young women entered the restaurant and walked toward me. One of them eyed me suspiciously. She was about my age, though she looked quite fabulous in a spaghetti strap dress that went halfway down her thighs and jeans and flip-flops. How do girls like her do this? If I wore something like that I'd look like Dumbo the elephant.

"This table is reserved," she said in a British accent.

It was? Then Sophie came back to save the day.

"Oh, Shauna, this is Drew's friend Amelia." Sophie hugged both women and kissed them French style, on both cheeks.

The two women, both tall and regal, regarded me politely and held out their hands.

"It's nice to finally meet you," the other one, Nicole, said. She spoke with a Dominican accent.

Apparently, this was their weekly girlfriend get-together, and I was intruding. But they were nice. They were all married, happily so it seemed. They talked about their kids. A lot. I thought they were hilarious. If I ever have kids, I told myself, I'd never talk about them around people who didn't have kids. It was so hard for me to care. I had to laugh when they laughed, oooh when they ooohed, and aah when they aaaahed. Then the conversation switched to husbands. Something else I didn't have.

"Oh, he had the nerve to ask me what I was cooking," Nicole was saying of her husband. "It's not even lunchtime yet and the man wants to know what I'm making for supper."

It was all harmless, softball married-girl complaints. They all looked so content in their wedded state. Neither Sophie nor Shauna worked, and Nicole was a part-time pediatric nurse at the Princess Margaret Hospital. I recognized the name of the hospital because it was where Drew had been born—he'd taken me there.

"So, Amelia, are you liking it here? Is the heat too much for you?" Shauna asked. I liked her. She was a bit haughty, but then how could anyone speak with a British accent and not come off that way?

"Not at all, I'm having a great time. I've only started going out recently. I plan to do a little exploring every day this week." Once again my mouth was making the plans as my brain idled by helplessly.

"That sounds good. If you need company, just call," Sophie said.

Then a woman, ample like myself, came out of the back with a huge tray.

"Okay, ladies. This is what I made for us today."

They all exclaimed at the plates of crab and vegetables. It was a visual and culinary feast.

"I'm Mona," she said, putting a plate, overflowing with stuffed crab, vegetables steamed in a spicy sauce, and brown rice, in front of me. God, it smelled so good!

"Mona owns this place," Sophie said as Mona, still wearing her cook's apron, joined us. "And she owns a spa out in the country and she's thinking of building a hotel, too." They all laughed.

"She's the overachiever of our group," Shauna said.

Mona waved her hand. "I just like to work. So, you're from Boston?"

I nodded as I dug into the food, trying to remind myself not to eat too much.

"I went to school in Boston," she said.

Mona explained she'd gotten her MBA from Harvard fifteen years ago and had worked as an investment banker in New York for ten years before moving back to Dominica. I was surprised by this because of all the women around me she seemed the most Dominican. There was no trace of New

York or Boston in her accent. Her mannerisms were all very pronounced and overly feminine like most Dominican women. I asked her about this in as polite a manner as I could manage.

"I couldn't tell that you'd lived in the States," I said.

She laughed. "Oh, I'm a chameleon, girl," she said. "It's good for business if I'm one of the people here. Dominicans hate it when people come back from abroad and try to put on airs as if living overseas is a big deal or something. The worst thing you could do down here is act too big for your britches."

Shauna arched her brows playfully. "Yeah, she's the veritable salt of the earth, our Oprah here."

Mona waved her hand again dismissively at Shauna. "And she's Ms. Prissy."

I was having a great time with these women, but two hours and several glasses of wine (for them, not me) later it was over.

"You should come again next week," Shauna said.

"Why wait?" Mona said. "If you ever run out of things to do, come and hang out with me. I'm always either here or at my spa out in the country."

I felt good as I got back in the Jeep. Full and finally welcome. Now I had to find a way to burn off this extravagant lunch. So instead of heading straight home, I walked around the capital some more. It was baking hot and my feet were dusty and parched, but I kept going even as sweat poured down my back.

I found an old cathedral and sat in the pews for fifteen minutes just to catch my breath and let its dark, holy aura wash over me. I took a few pictures of the beautiful flower garden that ringed it. There was a boys' high school across the narrow street and I walked into the courtyard. A few young boys were playing basketball and they looked me over curiously, then went back to their game.

I kept on walking, found a cemetery, and took some pictures of old, ornate gravestones, some almost totally covered by weeds, some dating to the early eighteenth century. I noticed that several of the names on these stones were French. St. Pierre. Beaulieu. Toussaint. Gosh, I was so hot and thirsty! Then I saw what looked like some type of recreational or country club. It wasn't huge but there were a couple of tennis courts and a clubhouse attached. Water!

I followed the main road through the cemetery and out through the courtyard of another building that looked like another school, but later I'd find out that it was the old barracks for the scraggly Dominican Defense Force.

By the time I entered the club, sweat was dripping from the sides of my head. I pulled my hair up in a ponytail. It was so hot!

There was no one in front so I walked into the foyer, which was air-conditioned and so comparatively plush that I just wanted to sit in one of those wicker chairs and nap for a good ten minutes. Before I could venture farther in, a black man hurried out to me, a look of worry on his face.

"What you doin' in here?" he demanded. I was taken aback. "Get out of here!" he roared.

"I just . . . I just wanted some water," I stammered, backing away.

Once he heard my accent his demeanor changed. "You're American? Tourist?"

I nodded, shocked by the sudden change in his behavior.

"Oh," he smiled widely. "Follow me."

He guided me into a large dining room where a few older men sat around a table, all white hair, large bellies, and pompous countenances, smoking cigars and drinking seriously. Movers and shakers? He sat me down at a table and then brought me a tall glass of water and asked if I wanted anything else. I was still very tired and so I decided to rest for a bit. I ordered a virgin piña colada.

Massive bay windows overlooked the tennis courts. A couple of guys played tennis while a few women watched. They looked like younger versions of the men at the table. Hmmmm, I thought. The Dominican ruling class. Wow. My American accent had gotten me into this place, but what if I'd been just a regular person? Would I have died of thirst out there? Maybe this place wasn't all paradise then.

Chapter 25

Drew's truck was parked outside as I pulled into the drive-way. It was only four-thirty—normally he wouldn't be home till about seven.

"Hey, babe!" I could smell something delicious; he was cooking. I loved that guy! He came out of the kitchen.

"I was worried about you. I called several times."

That technically was my fault for being home all day long every day since I'd come here. He had come to expect it. But still . . . Didn't I have a right to come and go as I pleased? Didn't he tell me that I should go out and explore?

"I was out doing a little exploring." He glanced at the bag in my hand. "And shopping."

"I know. I called Mom, and she said you'd had lunch with Sophie and her friends." He was smiling, but there was a look on his face that said that he wasn't all the way pleased.

"Yeah, I ran into her at the waterfront. . . ."

"Next time can you call me and let me know when you're going out?"

"I didn't plan to be out for long."

"Just call me and let me know so I don't have to worry that you're lost or something."

"I was bored." I followed him into the kitchen.

"That's why I've been asking you to come down to the site."

Why would I want to hang out at a construction site all day?

"Fine. I'll let you know when I'm going out next time."

Tension simmered as we ate and then burbled as we stood at the kitchen sink doing dishes together. This was supposed to be our special place.

"So, you had a good time with Sophie and her friends?"

"Yeah, they're a lot of fun. It felt good to interact with other people."

"What? Interacting with me is not enough?"

I laughed to ease the tension but thought, what a strange question. He didn't even seem to be kidding.

"Of course, it's enough. They come in a very distant second to you."

"So what did you all talk about?"

"Just girl stuff."

"Like what?"

I couldn't help but laugh. "They didn't tell me all about your sordid past if that's what you're worried about."

"I'm not worried. Just curious."

"Yeah, right. We were just getting to know one another. They talked about their husbands and kids and I listened and ate."

Then I told him about my strange encounter at the tennis club and the cemetery and the cathedral. "That guy at the tennis club was so mean."

"He's just doing his job."

"By being nasty to strangers?"

"It costs a lot of money to join that club; the members don't want people just walking in off the street."

I couldn't believe my ears. "What happened to you? I thought you were Mr. Populist."

"It's not that simple. Rich people's money keep this country functioning so that the poor don't starve to death. If that means giving them their own club, then so be it. Besides, you should have told that guy who you were up front and you wouldn't have had any trouble."

"Whatever, Drew. I don't see why a thirsty person can't walk into a place and get a drink of water."

"I don't expect you to understand."

"Right. I'm a spoiled American."

"Here we go," he laughed. "No fighting today."

"Fine. Can we go to the waterfront tonight?" I wanted to see the full moon shimmering off the water up close. But I also wanted to change the subject. It bothered me the way he always laughed at any political argument I tried to make. Like it didn't matter. Like I didn't know what I was talking about.

When night fell we rolled into the capital. I was anxious to see what it was like at night when the cruise ship was in town. From what Sophie told me that was when the capital truly came alive. And it was jumping—in its own reserved way. Drew and I watched tourists stagger out of bars holding bottles of rum in shaky hands. They roamed the streets, which were largely devoid of any local people, baying and carrying on as if it were Mardi Gras. The moon was huge in the black sky and it shone daylight bright on Roseau, putting the stars out of business temporarily. Music and laughter filled stray corners.

"European men sure love them some Caribbean women," I said as a ruddy-faced man in a garish Hawaiian shirt clutched a nubile Dominican woman outside a bar.

"It's just an adventure for them," Drew said critically.

"The men or the women?"

"Probably both."

"Did you ever do the nightclub scene down here?"

"Only if it was a business opportunity . . ."

"You're so serious, Drew."

"Ouch!"

"I don't mean it in a bad way. I just mean that you're so focused on your goals; it's like you don't think about anything else."

"I think about you. Oh, wait. You're just another goal of mine."

"Stop it."

"My mother thinks you're serious."

"Really?"

"Yeah, so does my sister. That means we're compatible."

"Uh-huh." Then I remembered his television interview. "So, you're going Bill Clinton on me? I'm just a good friend of yours who's staying in your home for the summer?" I was teasing him. I didn't mind that he had to lie to protect his and my name.

"Hey, I could tell them you're giving me some good, sweaty lovin' every night if that's what you want."

"No, thanks. But thanks for playing."

Later, I lay awake, just contemplating. It had been a good day. I'd gone out, done and seen some things. But I had questions. How was word of my whereabouts, feelings, aspirations, and seriousness going around so quickly, from Sophie to Vanessa to him? And how should I deal with all of this gossip and attention from Dominicans. Was I overthinking this? My imagination began to run wild as I fell asleep. That night I dreamed that I was Antoinette Cosway again. Locked up in some attic of some old plantation house and going crazy.

I was up early the next day to watch the sun rise from the back porch. Drew had gone out for his jog and I savored the time alone with just the laptop. I reread the e-mail from Whitney. She said I sounded lonely. She was right, a little bit. I missed her. I missed James and Kelly, who sent me pictures of houses they were looking at. But I was okay. I was content. I certainly wasn't living it up like she was, shopping on the Via Veneto and shuttling all over Italy from Termini.

I wrote her back, determined to sound more upbeat but not quite being able to swing it:

> Sometimes everything inside of me says stay here. I could become Mrs. Drew, teach school, hang out with Sophie and her girlfriends. Build a life parallel to Drew's so I wouldn't be so bored half the time. But other times I miss home so much I feel like running to the airport and taking the first plane out. I miss the South Shore Mall, Harvard Square, gourmet chocolate, the shoe department at Nordstrom. And I miss my Beetle, girl. I want to be with Drew but I don't know if I could be happy without all of the above. Is love enough to rough it down here? I don't know.

I hit send and watched the yellow sun rouse itself. Maybe. Just Maybe.

"So what's the adventure for today?" Drew asked as he unlaced his sneakers.

"I don't know. I was thinking I'd go with you today."

"Really?"

He looked genuinely pleased. I wasn't excited about sitting at a construction site all day. I had to remember to pack a book and a big straw hat because I just knew I was going to be hot, bored out of my mind, and would probably get sunburn again. But I was doing this for love.

He listened to BBC news as we drove the twenty miles to the village of Delices where the school was being built. My heart kind of lurched when I heard President Bush's voice over the radio. I had to be deathly homesick, then.

"Oh, I forgot to tell you," he said, turning down the volume. "I'll be nominated in a couple of weeks."

"For the education secretary thing? I thought you said that was just a rumor." Of course, I knew all along he'd get the job.

"At first it was." He looked at me. "Is that okay?"

"What? The nomination?"

He nodded.

"Yes, of course! It's huge, Drew. I'm really proud and happy for you."

"I'm glad then. Mom wants to throw a big party, but I told her to wait until after I'm confirmed."

Vanessa knew?

"When did you find out?"

"A few days ago."

Wonderful, I thought. *He's known this for a few days, Vanessa knows, and he's only telling me now. This news will affect what happens to us and he told Vanessa before he told me.* I had to check myself. I would not feed this little monster that was growing inside of me. I would let this go. I took a deep breath.

"I was thinking," Drew said. "We should probably start thinking about what's going to happen with us."

My heart leapt again and this time it kept right on thudding. "How so?"

"I mean our future." He glanced at me.

Our future? I could have jumped for joy or burst into tears.

"What, you mean, like the distance?" I didn't even know what I was saying.

"Yeah, that. And . . ." He paused. "Do you like kids?"

"What?" We'd already talked about this a long time ago, even before we met. I'd said I wanted two, he'd said he wanted five. But I never thought the issue would ever come up again. Okay, I didn't think it would come up this soon.

"I'm trying not to be sappy, Amelia. Help me out."

"I'm not understanding, Drew." The problem was I wanted this train to stop or at least let me off this instant. I just was not ready.

"I want to get married," he said.

Too late. The collision had occurred before I'd had a chance to escape. Again, the urge to either jump for joy or start bawling overwhelmed me. This is what I've always wanted, I told myself. A handsome, smart husband who loved me. But did I have to stay here to be with him?

"You're not saying anything?" This was the first time I'd ever seen him show any sign of insecurity.

"I'm speechless," I said. Then I reached to grab his free hand. We held hands for a few seconds.

"So, will you marry me, Amelia?"

Oh my God. What do I say?

"Yes, well . . ."

He pulled over. There was no breakdown lane so he parked in a thicket of spindly trees and wildflowers. It was another gorgeous morning, and I felt like we could have been in a picture for a *Condé Nast Traveler* spread.

"You don't sound too sure."

"I'm sure," I said. "I'm sure I want to marry you. It's just that . . . I'm not sure if I want to live here forever."

He looked at me. "You," he paused, "we could go to Boston anytime you want. It's not that hard."

"I know. I have to think about it some more, Drew."

"So, should I not give you your ring?"

He'd gotten me a ring? This was so unromantic, by the way. It was as if he'd expected me to say yes so he'd just jury-rigged this off-the-cuff proposal. As if reading my mind, he said, "I hadn't planned to do it this way. I was going to wait till this weekend and then take you out to dinner and all of that. But I just got too excited. Couldn't wait." He sounded rueful and I felt guilty. Romance is all subjective anyway.

"I want the ring. I mean, I want to wear it."

"I don't think that's a good idea if you're not planning to go through . . ."

"I want to marry you. I want us to have kids. I want us to be together. But Dominica is still growing on me, okay? I'd probably feel the same way if you lived in Cleveland."

"Really? So it's not because this is a small, Third World country without all of the comforts you're used to?"

Ouch!

"I have all the comforts I need right now," I said.

Then he opened the glove compartment and pulled out a box. I couldn't believe he kept the ring in the glove compartment. In the glove compartment?

He opened the box and a gorgeous marquis-cut diamond stared back at me. Oy! I let out a huge peal of laughter. I just couldn't help it. "Oh my God! It's . . . It's so me!"

"I thought you'd like it," he said, smiling. I put my hand out and he put it on my ring finger. And I let out another squeal.

Oh! I'm getting married! my mind exclaimed, but I tried to keep my excitement under control. *Ma is gonna lose her mind!*

We kissed for a long time. And then things began to get even hotter.

"Babe, do you think it's okay to do it here? What if someone comes?"

"They won't," Drew said as he pulled off my panties.

It wasn't working out well. He reclined my seat, the passenger seat, all the way back and climbed on top of me, and the seat creaked from both our weights.

"Drew, I don't think this is going to work."

He only groaned as things got hotter in the truck. It was good, but I tried not to move for fear that something would break. Then he swore. "Don't move."

"What?" I asked. "What is it?"

"Just don't move."

He eased himself up and then crouched down in a weird position. Then I heard voices. Female voices. There must have been at least four or five of them. They got closer and closer and closer.

"Oh, shoot! Who is it?"

"Just don't move," he said.

Thank goodness, he was still wearing his T-shirt.

But was the rest of him exposed, and would they be able to see?

"Hello. Good morning." He smiled and I could hear the thin voices of the women through the glass greeting him. He continued to nod and say good morning for a few more seconds that felt like hours and then they were gone.

I exhaled. "Did they see anything?"

He grinned and shrugged. "Let's pick up where we left off. I was almost there."

"No way, Drew. That freaked me out."

"Come on," he said. "You're going to be my wife. You're supposed to do what I say."

I didn't laugh.

"I'm kidding!" he said, laughing. "You American women are so sensitive."

"Whatever," I said.

Then we went back to fooling around. It was good, for him anyway. I couldn't focus because I was hearing voices. What in the world did I just do?

As we pulled up to the work site, he said, "Those guys like to flirt, so be careful."

"Yes, husband, sir," I teased.

"That's what I'm talking about, woman," he winked.

The work site was what I expected, messy with construction materials all about. The school was almost finished, from what I could see, except for the interior. I walked around with Drew and the foreman of the project, a white Australian who was a missionary as well as a businessman.

"Will you be teaching here?" he asked when I told him that I was an English teacher from America.

"I don't know yet," I said. If I were going to teach here I'd probably do it at the grammar school in town; it reminded me of my school back home.

I found a shady spot under a tree and spread out my towel. Drew had disappeared into the building with the foreman. I decided to reapply sunblock to my flaked-up skin. I needed to take better care of my skin else I was going to lose the top layer of my epidermis! I was doing my shoulders when a shadow darkened my little spot. I looked up. It was a young guy, probably in his late teens or early twenties.

"You need some help with that?" He looked at the bottle of sunblock in my hand; then his eyes traveled back to my face suggestively.

"I . . . No, but thanks."

"You sure?"

He smiled again and I could tell that this kid was used to having his way with the ladies. He had a nice smile, he was tall and good-looking. But I wasn't looking, and I was a bit too old for him.

"What are you doing sitting here all by yourself?"

"I . . ."

"Anthony!"

Drew appeared out of nowhere in front of the two of us.

"Get back to work!" Drew thundered.

Anthony, who was as tall as Drew, gave him a look that spelled pure hatred and resentment, and walked away.

"He was harmless," I said.

"I warned you," Drew said, still angry, but with whom, me or young Anthony? "I don't like you sitting all the way back here. Why don't you go sit in the office?"

"I'd rather stay here. It's too noisy where you guys are working."

"I need to be able to keep my eye on you."

"Why?"

"Listen, just do what I say and stop asking questions!"

"No!" I said. Where did he get off talking to me that way? "I'm staying here because I like sitting under this tree, and it's shady and quiet. Okay?"

He looked at me, exasperation on his face.

"Drew, I can take care of myself, okay?" I think this was the first time I'd ever raised my voice at him. "I'll scream if I need you."

He didn't think that was funny; he shook his head and walked away.

I didn't see him much for the rest of the day. We had planned to eat lunch together, but he never did come back to get me. I followed men's voices and found him eating some kind of sandwich with some of the workers. The radio was turned up loud, zouk music was blaring, and the guys were laughing and being rowdy. I could smell beer. He didn't even notice that I'd come in. A man nudged him.

"I'm busy," he said, then turned away from me dismissively, immediately going back to talking and laughing with the guys, who also acted as though I didn't exist.

I fumed all the way back to my spot on the blanket. We would have this out tonight. I ate my boring bologna alone and tried to concentrate on *Cry, the Beloved Country.*

A few hours later, I was bored with the book and tired of fighting away the mosquitoes that seemed to multiply in number the closer it got to dusk. Then a car pulled up. I craned my neck to see who it was but I couldn't tell anything except that it was black and shiny. Then I heard voices, and then there she was.

"Oh, Amelia!" Vanessa said, almost running toward me. She wore a long white sleeveless dress, brown sandals, and big brown beaded jewelry around her neck and arms. Mother earth with accessories.

"Vanessa?"

What in the world was she doing here?

"I heard the news. Drew called me and told me this morning."

The news? That I was going to kill him for acting like a jerk?

"I hope you're not upset with me for coming here but I was just so excited!"

I stood to greet her, swatting a mosquito on my arm.

We embraced and did the four kisses on the cheek thing.

"You know, the moment I met you I just knew you'd become my daughter-in-law," she gushed.

I said something equally gushy back and we embraced again.

It was a weird thing to be doing because right at this moment I was so angry with Drew that I could have given him his ring back. Had he called her this morning to tell her that I'd said yes? Does she always have to be there every time something important happens to him? To us?

"So, have you talked about a date?"

"Vanessa, he just asked me this morning."

"I understand that, of course, Amelia. But you must have some idea of when . . ."

"Right now, it's just kinda sinking in. I can't think further than today."

She grabbed my left hand. "What do you think of the ring?"

"It's gorgeous."

She smiled triumphantly. "I went with him to the jewelry store, but he picked this one out all by himself."

Oh, geez! Did he pick out his underwear all by himself, too, Vanessa?

"Don't tell him," she whispered, "but I think I'll give you two his father's and my wedding bands. I still wear mine, but I guess I can part with it. Of course, my ring size is a bit smaller than yours. . . ."

"It's still early to be thinking about that, Vanessa."

"I know, Amelia. But it never hurts to plan."

"Right. So you drove all the way up here just to congratulate us?" I tried to sound as friendly as possible.

"I did! Besides, I was bored. My best friend, Jean, is in the States this weekend visiting her grandbabies. Her son just had twins. I'm so jealous."

"But, Vanessa, you already have grandkids."

"I know that, Amelia. But it's different when they're your son's."

Did I even want to ask how so? No. Drew was here.

"Mom, I can't believe you let that old guy drive you all the way up here."

"He's not that old. Anyway, I was just about to leave."

"You'd better get on the road before it gets dark and old boy goes blind."

She kissed him on the cheek and looked at me. "Isn't he awful, this son of mine?"

I waved to her as her 90-year-old driver took off at a raging fifteen miles per hour. The guy was really old. You could hardly see his little gray head over the steering wheel. The whole scene reminded me of *Driving Miss Daisy.*

"Ready to go?" Drew asked as I gathered up my things.

"I can't believe she came all the way out here. . . ."

"She's really excited," he said shortly.

And I took that to mean that she was obviously more excited than I was.

He was silent as we drove home, but I had a lot to think about. How would I tell Ma that I was now engaged? Whitney would definitely have a lot of questions. James and Kelly would be thrilled. Gerard would be skeptical. Ma, I just could not anticipate what her reaction would be.

"I don't like what happened today," he said out of the blue.

"What?" I knew full well that he meant the episode under the tree. Later we would call this our tree fight.

"You're in a foreign country, a different culture. When I say you shouldn't be in a certain place it's because I know what can happen to you. I'm not trying to control you."

"I didn't say you were."

"No, but you're thinking it."

"If you know me so well, then how come you didn't know that I'm perfectly capable of taking care of myself."

"I do know that. But those guys up there don't know that. The guys here . . . They're always putting people to the test . . . especially foreigners. I had to go through hell when I came back from the States just to prove I was one of them and not some money-hungry Yankee. That kid who came up and talked to you today, that wasn't just a coincidence. They're using you to test me. To see how far I can go."

This sounded like some caveman, male-posturing stuff to me.

"I don't know why I should get caught up in that. How was I supposed to know . . ."

"You don't get it," he said testily. "They're going to measure me based on how they see us interact."

Clarity was dawning. "Ohhhh," I said. "So if your little woman doesn't obey you, then they won't respect you?"

"Sarcasm." He shook his head. "We'll talk about this later."

"No, let's talk about it now. Just because those guys hold antiquated ideas about women doesn't mean that I should change who I am to . . ." I stopped as the full force of my words hit me.

"To make me look good?" He glanced at me. "That's not what I'm asking you to do. But if I were, would that be a huge problem?"

I gulped. I didn't know what to say. He was my man and

I loved him, and of course I wanted him to look good. But . . .

"It wouldn't be a problem. I just wish you'd explain things to me instead of just ordering me . . ."

"When did I order you to do anything?"

"When you told me to move earlier today . . ."

"Come on! I didn't order you to go into the office."

"You sort of did," I said. "And you were really rude at lunchtime when I came in to speak with you and you said you were busy."

"I was busy!"

"You were laughing and talking with those guys!"

"That's what it looked like to you, but it's more than that."

"Oh, please."

He sighed and muttered under his breath. "Do you know what those guys think of me?" I didn't answer because I didn't care.

"They think I'm some rich foreigner who thinks I'm better than they are. If I have to get them to think otherwise I have to work as hard as they do, talk like them and with them, okay? Do you think I need to be out here every day doing this work?"

"This is what I don't understand, Drew. Why is it so important that everybody likes you? It's like you're running for president or something."

"I might want to do that someday. I told you that. And it's not about people liking me. It's about me doing something good for my country and gaining other people's respect."

What could I say to that? He was the noble statesman and I was just a whining woman.

"I don't expect you to understand," he said.

"Why, because I'm American?"

"No, because you're a little spoiled and selfish."

"Excuse me?"

It went further downhill from there.

"You think everything's about you. . . . The whole world revolves around your needs, Amelia."

"That is not true! I'm not the one who grew up with a maid at my beck and call."

"You think that's what makes a person spoiled? Try being so self-centered that you feel threatened by a housekeeper doing her job!"

The housekeeper? Celeste? Why was he bringing that up?

"She . . . I'm not threatened by her. I told you I could do the cleaning while I'm here."

"You said you didn't feel comfortable around her."

"Sorry, but I don't. She's weird."

"She's weird? She needs that job, Amelia. Did you ever think about that?"

Actually, I had. Once I'd met Celestine and George I'd stopped asking him that he give Celeste the rest of the summer off.

"That's the thing, Amelia. You don't feel comfortable around her and other Dominicans. What do you think they're gonna do to you? You don't even like Jimmy Wilkes and he's only seven! And you never talk to the neighbors."

"What are you talking about, Drew? I never even see your neighbors!"

"That's because you never leave the house. It's like you came down here to watch CNN and read."

"I went out yesterday and I came out today, didn't I?"

"And look what happened. Maybe you should have stayed in. . . ."

That really hurt. I shut up then. I wanted to cry, and I wouldn't do it in front of him. He would only think me even more self-centered and narcissistic. Ugh! Where did he get off? Mister-I-have-to-run-thirty-miles-a-week-else-I'll-go-insane?

We drove the rest of the way home in silence. That fight had been like a hurricane—forceful, loud, and destructive.

The eye passed over during dinner; he ate, but I didn't. Then the winds started up again when Vanessa called and he spent a half hour on the phone with her, outside on the porch, where I couldn't hear him vilifying me.

"What did Vanessa say about me?" I asked.

"Just go to bed, Amelia. I don't want to deal with this anymore."

"Mama's boy," I muttered and walked off to the bedroom.

He snickered. "That's funny coming from you. You can't even take a vacation without worrying about who'll buy your mom's groceries."

"My mother's none of your business!"

"You have some serious issues, Amelia." And the way he said that made me want to hit him. I ran to the room instead. How could he be so mean? Didn't he just propose to me this morning? Did he want his ring back?

I heard him leave a few minutes later. He probably spent the night at Vanessa's, probably cradled in her arms. Mama's boy.

Chapter 26

"So you got engaged and then promptly got into a huge fight," Whitney said. "How romantic."

"I hope I'm not making a huge mistake," I said.

"Ah well. He might be a good starter husband," she said.

"Whitney, I'm being serious. He might want his ring back after last night anyway. I can't believe I called him a mama's boy."

"You've been thinking it for a good few months now."

"It's just that he can be so dense sometimes. I mean, like the way he was keeping the ring in his glove compartment. And then he's so. . . . Ugh! It's like he needs adoration from everyone he comes in contact with."

"And what's wrong with that? Most politicians are like that."

"I never thought I'd end up with one."

"Stop tripping, Amelia. The guy sounds like he's madly in love with you. You just gotta accept him. And his mama. And your role as the 'woman behind the good man.' That's all."

"I don't know, Whitney. I don't even know if I can live here. That's why I didn't want to take the ring."

"How? What do you mean?"

"It's like I said in my e-mail. I don't know if I could do without spin class, Nordstrom . . ."

"Girl, please. You can come to the States anytime you want."

"That's what he said, too. But down here, it's a whole different lifestyle."

"Oh, right. It's warm every day, you live in a cute house out in the country with big trees in your backyard, you have a waterfall singing you to sleep every night, there's no crime in your neighborhood, no George Bush, no genteel New England racism. Come on, girl! If you want, we can switch places."

On her good days Whitney had a gift for making things seem much better than they actually were.

"Aaargh! Enough about me. How you doing?"

"Eh, I can't complain. I'm starting to work again in a couple of weeks."

"I thought you said you'd spend the whole summer in Rome?"

"I am. But I'm bored. I need to start using my brain. I can always work from here."

"What happened to, er . . . Rodolfo or whatever his name is?

She snorted. "He's gone. Ugh! That fool tried to get into a debate with me about intelligent design."

"Intelligent design? You were talking about evolution with him?" Oh, no. That was one subject that got Whitney so up in arms she'd wrestle anybody to the ground who disagreed with her. She'd read some book by some scientist about why there had to be a God, and from that moment on she became a crusader for Genesis 1:1. It was one of her life's goals to make the rest of her nerdy fellow men see the light. So to speak.

"He actually told me that those scientists I was talking about weren't real scientists . . . and he was raised Catholic!"

"Uh-huh.. Anyway . . . So you guys just broke up?"

"There was nothing to break up. . . . I just don't take his calls anymore. I really need to start working again. That's all I'm concerned about right now. My brain muscles are starting to atrophy. I need a challenge."

That sounded good. She was always a better person when she was excited about work and not about some random guy. "Sorry it didn't work out."

"I'll be fine. Hey, guess what?"

"What?"

"I made contact."

"Contact? With whom?"

"Mr. Stevens."

"What?" I couldn't believe it. She'd actually spoken with her father.

"When? How?"

"I guess he had some kind of spiritual awakening or something. He called me and left a message on my voice mail back home and I called him back. He told me you spoke with him a few months ago?"

Oops. I'd hoped she wouldn't find out. "Yeah," I faltered. "When you . . . Well, I thought it would be good if he knew what was going on. I mean, you're his daughter." I'd called Whitney's father when she was admitted to McLean, hoping that he might go visit her. But he'd said he was too busy.

"It's all right," she said. "I appreciate it. Just tell me next time."

"What did you two talk about?"

"Mostly my health. He said he felt guilty and partly responsible. I'm like, dude, get over yourself."

"You didn't tell him that!"

"No, I told him it wasn't his fault, that he was the best absentee father in the whole world."

"Whitney!"

"He asked me to have dinner with him and his family when I get back to the States."

"He told them about you?"

"Apparently."

"Wow, girl. You're gonna have a white stepmama."

She laughed. "Nah, I told him I'd rather do it one-on-one; then I'd think about meeting his family afterward."

"So, wow again. What else did he say?"

"He seems really mellow now. Like he's gone through some type of metamorphosis or something."

"A midlife crisis?"

"Maybe. Sounds more like he got religion, though."

"Girl, I'm happy for you. Things are looking up."

"Yeah, for you, too. I can't believe you're getting married before me!"

"Well, let's not get carried away here. As of now, my husband-to-be is not even speaking to me."

"You guys will work it out."

I hoped she was right.

"Listen, I have an idea," I said.

"What's that?"

"Why don't you come down here for a few days?"

"To the island?"

"Yeah, come keep me company for a weekend or something. Drew's been dying to go off to Barbados to play golf with his buddies anyway."

"And you wouldn't want to go with him?"

"Heck no. I'm not going anywhere near a golf course."

"Even if it's on Barbados? Do you know the kind of golf courses . . ."

"Why don't you go with him then, Whitney?"

"All right. Okay, that sounds like a good idea."

"Yeah!"

"Make sure you have a fine Caribbean man waiting to pick me up at the airport."

"I'll work on it."

I was so excited! Whitney and I could get into all kinds of

trouble down here. I knew she wouldn't be timid or scared to do the things that I wanted to do. Maybe I would end up going diving again if she went along with me. Finally, something to look forward to!

The next order of business was Grace Wilson, who was in a foul mood.

"Amelia, I ain't heard from you in two whole weeks. Where you been?"

"Ma, you have my number. You could have called."

"You know how expensive those calls are!"

All of a sudden I didn't miss her much anymore.

"Ma, Drew asked me to marry him and I said yes."

There was silence on the other end.

"Ma?"

"Amelia, are you stupid or crazy? You just met this boy a few months ago and you gonna marry him?"

"Ma, he's not just some boy I met a few months ago . . ."

"If he's everything you say he is, then why he ain't marrying one of his own kind? Why you?"

His own kind? Why me?

"I thought you liked him, Ma!"

"Of course, I like him. I just don't understand. . . ."

"You don't understand what he would see in me?"

She didn't answer.

"Okay, Grace," I said. "I just wanted to let you know what was going on. I'll call you again in a week."

Fifteen minutes later, the phone rang. It was Gerard, calling collect.

"Hey, sis, I hear you getting married."

"She told you?"

"Yeah, girl. Don't mind Ma. She's just mad she won't have you to push around no more. Hey, can you hook a brother up? Send me a ticket so I can come down there and chill."

"Gerard, you're on probation for three more months. You can't even leave Massachusetts."

"Dang, that was low, Amelia. How you gonna talk to a brother like that?"

"I'm just playing. But, hey, if you really wanna come down, I can hook it up."

"Serious?"

"I'm serious. But you gotta buy your own ticket."

"Daaaang! You are mean, Amelia. For real."

We joked around and Gerard asked about the women on Dominica. "I don't think they're your type."

"Why not?"

"They like to be taken care of. They like men who take charge and stuff."

"What??? But that's me! I take charge of my girls. Listen, I gotta come down there!"

Gerard was killing me. I hadn't laughed this hard in a while. I even forgot about how mad I was at him for trashing Ma's car and not telling her about it. When we finally hung up I felt longing. I didn't miss Ma's foul moods; I missed her. I missed Gerard, too. I could see him living down here. Without all his personal and criminal baggage, plus all the other distractions of Boston, he could probably even make something of his life.

The day seemed to be crawling by. It was raining heavily, and I knew that Drew would not be working. But he still hadn't come home. I missed him terribly. I wanted this awful gulf to be bridged. I walked into his closet, running the back of my hands against his shirts. Who was I kidding? I'd go to Timbuktu if that's where he was. I loved this man. Everything about him said strength and stability. When I was with him I felt safe and cared for; I hadn't had that feeling with anyone except my dad. The memory of my father was suddenly sharp and painful. I saw his face in front of me. I smelled him and I had to turn around to make sure that he wasn't there. What would he think of Drew? Would he like him? I could see them getting along, having long talks, probably about politics. I had to close my eyes just so the image would go away. I didn't want to feel this anymore.

I went to the exercise room and worked out for two hours, one hour on the bike and another walking on the treadmill. Sonny would have to amuse himself on his own this rainy day.

I hadn't weighed myself in over a month but I didn't have to. None of my clothes fit anymore. Not even my bras. I'd been stuffing them with tissues for the last two weeks. I needed some new clothes, and I couldn't even order them online because the only company who shipped here was FedEx, and it was just too darned expensive.

I thought of calling Sophie and asking her to take me shopping in Roseau, but that seemed unreasonable considering the downpour outside. She probably was up to her ears in her kids anyway.

As I dried myself off after the shower I heard footsteps in the house.

"Amelia!"

"I'm in the shower," I called out.

He walked in as I was slathering lotion all over my naked body.

"Wow, you've really lost a lot of weight." He looked surprised, as if he hadn't been sleeping with me every night for the past six weeks.

"You're only noticing now?" I pulled the towel around me. I felt naked inside and out under his intent eyes.

He nodded, a look of surprise still on his face. "Was it something I did?"

"What do you mean?"

"I don't know." He cocked his eyebrows. "Don't lose any more. Especially up there," he said, looking at my breasts.

"Oh, yeah. Like I know how to control that."

"Just don't lose any more. You look better with more meat on your bones."

So, we were talking? What had happened to our big fight?

"Where were you?" I asked. He couldn't have been working at the site because the rain had been coming down in sheets all day. He hadn't even called.

"At Mom's."

I wasn't surprised. Ironically, he could run to his mother when something went wrong and I did the exact opposite thing. I couldn't imagine calling Ma and expecting to get any comfort when I was in trouble.

I leaned against the sink. "I'm sorry. For the stuff I said."

He didn't say anything. Wasn't he going to apologize, too?

"I think we should set a date."

Set a date? Was that what Vanessa told him to do?

"Aren't you going to apologize first?"

"For what?"

"For being mean to me in front of those guys. For calling me selfish."

"I wasn't being mean to you. But I'm sorry, okay? I'm sorry. Do I get down on my knees now?"

"That would be a good start. But I'll settle for a makeup session." I unbuttoned his shirt.

"Okay. You win."

A half hour later, we were lying in bed and the question came up again.

"So when do you want to do this?"

"I bet Vanessa really wants to know so she can start planning, right?"

He sighed. "Do you want to marry me, Amelia?"

I turned to him. "Yes. Yes, I do, Drew."

"Then why all the stalling?"

"I don't know," I said, stalling some more. "I just feel like it's happening so fast. And I'm so far away from home."

"Okay, fine. We won't set a date then," he turned away. I could tell that I'd hurt his feelings and I couldn't live with that.

"How about in December?"

He turned to me. "This December?"

I nodded. "That'll give me enough time to tie things up back home, with school, my family and everything."

He smiled and kissed me on the lips.

"Drew?" I'd been thinking about this for a while but I thought now was a good time to ask. "Do you think it would be easy for me to work here? As a teacher?"

He propped himself up on one elbow. "You really want to do that?"

"I need to work. For my own sanity."

"I guess you could. But those jobs are not easy to come by. There are a lot of overeducated unemployed people here. . . ."

"But you have a lot of influence, you could help me. . . ."

"I could . . . But there are poor people who need those jobs more than you do. They need to work—for money, not just because they're bored."

I decided to ignore his last statement. Was I not poor, too? "How about when the new school opens up? There'll be more jobs to go around."

"Amelia, that's way out in the country. You'd have to drive up there alone every day."

"So what? I've been driving around. I think I'm getting used to the roads."

"I guess I could get you a driver. . . ."

I punched him in the arm. "Did you hear what I just said?"

"I heard you," he said. "But those roads are tricky. On a day like today when the rain's coming down real heavy you don't want to be out there by yourself. I just drove past a huge mudslide on the way here."

I decided not to push it anymore. I was starting to think that this would always be a point of contention between us. I little woman who can't drive; he big man who will protect little woman. At least the sex was good. And he was cute. And he wanted to marry me. You can't have it all, Amelia. You just can't. But he had to know how I feel.

"Drew?"

"Mmmm mmmm?" He'd already begun to nod off.

"Can I say something?"

He didn't answer and so I went ahead.

"Sometimes I think . . . I feel that you don't have a lot of confidence in me, my abilities . . ."

He lifted his head from the pillow and looked at me.

". . . as a woman." There, I'd said it and there was no taking it back.

He sat up in the bed and sighed.

"Where is this coming from?"

"Nowhere," I said. "It's just an observation."

"So, this is what you've been thinking? That I'm some kind of chauvinist? That's why you started this huge fight?"

"I did not start a huge fight, Drew. And no, I have not been thinking all along that you're a chauvinist. I just think . . ."

"What?"

"Well, when you say that I can't drive myself . . ."

"Amelia, you yourself have said how bad and dangerous the roads are."

"I know, but . . . At least give me the benefit of the doubt. I'm not some little kid. I've lived on my own since college." Did that sound whiny? Every time someone had to declare that they were not a little kid it was probably because they were acting like one.

"Okay, fine," he said. "Drive anywhere you want. Just be careful."

"It's not just the driving. . . ."

"What else?"

"I don't know. I want you to think of me as a capable and strong person."

"Amelia, I think you're very capable. And I'm not just saying that because I'm tired and I need to get some sleep. You've surprised me. We hiked mountains together, went diving . . . I didn't think you'd want to do those things. You didn't think you'd want to do those things. Now you're hiking with the dog every day. I think that's really cool and brave. Not to mention the fact that you left your family and your friends and came down here to be with me."

I felt better. I hoped he meant what he said.

"So don't tell me what I think, okay? Stop trying so hard to get inside my head. It's freaking me out."

I looked at him, surprised.

"Yes, you heard me," he said. "Stop thinking you can read my mind. You don't know what I'm thinking, so don't just make it up as you go along. Give a guy a break."

"Okay. Sorry," I said.

"Can I go to sleep now?"

"Sure."

Well, that turned out nicely, I thought. If he won't treat me like the little woman anymore, then I won't try to get inside his head anymore. But the battle was far from over.

Chapter 27

Sophie and her girlfriends were growing on me so much I began to think that they were my girls, too. I'd never been the type to run in a pack of estrogen, but I was enjoying these weekly lunches with these sisters. Their lives were so drama-free compared to Whitney's and mine. No visible mental illnesses, eating disorders, troubled marriages, alcoholic mother enabling issues. How did they get so lucky? Did it have something to do with living on a tiny, uncomplicated, sunny island? People here just seemed to let the troubles roll off their back like beads of sweat.

We'd spent the morning clothes shopping, and I was surprised at the tiny tops and shorts that fit me. I was now a size 8. A European size 10. That meant something, right?

Sophie was so bubbly. "I'm so excited!" she'd said. "I'm going to have a sister-in-law. Girl, you don't know how long my mother's been trying to marry this boy off."

I'd suspected it had been a long time, judging from the number of calls I'd received from Vanessa over the past few days. She'd called while Drew and I were off walking Sonny one morning, asking how many people I expected to invite. She'd automatically assumed that it would be held on the island and not in the States. She'd suggested that we have it at the Fort Young Hotel, since that's where most of my guests would be staying. Though she really wouldn't mind if I decided to do the whole thing at her house. "I have the room," she'd purred.

Then she'd told me about her friend who worked at some fancy schmancy boutique in New York who could get me a good deal on a designer gown. This conversation took place halfway up Mount Diablotins, at 3,000 feet, on Drew's crackly cell phone. He finally intervened and told her that we had to get going before darkness hit us at the top of the mountain.

"She's gonna drive me crazy," I told Drew. And this time he did not laugh it off. "Just tell her you're busy when she calls," he'd said. Was she getting on his nerves, too? Could it be possible that I was having a breakthrough here? Was the wedding planning exposing Vanessa for the nag that she was?

But back to the present. "So, you know Vanessa's going to make this as lavish and pretentious as possible, right?" Shauna laughed as we ate mussels marinated in white wine, another one of Mona's culinary masterpieces. This woman could cook her behind off! She'd laughingly told me that Vanessa had called her a week ago, informing her that she might be catering my wedding reception and that she should keep her calendar clear for the month of December. That had been news to me, too.

Sophie was sitting right there so I didn't want to badmouth Vanessa, but there was so much I wanted to say. Vanessa had not even asked about my mother yet. They'd never even spoken. Vanessa had taken the reins, assuming that everything was going to happen on her own turf and on her own terms.

"So, what do your folks think about all this?" Nicole asked. We'd been talking a bit lately and I liked her a lot. She was a pediatric nurse and she reminded me a lot of Whitney, very career-focused but with a quirky, offbeat personality that made her more interesting than the average corporate worker bee.

"Well," I paused. How to say this nicely? "My mother is still warming to the idea. She thinks it's a bit soon."

"Our mothers always think they know what's best for us."

Actually, no, I wanted to say. My mother had never pretended to know what was good for me. She just would never agree to anything that didn't leave me in close proximity to her and her needs.

"Does she know about Drew's nomination to education secretary?" Shauna asked.

"She knows. But it doesn't really mean a whole lot to her. She's in her own little world."

"Most Americans tend to be that way," Shauna said, adding quickly. "Not you, of course."

I laughed it off. She'd get along famously with James and Kelly.

"You're going to become an old married woman like us," Sophie said. "Soon, you'll be worrying about diapers and breast-feeding."

Diapers and breast-feeding! I hadn't really thought about that! I mean, I wanted kids, but I'd never, ever thought about diapers and breast-feeding. I just wanted to keep thinking about Drew and sex. And all the clothes I was going to buy at Arden B. once I got back to the States. Man, I used to hate that store! Every time I'd walk by there would be some cute top that I couldn't wear because my boobs were too big or some hip-hugger pants that were oh so cute but oh so tiny. But I was a European 10 now, which was probably a U.S. 8. Ha! I couldn't wait to go back and show them all. I'd be sure to pay a visit to that Lord & Taylor again and hope I run into that rude salesgirl. She'd think twice before telling my skinny butt to go to the women's department!

"What are you thinking about?" Sophie asked, laughing. "You just wandered off in the middle of the conversation."

"She must be making wedding plans in her head," Nicole said.

I laughed with them. "I'm just thinking about how I'm going to get my folks and my friends down here for the wedding."

"Oh, you won't have a problem convincing them," Mona said. "Who wouldn't want to leave Boston in December? Especially for a trip to the islands."

"Right," I said.

Sophie looked at me. "Don't let Mom bully you, Amelia. If you want to have your wedding in Boston, go ahead and do that."

"Oh, no!" I said. "I want it here."

She patted my arm. "Just don't let her bully you. She tried to do the same thing to my sister and me. We're always having to put her in her place."

"Yeah, Vanessa's a pit bull until you stand up to her," Shauna said.

Sophie laughed. "See, I let them talk about my mother like that."

"You know she ain't lying," Mona laughed.

Good. Great. I didn't feel so alone then.

Drew had not made it home yet when I turned my key in the lock but I could hear noises inside. "Celeste?"

"Yes, Amelia," she said, surfacing in the living room.

"Just wanted to make sure it was you."

"Who else would it be?" She put a hand on a hip.

"Uh . . . no one. It was just a figure of speech."

"Hmmpf!" She waddled back to the kitchen.

I'd have to stay out of her way; hopefully, she'd be finished soon. I had to make room for my new clothes so I began to move some of Drew's things around. How many white T-shirts did one person need, I wondered as I cleared out one drawer. I stopped as I hit its oak bottom. Two passports spilled halfway out of a white envelope. U.S. passports. I opened one, curious to see his photo. On the first page Drew's serious face stared back at me from the square, laminated box. I looked at the name next to it: Steve Harrison, it said. Born November 30, 1969. How? Drew was born in 1976! I picked up the other passport and opened it; that one looked normal. His name, his picture, his birth date, was correct, at least according to what he told me. What was going on? Why did he have two passports? I felt eyes piercing into me and looked up. Celeste stood at the door, a bag in her hand. I almost jumped out of my skin.

"I'm finished for the day," she said, an accusing look in her eyes.

"Ye . . . Yes," I stammered. "I was just putting my new clothes away."

She turned on her heel and left, not even bothering to say good-bye.

I put the passports back at the bottom of the drawer and began replacing the T-shirts. My heart was galloping out of my chest. I didn't want him to know that I'd been in here, in his personal things. But why? Why did he have two passports? What was going on here?

I could hear his key turning in the lock. He was home early. I quickly put the last of the T-shirts in the drawer and slammed it shut.

"Hi, sweetheart," I said, almost running to meet him at the front door.

We embraced quickly. I could ask him about it, but then I'd have to admit that I'd been snooping. But I hadn't been! I was only looking to put away my new clothes. He would understand. But what if I was not supposed to know? Who in the world was Steve Harrison?

"Know why I'm home early?"

"Why?" I hoped my voice sounded normal.

"Because I'm taking you to the flower show."

"Oh." It took a minute before it sunk in. I'd begged him to take me to a flower show I'd seen advertised on TV, and he'd flat out refused at first. "Those things are kind of boring; I'd be the only guy there." He wanted to go diving instead, again. And I'd given up, not wanting another fight. But something must have changed his mind. I thought it was sweet that he was trying to smooth things over after our big fight.

"You do still want to go, right?"

"Of course, I want to go." I took a deep breath.

"Are you okay?"

"I'm fine. Celeste was just here."

"I saw her driving down the hill. Did you two argue?"

"No! I'm fine. I have new clothes." My mind was reeling and I couldn't focus. "I'll go get ready."

The show wasn't far away, and he was in a talkative mood. He'd found another site to build on, this time a clinic, in some tiny village near the Carib Reserve. I had yet to visit it, but I'd heard it was much like a Native American Reservation. It was so ridiculous to me that even on Dominica indigenous people still got the shaft.

"That's so great, Drew," I said. "Are there enough doctors who'll want to go all the way out there?"

"I'm hoping there will be. We'll have to bribe them with money. . . ."

He was so good-hearted. There had to be some simple explanation for this Steve Harrison passport. It was probably some gag or joke thing. Drew was too noble, too good to be up to anything nefarious. I tried to relax and take my mind off it.

Vanessa's car was among a few parked in a dirt lot near a gaggle of stands off a main road that showcased the most beautiful flowers and fruit I'd ever seen.

The Giraudel-Eggleston Flower Show was a festival put on by two villages known for having relentless rainfalls, and therefore wild bursts of colorful flowers all year long. Bougainvillea and poinsettia lined the road leading into the villages, and the air smelled sweet and clean. It was not quite as hot up here, although the sun was huge and bright in the sky. The air felt clean and dewy.

It would have been so perfect had it not been for her, dressed in her trademark all white, this time a pantsuit, and huge silver jewelry. She was haggling loudly with a flower vendor. Drew called out to her, and I cringed. Why couldn't we have this beauty to enjoy by ourselves? Did she know about Steve Harrison? Was there anything to know? I had to get my mind off this. She waved us over, and I went reluctantly.

"I'm so glad you could make it." Her Chanel No. 5 was at its most blossomy, competing with the aromas of the other flowers.

"You're losing too much weight," she said, suddenly pushing me at arm's length. "What are you doing?"

"Hiking in the hills behind the house," I said.

She looked at Drew disapprovingly. "You make her go out there in the hot sun?"

"I don't make her go. She goes on her own while I'm at work!"

"Don't let him turn you into some adventuring type like himself," she said. "You don't want to become like those sweating tourists . . . It's so unladylike."

Okaaaay. "Vanessa, everyone sweats here; it's so hot."

She looked at me surprised. "I don't. I never perspire."

And it occurred to me that she didn't. I'd never seen even a sheen of liquid on her forehead on the hottest days. Her face was always a matte mask of makeup and serenity. *Scary,* I thought. *Is she even human?*

"These flowers are beautiful." I was dying to change the subject. She relaxed again and said something to the vendor in the French patois spoken by older Dominicans and those who lived in the villages. The woman nodded and handed her a huge bouquet of flowers. Vanessa passed the woman twenty dollars.

"These are torch lilies, my favorite," she said, caressing the pink, hardy-looking petals. I remembered seeing several in her home. "And these are anthurium."

An older couple approached and immediately began to congratulate Drew on his nomination. Vanessa beamed widely and insinuated herself into the conversation. Then she introduced me as "Amelia, Drew's bride-to-be." I smiled and did the four-kiss thing with the couple. But I was pissed. It was as if Drew had forgotten me again. He had gotten so caught up in those people's adulation that Vanessa had to step in and remind him that I was standing there! And that was just the beginning. It happened again and again as we ran into more and more people who wanted to shake his hand.

I should have been enjoying this outing, but it was so difficult. Steve Harrison was on my mind and we were stopping every five minutes to greet more people. Between those meetings, Vanessa acted as a chatty guide, pointing out heliconias, bird of paradise, orchids, yellow allamandas, pink chenille, and lavender morning glory. I took pictures, hoping I'd get to observe them more closely when I was in a better mood.

When she grew tired of walking we sat down to eat in a makeshift outdoor restaurant. Drew ordered beer and fish and chips. I drank sorrel juice, which tasted and looked like fruit punch—but with more fruit than punch. I decided to go out on a limb and try the fried bread-fruit with smoked herring. It tasted delicious, but Vanessa wrinkled her nose with distaste, and I began to feel self-conscious.

"That smell is going to stick to your clothes all day," she said.

"Mom, leave her alone!"

I was shocked, both by Vanessa's statement and Drew's retort. He shook his head and walked away with his beer in hand.

"It's okay. I wasn't offended," I lied.

"Why would you be?" Her eyebrows shot up. "I don't know what his problem is, but herring stinks. I wasn't telling a lie."

I sighed. "I just wanted to taste it."

"You could have asked about it first."

"Vanessa, it really isn't any of your business what I eat."

She put down her glass of water and looked hard at me. I glared right back. I would not lower my eyes, and I was ready to go at it if she said just another word. This staredown lasted for a minute or so, and she blinked.

"I'm going to buy some more flowers," she sniffed and walked away. I happily ate the rest of my stinky herring. But she was right. I did need to wash up a few times and brush my teeth for a good five minutes before the stench went away. Still, I'd like to think that the balance had finally begun to tip between Vanessa and me. She didn't linger much after that, so Drew and I hung back for a couple of hours enjoying the sights of the small village as more and more people drove up to see the show, to buy and sell flowers, fruits, and vegetables. With Vanessa gone, everything looked prettier, smelled so much purer.

I clicked through my photos in the camera as we drove back. "Thanks for sticking up for me, husband."

"I really wasn't. It's like she's become another person since this wedding thing came about. I think I need to find her a boyfriend."

"That's a great idea! Do you know anyone?"

"I'm working on it."

"That would be the best thing that could happen to me. I mean to us. I mean to her."

"It's okay. I know what you mean."

"I can't wait till Whitney gets here."

"Yeah? Try not to end up on *Girls Gone Wild.*"

"Who? Me? Sweet, innocent me?"

"Yeah, right."

"When have I ever acted wild?"

"It's not you. It's your friend and what you've told me about her I'm worried about."

"I was just trying to be entertaining. Whitney's not half as bad as I make her out to be."

"I hope not."

"I'll defend my virginal reputation. I promise."

"Virginal reputation? That went out the door a long time ago."

"Thanks to you," I said.

"You forced me. . . ."

"Of course, I did."

And as we joked around I put Steve Harrison and all those questions out of my mind. Whitney would be here soon and we'd find Vanessa a boyfriend. Everything would work out just fine.

Two SUVs were parked in front of the house when we arrived. "Who's that?"

He narrowed his eyes. "Looks like my lawyers."

"What are they doing here so late?" It was almost dark.

"Something must have come up."

Two men were waiting for us on the porch. One I recognized. He was the ex-New Yorker Drew had introduced me to my very first week on Dominica. The other was a white guy in his thirties. They both wore shorts and golf shirts.

"What up, dude," the white guy said, and I immediately recognized his voice. He'd called my cell phone while Drew was visiting me in Boston.

"What's up?" Drew asked as he opened the door. He introduced me to the white guy, Jason.

"You're from Boston?" he said. "I spent some time there

in the nineties." Jason was from Atlanta; he and Drew did business together while Drew lived in the States. The other guy, Phillip, was serious and unfriendly and only said a curt hello. Was something wrong?

"You remember Phillip, right?" I held out my hand and Phillip shook it noncommittally. There was something a bit too familiar about him.

I decided to make myself busy in the kitchen; they obviously wanted me out of the room. I asked if they wanted drinks but they all declined. Fine. I'd go sit on the back porch and hassle Sonny.

Ten minutes later, I could hear engines pulling away. Drew was sitting on the couch in the living room, a troubled look on his face. "What's wrong, babe?"

He looked at me intently for a long few seconds, then said, "Nothing. Nothing's wrong."

"Are you sure? Is your golfing trip still on?"

"Yup. Let's go to bed. I need to be up early for my flight tomorrow."

"Drew, there's something really weird about that Phillip guy."

"Weird?"

"Not weird. Familiar."

"You mean the fact that he looks just like Celeste?"

"Oh, yeah! That's what it is!" It finally made sense. They had the same eyes, taciturn expression, and grimacing lips.

"That's her son. I thought I told you that."

"You didn't. Wow. Everything's so six degrees down here."

"Right. You should be careful. You never know who's who."

I thought he was joking.

Chapter 28

I sat in the airport waiting for Whitney's plane to land. Drew had left earlier in the morning with three of his friends. He'd been acting strange since his two lawyer friends visited, but I chalked that up to his relief about getting away from me for three days. We'd been in each other's faces constantly for the past two months and it had begun to get claustrophobic in the house. Hopefully, when he came back from playing golf at Sandy Lane in Barbados, we'd both be in a better mood.

I paged through the *Chronicle,* perusing the headlines and the shorter stories. As I paged through the middle, I saw Drew's picture in black and white. I did a double take. The headline did not mention his name. I imagined that the story concerned his appointment to the Ministry of Education. I read it anyway, though I really wasn't interested in all that political stuff. My eyes popped open the more I read of the story, which read like an opinion piece, but journalism in Dominica tended to favor the dramatic over the factual. One paragraph, in particular, grabbed my attention:

Anderson, 31, was also romantically linked to Shauna Woodson, a British citizen who has roots in

Dominica. She is now married to Michael Woodson, a businessman who is also British. It seems that our soon-to-be Minister of Education may be holding a grudge against Dominican women. His current fiancée is an American import, a teacher from Boston who is hidden in his Castle Comfort home. The few times she makes appearances in public she's surrounded by Mr. Anderson's sisters or his mother. Neighbors in Castle Comfort say she never leaves the home without Mr. Anderson's dog, Sonny. What does she think? She needs protection from us savages? Our prime minister might want to rethink Mr. Anderson's appointment to such an important ministry. If our own women are not good enough for him, then how well can he serve us as Minister of Education?

Allrighty, then! Ugh! I closed the paper and looked around. At least they hadn't put my picture in their rag. Ugh. Drew! Why didn't he tell me that he and Shauna had been involved? More than anything in that ridiculous story it was driving me insane. Yes, she was happily married, but somehow that made it worse. That could mean that she'd ended it and that he might still have a thing for her. Grrrrrr . . . Shauna.

I heard the noisy engine of a Cessna and turned toward the gate. Whitney's plane had landed. I'd made sure she came into the Canefield airstrip instead of the Melville Hall airport, which was three hours away. That way I wouldn't have to drive her across the entire island.

Whitney waved to me as she checked in with immigration and I had to laugh. She had on her movie star sunglasses, these huge, black, Jackie O things, a tiny pink halter top and some white short-shorts, with pink high-heeled wedge espadrilles. She looked amazing.

"Look at you!" she said as we embraced. "You're so skinny now! Don't lose any more weight!"

"Why do people keep telling me that?" I hugged Whitney tightly. "You look so amazing, girlie."

"Well, dahling, I wanted to fit in. . . . That's how they do it in the islands, right?"

Whitney spoke loudly, and she was attracting a lot of attention. It was fine with me, but the Dominicans were watching her suspiciously, disapprovingly. They didn't like it when women dressed that way in public, nor did they like it when women called too much attention to themselves.

A man approached us. "Do you need a taxi?"

"No, thank you," I told him.

"Oh, you're the American girl Drew's marrying?"

He held out his hand and I shook it as he told me his name. He smiled at me and quickly turned his attention to Whitney. He beamed at her kindly, and at first I thought he was going to hit on her; instead, he shook her hand and said, "I deal with a lot of tourists here, young lady. So let me give you some advice. Don't go out in public looking like that else you're going to have a hard time down here. Okay?"

He turned and walked away quickly enough before Whitney's mouth could close.

"Did he just say what I think he did?"

"I wouldn't worry about it, Whitney," I said, guiding her to the exit.

"What is this place, freaking Saudi Arabia?"

"It's not a big deal. They're just conservative. It's kind of weird, actually. They don't mind when white women do it. It's just black women they don't want walking around too exposed."

She sighed. "Why did I let you . . ."

"Whitney, we're gonna have fun. Relax. We're going diving."

"Now?"

"Yup."

Since when had I become the director of fun? I didn't know but it sure was fun playing one. I drove Whitney around for a bit, and she, as I did on my first days in Dominica, snapped pictures, exclaiming about the stark contrast of beauty and poverty before her eyes.

"Someone should buy this place and fix it up," she said. "They could turn it into this eco-resort. . . ."

"Nah, I think the people like it just the way it is."

"But if it were more like St. Thomas, they'd get more tourists."

"It wouldn't be the same. These people like their lives the way it is. I don't think they wanna see a bunch of glossy American stores in their downtown."

"I thought that's what you missed the most."

"It is. But I don't want to see a Gap or Starbucks down here. It just wouldn't fit."

"Oooooh, Amelia. You're starting to sound like you love it down here."

I shrugged. "I like it. It's not perfect, but I like it. There, I said it."

She smiled and spread her dreadlocks on her shoulders. "It's a funky little place." She snapped more pictures as we drove through Roseau. "It's a nice change after being in Rome for the last month."

"So did you finally kick Rodolfo to the curb?"

"Girl, you know I did. But guess who keeps e-mailing me?"

"Who?"

"Duncan, that fine lawyer . . ."

"I remember. Big D."

"Exactamente! I think ol' dude is catching feelings for your girl."

"Ooooh. What you gonna do?"

"I don't know. He's kinda sweet. He's like one of those reformed players who's finally ready to settle down."

"Hmmm . . . You guys would be perfect for each other then. Though I wouldn't call you reformed."

"Chile, I'm not ready for all that. I'll see how things go when I get back home. He is cute, though. With the e-mails and all."

Oh, boy. Did she even listen to herself? With Whitney it was always one down, on to the next guy. She always managed to convince herself that each new fling or relationship would be so new, different, and exciting. That's my girl, though. Ms. Optimistic.

Once we arrived at the house she ooohed and ahhed over the magnificent view from the front porch and the lush trees and bushes in the back. "This place is amazing! Amelia, I wanna stay forever!" she said over and over again.

"Shhhh!" I told her.

"What's that?"

"It's the waterfall."

"I hear it! I hear it! That is so cool!"

"We'll go see it later."

We had a quick snack then jumped back into the Jeep, heading for the dive lodge.

"So did you get your certification?" Whitney asked.

"No, not yet."

"How come? What you been doing all this time? I thought you'd be a dive instructor by now."

"I just haven't gotten around to it."

She looked at me as if I were crazy. "It's not like you've been busy with work. . . . You can spend all your time playing."

"I know. I know. I just didn't want to go by myself."

"You're so weird, Amelia. You really are."

"Not weirder than you."

"Yeah? At least I know how to have a good time."

"Whatever, Whitney."

We arrived at the dive lodge just as a group of tourists were getting their dive equipment together. It was another sunny, colorfully gorgeous day, and I wanted to smack myself hard for not doing this earlier. I could have been out here every day diving if I hadn't been such a wuss! Now Whitney was going to have all the fun while I stayed back and snorkeled with the 9-year-olds and old ladies.

She joined up with the group of about twenty people who'd lined up to rent equipment. The dive master waved to me cheerfully.

"You're not joining us today?" he asked, coming up to greet me with a big hug. I had only met him once, with Drew.

"Nah, I'm gonna do some snorkeling instead."

"The whale-watch guy is leaving in a few minutes. You should go with them."

"Really?" Now that I could get into because it didn't require any talent or skill.

"What's your friend's name?" he asked, following Whitney's butt with his eyes.

Oh, here we go. "You should ask her."

"I think I will," he said, eyeing Whitney inquisitively. She was quickly making friends with the group of divers boarding the boat. Darn! I envied them. I made a vow right then and there: I would take the stupid scuba class. I WILL take the scuba class. By next year this time I will be an expert diver. EXPERT!

I ran off to the other boat that was almost finished loading.

"Whale watch! Whale watch!" a burly man called out from the deck.

"Oh, you're Drew's girl," he said when I got near the gangplank.

I nodded and introduced myself. "Tony," he said, shaking my hand. "I'll take good care of you."

As the boat pulled off, I pulled out my camera. The Caribbean Sea had a clean, salty smell and was so blue it hurt my eyes to look. There was a light breeze off the ocean that balanced out the steady rays of the sun. I could see birds clipping across the sky in brilliant formations, and the little dock getting farther and farther away. Amelia, I thought, you're doing something fun. On your own! Whitney was probably raising hell with her group of divers. But I was having a good time, too. I was still snapping pictures of distant mountains, when a woman cried out behind me. "Oh my God!"

I turned and there was a huge black shape in the water. It flashed its flukes in the air and a plume of water shot up. The woman, an older American, shrunk back. Her husband laughed at her. "That's a sperm whale," he said.

I tried to get a picture, but it had already dived back under the surface. From that point on, my eyes never left the water. And a few minutes later I got lucky as the same whale, I think, resurfaced. This time, a few of us were ready, and our cameras all responded in unison. I wished my digital camera was as fancy as the one belonging to the Japanese couple next to me, but I just had to make do.

The time went by quickly, and it seemed that the farther out we went the more common whale sightings became. I saw two dolphins leap into the air, and I caught that on my camera. I snapped a Pilot, a False Orca, and two Spinners. I knew what they were because Tony, our guide, could tell them apart. To me, they just looked frighteningly huge and awesome. By the time we turned around to head back my heart was pounding. We had gotten so close to the dolphins, they'd seemed within arm's reach. I was so pumped up. I couldn't wait to tell Whitney all about it.

When we returned to shore, the divers had not returned so I decided to go snorkeling with the elderly American couple, the Smiths from Kansas City.

"Is this your first time on Dominica?" the woman asked me.

"Not really. I'm here for the summer."

"Oh, how fun. Do you have family here?"

"Uh . . . sort of. My fiancé lives here."

That sparked the requisite showing off of my engagement ring, questions about the wedding date, etc.

"So, you'll be moving here permanently?" Mr. Smith asked.

"I intend to."

"We thought of retiring here. But my wife felt it was too isolated."

"I like to shop. The shopping here's not that great," Mrs. Smith said. Finally! Someone who got where I was coming from.

"There's great shopping on Guadeloupe; it's only a ninety-minute ride on the ferry."

There was? And why hadn't I heard of this before?

"Yeah, but you have to pay in euro. It's too expensive," Mrs. Smith said.

They went on and on like this until I managed to escape them and headed underwater. They'd been married fifty-four years and they still looked pretty happy. Hell, they were still hanging out together. That wasn't a bad thing, I thought as I sank lower into the warm water. I'd brought my camera with me this time, and I was hoping to find a hawksbill turtle. If I found one, I'd frame that picture and put it above my bed. Thirty minutes later, I had seen plenty more exotic fish and other marine life but no hawksbill turtle. Guess I'd have to come back.

When Whitney and I finally headed back to the house we

were salty-haired, giggling, and exhausted. It had been a long day, but Whitney wanted more.

"So, what are we doing tonight?"

"Tonight? Aren't you tired from traveling all day?"

"Not really. My happy pills give me boundless energy."

"I don't know how you can joke about that stuff." I'd made us tuna melt sandwiches, her favorite. I hadn't had one in what seemed like years and, boy, they tasted good. Aaaah, American food.

"I'm not ashamed."

"Not saying you should be."

"Then why wouldn't you joke about it?"

"Because . . . it's serious."

"What's serious?"

"Your . . . your . . ."

"Mental illness? Psychosis? Craziness?"

"I thought we were just gonna have fun this weekend."

"We are, Amelia. But let's get this straight, I'm not going to act like I'm some fragile little creature who takes herself so seriously that I can't laugh at being on these meds. That's not who I am. And you should know that by now."

"I do, Whitney." God, she was in a mood today. "Sorry if I made it seem otherwise."

She looked at me and then shrugged. "Are there any bars nearby?"

"Well, the Fort Young Hotel has a happy hour that's supposed to be really hot."

"Good, I'll go get changed."

She ran off to the bathroom, leaving me at the kitchen table. I wondered if I should call Drew and let him know that I was going to be out with Whitney for the night. I didn't want to bother him on his golf weekend. He'd been dying to go all summer long, and I was the reason he hadn't been able to go. Besides, he'd probably expect that I'd be showing Whitney around anyway. As I cleared up the table I wondered if I should tell Whitney about the Steve Harrison discovery. Knowing her, she'd make a huge deal about it. Probably make up some crazy story in her head full of intrigue and CIA agents. No. I'd try to keep my mouth shut for once.

When we walked into the darkened bar I could feel about fifty pairs of eyes on us. Whitney, of course, looked smashing in slim white capris and a fuschia halter. I was wearing a spaghetti strap aquamarine dress that dipped way down into my cleavage. I was a little worried when I put it on. Drew would probably think it was too revealing, especially since he wasn't there. But Whitney had said, "Since when did you join the Taliban?" And that had been enough to make me wear the dress. And I looked good in it, too.

I noticed the bartender from a few weeks ago and I waved to him. "Let the fun begin now that the diva's in the house!" Whitney said and hightailed it for a bar stool. There was jazzy calypso playing and a few people were dancing on the terrace that overlooked the ocean. It was a gorgeous evening. I felt like I was in South Beach. There were quite a few tourists mixed in with the crowd of locals, which looked to consist mainly of the young professionals and probably students. I thought I saw Jason, Drew's lawyer, in the crowd, but that couldn't be. He was in Barbados playing golf with Drew.

"You're Drew's girl?" A girl came up to me as I sipped my virgin piña colada. Whitney was busy chatting with some French guy who had sidled up to her.

"Yes, I'm Amelia." I held out my hand.

She ignored my outstretched hand and didn't return my smile. "Couldn't you find a man in your own country?" she snapped, and walked away, shaking her head in disgust.

What? What the heck was that? I put my drink down. I felt really shaken up. First the story in the paper and now this? What was happening here? I had all of a sudden become a celebrity in this place and people hated me. Why didn't Drew warn me about this?

I turned to signal Whitney that we should leave, but she was giggling along with her Frenchman. I elbowed her in the ribs anyway. She whirled around.

"What's up?"

"We need to go."

"What? Why?"

The guy looked at me. "Is something wrong?" He had a French accent that was only slightly European. He was probably from one of the neighboring French-speaking islands. He smiled. "I'm Pierre." He said his last name but it was something that I couldn't pronounce. I smiled and shook his hand.

"I know you. You're the American girl Drew Anderson's marrying."

So, maybe it had been a good thing that I hadn't gone out in public much. Everyone knew me. It then occurred to me that there had to have been a picture of me somewhere since all these people recognized me. I mean, they may have seen me driving around with Drew. But was I that memorable?

"He's a lucky guy," Pierre said. "A rich, lucky man."

Rich? Lucky? Drew wasn't that rich.

"Everyone knows you around here," Whitney said, a big smile on her face.

"Yeah, that's why we need to go now."

"No way! We're just starting to have fun."

I grabbed her arm. "Excuse us, Pierre."

She hopped off the bar stool reluctantly and I pushed her toward the ladies' room.

"Some girl just came up to me and gave me some attitude!"

"Oh, I heard her."

"You heard her?!"

"So what? You know girls gonna be hating on you. You stole their most eligible bachelor."

"She looked really mad, Whitney."

"Oh, please. We're from Dorchester, remember? We'll take her ass outside and . . ."

Just then a stall opened and the same girl walked out, her eyes were blazing with anger.

I stopped breathing and Whitney must have gotten the drift from the look on my face.

"So you got a problem, sweetie?" Whitney asked the girl, who was at least my height, so a good three inches taller than Whitney.

She walked up to Whitney, leaving about a hair's distance between them. "You want to do something about it, midget?"

Whitney put her hand on her hip. "Did you just call me midget, Bigfoot?"

I grabbed Whitney's arm. "Whitney, let's go."

"Yeah, get out my face before I break you in two," the girl yelled, taking off her earrings.

"I can take my earrings off, too!"

"Whitney, let's go," I said, dragging her behind me as I half ran, half walked out of the ladies' room. My heart was pounding. I'd never been in a fight before and I didn't want to start now. Not at my age.

"Whitney, we really need to get out of here."

I noticed that the girl who would break Whitney in two was now talking animatedly with two other girls. One of them had to be at least two hundred pounds. Oh, Lord, help me!

"Let's go find Pierre. He'll protect us." Whitney laughed out loud, looking straight at the three girls.

"I can't believe you think this is funny. Those girls look like they're about to kill us."

"They can't do anything."

"How do you know that?"

I noticed Pierre approaching. Great, now was the perfect time for Whitney to get her flirt on. Right before we got killed.

"Hey, babe," she said, calm as day.

I followed them back to the bar. "We're actually just about to leave," I said.

"Oh, that's too bad," Pierre said, signaling the bartender. Whitney rolled her eyes at me.

"So, what time do you girls want to leave tomorrow?"

Leave tomorrow?

"Oh," Whitney said. "Pierre's gonna give us a ride on his sailboat over to Guadeloupe. You said you wanted to go shopping, right?"

"Um . . ."

"How about nine-ish?"

"Good," he said.

"Oh, sweetie," she leaned into him. "Can you walk us out to our car? It's so dark outside."

He straightened up on his stool, all gallant and gentlemanly. "Yes, of course."

And off we went. I stole a glance back and noticed the three girls glaring at us. Thank God for big, burly Pierre. Those girls would have stomped us on the sidewalk. I could see it in their eyes.

As we drove home, I kept looking in the rearview mirror.

"Chill, chica, those hoes ain't gonna follow us."

"I don't know, Whitney. I'm the one who has to live here, not you."

"Relax, Amelia. No one's gonna touch you. Those girls know better."

"I hope you're right."

"I'm always right, babe."

The farther away we edged from the capital, the more secure I felt. It didn't even bother me that it was pitch-black outside and I was driving on those hilly roads leading up to the house. I was just so glad to be away from that situation. It was kind of funny when I replayed the scene in my head. I started to laugh.

"What would you have done if that girl had tried to do something to you?"

"Run for my life," Whitney said without missing a beat.

"I was so sure she was gonna start something when she took off her earrings. . . ."

"Girl, I was, like, I haven't been in a fight since I was nine years old, but I was ready to fake it!"

We howled with laughter.

"Drew would be so mad at me if he found out," I said as we walked into the house.

Sonny ran to the door, licking at Whitney's knees. "Hi, baby. You missed me?" Sonny was already in love with Whitney and had forgotten all about me.

I called Drew's hotel room while Whitney got dressed for bed.

"Hey, babe," he said, sounding happy to hear my voice. "What are you guys up to?"

I wanted to tell him everything that had happened. Instead, I gave him the *Cliff's Notes* version, telling him about the whale watch, snorkeling, and leaving out the part about the happy hour at the Fort Young, especially the part about the fight.

"I'm glad you're having fun, but I miss you."

"I miss you, too," I said. Whitney walked out of the guest bedroom, rolling her eyes. I miss you, she mouthed, making a face.

I heard male voices laughing in the background. I didn't feel too guilty then. We were both getting a well-deserved break.

"Love you," I said.

"Love you, too," he whispered back. Oh, that's right. His friends were right there.

"Coward," I teased.

"Yeah," he said. "Good night, babe."

Whitney looked at me, hands on her hip, shaking her head. "Look at you, with that stupid goo-goo look on your face."

"Oh, stop it. You're so not romantic."

"I'm plenty romantic. You're just pathetic."

"Whatever." I could take Whitney's ribbing. It was actually fun. It felt just like old times, back in high school when she teased me about having crushes on guys I never stood a chance with or in college when I agonized over what a single phone call from a guy meant. Whitney had always been the one steady thing in my life, steadier than my mother, my brother, and anybody else. I was just so glad to have her here with me.

"So we have to be up early tomorrow. We're gonna burn some plastic in Guadeloupe!"

"Ooo weee!" I said, rubbing my hands. "I can't wait. I haven't spent much money this summer so I'm due for a huge spree."

"Pierre said you can get all these European brands at a discount. I think I'm gonna get me a Hermes scarf."

"Well, my aspirations don't go that high. But I'd like a couple of new outfits."

"We're gonna burn up that sucker tomorrow," Whitney said.

"Yeah, baby!"

Chapter 29

I was still groggy when we boarded Pierre's boat at nine o'clock the next morning. Maybe it's because I'd missed my usual early morning walk with Sonny, or maybe it was all the excitement from the night before. I wanted to see Guadeloupe. And I wanted to shop!

Two hours later, we disembarked Pierre's sailboat at the Marina Bas Du Fort, which was so alive with people, shops, and activity I thought I'd just landed in some tourist overrun section of Orlando, except this place was less pristine, had tons more character, and everyone spoke French.

"Wow!" Whitney said. "Looks like there's a lot going on here."

Pierre nodded. "Yes, a lot of shopping . . ."

We needed to ditch this guy, I thought. Whitney read my mind.

"Well, thanks for the ride. Maybe we'll catch up with you later," she said, throwing her arms impulsively around Pierre's neck. That seemed to make his day, judging from the huge smile on his face as he hugged her back.

We said our good-byes and almost ran off in the direction of the shops.

"Oh, how are we gonna get back to Dominica?"

"There's a ferry. But I have Pierre's cell just in case."

"No, let's take the ferry. I don't think I want you hooking up with that guy. He looks dangerous."

Whitney laughed. "Come on, I'm leaving in one day! I can't get into any trouble, can I?"

"Riiiiight."

Pointe-a-Pitre, the capital of Guadeloupe, was bustling, crowded with thousands of local people, tourists, street vendors, and tiny, toylike European cars speeding through its narrow streets. "This is so exciting!" I said again and again.

"Yeah, it's kinda like eastern Rome," Whitney said.

We attacked a row of shops on rue Frebault, the main shopping strip, and immediately went to work. I hadn't spent money all summer so I felt entitled to splurge. Whitney, on the other hand, was her usual self, grabbing as much as she could. It was steaming hot outside, and I was beginning to sweat. I had three shopping bags and Whitney had twice that amount. We'd only been out about an hour.

"We should probably find a place to sit and cool off," I said, fanning my face with my hands.

"I know," Whitney said. "There's a salon near the waterfront. We should go see if they do spa stuff."

"Are you serious? I don't think I could afford that."

"I can."

We left the rue Frebault, looking back longingly at the stores, and hailed a taxi.

The waterfront was a huge terminal with a built-in mall, restaurants, movie theaters, and anything else a tourist would want.

Twice I pulled Whitney away from a clothing store. "These clothes are sooooo cute," she said, caressing a white linen dress with red piping at its seams.

"After all that money you spent on that Dior stuff on rue

Frebault, you probably shouldn't buy anything else. Plus, you've been shopping in Rome all summer."

She pouted. "I know. You're right."

When we got to the salon there were three or four women waiting to be served. "I don't think they do any of that fancy stuff here," I told Whitney.

A woman came up to us, speaking French. I smiled and tried to make sense of her words. Whitney, who knew French but was nowhere near fluent, managed to ask the right question. The woman immediately broke into English.

"You're American? Good!"

I guess the aura of dollar signs on Whitney translated well into every language. She ushered us into a back room, where we undressed and put on big, fluffy robes. It was freezing and the robes felt warm and comforting.

Three hours later, we walked out, scrubbed and buffed, made up, and blow-dried. At least I had gotten my hair blow-dried and straightened. Whitney just pulled her dreads back into a ponytail.

"I don't want to go back in the sun. I feel so cool and relaxed."

"Okay, cool. Let's go catch a French movie before we get back on the ferry."

"But we won't understand what they're saying."

"So what? Amelia, it's all about the moment, the experience," Whitney said, letting her hands signal whatever it was she meant. "You don't have to understand the words to enjoy it. Just think of it as a silent movie."

"Whatever you say, Whitney."

So we went into a movie theater. Luckily, they were playing a blockbuster from the U.S., so I read the lips and ignored the French voice that was dubbed over. It was funny and fun.

"Wow, the day sure went by quickly," Whitney said as we strolled toward the ferry headed back to Dominica.

"I could use a nap." That massage had really done a number on me.

"So, no partying tonight?"

"No way. Tonight we're going to bed early. You have an early flight, remember?"

"I hate the thought of going back to Boston after all of this. You're lucky. I wish I was going to be living down here."

Her being here had made a huge difference; who knows what would happen after she left? I was so disappointed in myself for not being more like her—not being able to just enjoy "the moment."

"So what are you gonna do when you get back home?"

"Finish my project. Fly out to Redmond for about a week for some meetings, then it's back to Boston."

"I wonder how Ma's doing."

"I'm sure she's fine. You always think of her at the weirdest times."

"I know. I just worry much more than I should."

"I won't argue that," Whitney said as we boarded the ferry.

"I'll be home within a couple of weeks myself."

"Ah, just stay. I'll send you your stuff."

"Ha! It's not that simple. I need to work one more term before I can cash out of the working world."

"Please, Amelia. Drew's got money. He seems like he wants to take care of you."

"Who said I wanted him to take care of me?"

"Isn't that a given? You're not going to work, are you?"

"I'm not one of those traditional Dominican women, am I?"

"You'd better keep your voice down or we're gonna get in another fight," Whitney said, eyeing the rest of the passengers who were not paying attention to us.

* * *

Drew's truck was parked in its spot in front of the house. Strange. I didn't expect him back for at least another day.

"Drew's back," I told Whitney. "Looks like you'll get to meet him after all."

She smiled halfheartedly. She was still angry that I'd told him she'd been hospitalized. But I so wanted them to meet. I had a feeling they would hit it off.

Sonny came bounding across the yard as I opened the gate.

"Hi, babe. You miss me?" I petted him, but he went straight for Whitney, almost knocking her down.

Drew walked around from the back to the front of the house. He was wearing a golf shirt that I hated (I hate all golf shirts; they are a fashion abomination) and cargo shorts.

"You're back early," I said. I hugged him and kissed him on the lips eagerly.

"This is Whitney," I smiled.

"I've heard a lot about you," he said, shaking her hand.

"Likewise," she said. Then there was an odd silence. Even Sonny looked embarrassed.

"Let's go inside," I said. Oh, man. Maybe they wouldn't like each other? Drew seemed to be in a weird mood.

"So, did it start raining or something in Barbados?"

"No," he said.

I looked at him, trying to get a clue as to why he was being so quiet.

"Have you all eaten yet?" he asked.

"No, actually we were going to make tuna melts . . ."

"Mona's expecting us at her restaurant," he said.

"She is?" What?

"Yeah, I told her your friend was in town so she said we should come down."

"Well, Whitney's kinda tired. . . . Her flight's really early."

"Oh, I don't mind," Whitney said, smiling a little too

brightly. She looked really uncomfortable. Could she sense that something was wrong? I could, too. But I had no idea what it was.

"Guess we could just go now . . . so we don't have to be out too late," Drew said.

"Sure."

Sonny barked at us as we drove off.

"Did you enjoy yourself today?"

"Yeah, we went shopping on Guadeloupe. It's so different from Dominica. I mean, you're here and it's so . . . so quaint, and then you're in Pointe-a-Pitre, which is like a huge metropolis in some ways. . . ." I couldn't stop talking, else that ungodly silence would descend on the car again and it would make me just want to die. Drew sure wasn't being his usual charming self.

The restaurant was crowded, but Mona had saved us a nice table.

"This place is really cool," Whitney said, still in her overly polite voice.

Mona came rushing out as soon as we were seated. "Amelia, it's so good to see you." We kissed on the cheeks, and she did the same with Whitney as I introduced them.

"I love your hair," she told Whitney. "How long did it take you to grow them that long?"

Whitney loved talking about her dreads so she and Mona were off into their natural hair utopia for about five minutes. I nudged Drew with my thigh, but he kept looking straight ahead.

"What's wrong?" I whispered.

"We'll talk about it later."

"Did I do something wrong?"

"We'll talk about it later," he said.

"So what can I get for you kiddies tonight?" Mona asked.

Drew wanted a giant burger and fries.

"Oh, can I have the same thing?" Whitney asked.

"Whitney, they have all these great seafood dishes you should try," I pleaded.

"No, let her have my burgers and fries," Mona said, smiling. "They're the best in the world."

"She's confident like that," I told Whitney.

"You know it," Mona said, disappearing amid the tables to chat with other diners. I noticed that other people were looking at us curiously, but it really didn't bother me much, especially since Drew was here. There was no way some crazy girl could come stepping up to me with him sitting right there. Right?

"So, you work for Microsoft as a programmer?" Drew asked Whitney.

She explained that she did a lot more, and I hoped he understood because I never did. When it came to Whitney and her work, my brain had its limits. They seemed to connect on that and I was left out of the conversation. Not an entirely bad thing since I was desperately trying to figure out what I did that had made Drew so angry that he would cut short his golfing trip. Was it the trip to Guadeloupe? And how could he know about that from over there? Were people spying on me?

I ate silently as they talked about computers and programming in a polite, reserved rapport. I didn't like it one bit; it sounded like a job interview. I knew Whitney too well to miss the fact that she thought he was too staid. Too safe. Boring. That's exactly what she was thinking. She talked to him the way she would a preacher or an older man whom she respected. Well, that was just fine by me. I loved Drew for what he was. I was not the type to go around dating potential terrorists. Nah. I liked them safe and law-abiding. But I couldn't figure out why he was that way with her, too. I wanted the meal to go by quickly; I had long lost my appetite. I played with my pumpkin soup.

A couple walked over to our table and Drew's face lit up. He introduced us all around to Dr. So and So and his wife. The wife was pretty and well put together and pregnant. "I have been very eager to meet you," she said very slowly and properly, leaning down to kiss my cheeks.

"It's great to meet you," I said.

"It must be strange to have all this attention on you," she smiled.

"Yes, sometimes." Especially when people bring it up when I'm trying not to think about it.

"We should probably have lunch sometime," she said.

I nodded. Who in the world was this woman?

After the genuflecting and paying of homage Drew seemed in a better mood. This ego-stroking thing was like crack to him, I realized.

I yawned dramatically, hoping to send a message.

Whitney got it. "Actually, I'm a bit exhausted. It's been a long day."

"I'm sure it has," Drew said.

"I like your hair like that," he said as I climbed into the truck's passenger seat.

"Oh, thanks. This French lady blew it out." I touched it self-consciously. I hadn't been to a beauty salon in months. I must have been looking like hell the past few weeks, I realized. Thank God, Whitney came down. At least now I had some decent new clothes, new makeup that matched my browner skin, and waxed eyebrows.

He turned up the radio to the BBC, thankfully, so no one felt the need to talk. Once we got in the house Whitney almost ran to her room; she must have sensed the tension. "I'll see you guys in the morning," she said.

I followed him into the kitchen. "So, what's going on?"

"Let's talk about it tomorrow."

"Drew, I can't wait till tomorrow."

"Your friend can hear us."

"So what? She's my best friend."

"I'm not ready to talk about it now. Go to bed." He held a beer in his hand and looked at me, scowling. "Go to bed. I don't want to talk right now."

"So, why do I have to go to bed?" I didn't like his tone.

"Because this conversation's over."

"Why are you so angry?"

"Why are you always challenging me?"

"I'm just . . . I just want to know what's bothering you."

"And I don't want to talk about it now, Amelia!"

"Is it because we went to Guadeloupe and I didn't tell you in advance?"

"Did you not hear what I said?" He put down the beer and grabbed his keys. "I'll see you in the morning."

I followed him out of the house and onto the porch.

"What are you doing, Amelia?"

"You're not gonna just walk out on me like that, Drew. Let's talk about whatever's bothering you."

He stopped at the gate and turned around. "Okay, fine. You want to talk? Fine."

I folded my arms across my chest, waiting.

"Why didn't you call me the other night? Before you went to that place?"

"What place?"

"The Fort Young Hotel."

"I . . ." My mouth opened but no sound came out.

"Do you know what they wrote about you in the paper the next day?"

"No, I haven't seen the paper."

He shook his head.

"What did they say about me?"

"What do you think they said? You were there, right? You were flirting and carrying on with strangers, even getting into shoving matches with other women?"

"What!" I shrieked so loudly I thought I heard Sonny growl.

"That's what it said," he said. "I have a copy in the car."

"And you believe it?" I was in total disbelief.

"Not really. Not all of it. What I don't believe is that you'd put yourself in a position you know would embarrass me. And to go off on some guy's boat. Someone you don't even know?"

"He just gave us a ride."

"Amelia, that guy, Pierre, is a notorious drug dealer and gunrunner."

Again my mouth opened and no sound came out. I felt stupid and angry at the same time. I had screwed up big time, but he was making it seem like it was my fault. I didn't mean for any of this to happen.

"You just don't think, Amelia. No matter how much I warn you about being careful . . ."

I didn't know what to say. I wouldn't say I was sorry. I didn't do anything wrong, did I? I had probably used bad judgment, but who hadn't. Why did he expect me to know that everything I did would end up in some gossip column?

"What do you want me to say?"

He shook his head. "What do I want you to say? There's nothing you can say. You can't undo the damage that's been done."

"What damage? It's just a bunch of gossip, Drew."

"It makes me look bad, Amelia. These people have been looking for a reason to discredit me from day one. You gave them one."

I was shocked he would say something like that. "Are you saying that you might lose your appointment because of me?"

"I'm not saying that at all. I'm saying that my reputation is tied to yours, and if you come off as this wild party girl it makes me look less deserving of my position."

All of a sudden I felt tired. "I'm going to bed," I said. "I'm sorry I ruined your reputation or whatever. I just can't keep up with all these rules and regulations. Maybe this is a big mistake."

I left him standing there and went to the room. I didn't start crying until I heard the engine start and his truck pull away. Yeah, off to Mommy's house.

I didn't belong here. Maybe I should just go home with Whitney. I'd never get it. First he said I should go out and explore; then when I did he got upset. Then I couldn't talk to other men because it somehow challenged his manhood. And then this whole Whitney thing. Who was I kidding? I was not Vanessa, nor did I want to be.

Chapter 30

A tapping on my shoulder jolted me awake and I opened my eyes to look into Whitney's face. My mind was foggy and my eyes were cloudy.

"Amelia, we have to leave for the airport," she said. She was fully dressed.

"Shoot, what time is it?"

I had overslept. I had stayed up till four A.M. feeling miserable and doing my best not to call Vanessa's house and command Drew to come home. I guess I must have cried myself to sleep.

"All right. Gimme a minute."

I threw on some shorts and a T-shirt and ran to the bathroom to brush my teeth. We were in the Jeep in ten minutes.

"Where's Drew?" she asked.

"Probably at his mom's."

"I heard you guys last night."

I didn't answer.

"I'm sorry. It's my fault. I shouldn't have made you do all that stuff."

"Please. You didn't make me do anything. I wanted to go out. I've been cooped up in that house all summer."

"He sounded really mad. In his controlled way . . ."

"You don't like him, huh."

"No. I mean, yes, I like him. He's just so formal."

"People are like that down here."

"I know. It's so different. . . ."

"I know, Whitney."

She shrugged. "That's just me, though. He's perfect for you."

"You think?"

"Yeah, he's really into you. He looks at you a lot when you're not looking at him."

"Really?" I hadn't noticed that. "Are you just saying this because you know how miserable I feel about last night?"

"Yup," she said, and we laughed. "But it's true. You guys will get through this."

"I don't know, girl. It drives me nuts the way he's so concerned about what people think about him."

"And it probably drives him nuts the way you don't. I'm so glad I'm not in a relationship," Whitney said. "All this drama . . ."

"Sometimes I think it's not worth it. I'm gonna have to give up so much to be with him."

"Don't look at it that way."

"How should I look at it, then?"

"Well, what exactly are you giving up?"

I thought for a minute.

"Not much, huh?" She looked at me and started to laugh. "I think your life is less pathetic now than it was before you met him."

"My life wasn't pathetic!"

"Okay, it wasn't pathetic. But it wasn't that great. You've always said that all you want is a handsome husband, two kids, and a nice house. You're no career woman. You hate your job. So don't come at me with this 'What am I giving up?' crap."

"Whitney!" But what she said was true. Sort of. But I'd

still want to teach. I could do that here. It could work out. That is, if Drew still wanted me. And there was a huge question mark there.

"Besides, I need you to stay down here so I can have somewhere to go diving every year."

"I knew you were only thinking about yourself."

"Did I say I wasn't?"

"I don't know. . . . There are still some things I'm worried about," I said.

"Like what?"

I really hadn't planned to talk about it but I did. I told Whitney about the passports and waited for her reaction.

"Why didn't you ask him about it right there and then?"

"I don't know. I was scared."

"Of what you might find out?"

"Maybe."

She sighed. "Well, he is Drew Anderson; that you know for a fact. Why don't you Google him and see what you come up with."

"Oh, I never thought of that!"

"Girl, every time I go out with a guy that's the first thing I do."

"Yeah, but I'm not you, Whitney."

"That's your problem."

I nudged her. "So you don't think I should worry?"

"I don't know. He's so . . . I don't think he's the type to do anything bad."

"Right. He's just too boring," I kidded her.

"I didn't say that!"

We rushed to the airport terminal, entering just as the flight began to board. "That was close," I said breathlessly. "We almost didn't make it."

"Gimme a hug, sweetie," Whitney said.

"I'll see you in a few weeks, girlie," I said. "Thanks for coming down and showing me a good time."

"Yeah, I hope you and Drew work things out. And have great make-up sex."

"If I can get him to leave his momma's house first." I hugged her again and waved good-bye as she tore off to her gate.

As soon as I got back into the Jeep I called Drew's cell phone. He didn't answer. I didn't bother leaving a message. Instead of going to the house, I decided to drive to Vanessa's. He couldn't hide behind her forever. His truck was not in her garage when I got there and I almost turned around, but she'd already seen me. She was standing in her flower garden with a tall, dark, gray-haired man. She waved, bracelets jangling, but did not smile. I pulled over reluctantly.

"Hi, Vanessa," I said, hoping this meeting would be short.

"You just missed Drew," she said. "Did your friend make her flight all right?"

Of course, she knew what I was doing at every second of the day without my having to tell her.

"This is Mr. James," she said, and the tall man shook my hand firmly.

"How do you do?" he asked.

Wow, I thought. Were all of Vanessa's friends so straight-backed and formal? I made small talk with Mr. James for a couple of minutes. Turns out he was another retired politician who had known Drew's father well and was likely now one of Drew's mentors. Ah, well. Guess I'd be seeing more of him in the future.

"Amelia, let's go inside for a second," Vanessa said.

"Actually, I should get going." But she wouldn't let me off that easy.

"Just for a minute," she said.

I followed her inside, feeling that I was walking to the electric chair. Dead woman walking. Drew must have told her everything. So in addition to the tongue-lashing from him, I'd have to get one from her, too. Swell!

"Can I get you something?"

"No, Vanessa. I'm fine."

She clasped her hands together. She was wearing rings on all ten fingers.

"You know, it was really embarrassing to me, and to Drew, that trash they printed in the paper."

I folded my arms. I was so not having it today.

"I don't know if what they printed is true or not, and frankly, I don't care. But you should understand that appearances are very important down here. A lot of eyes are on you."

"Vanessa, I don't feel comfortable talking about this with you." I used my firmest voice.

She looked at me, surprised. "I . . . I'm just giving you some friendly advice, Amelia. You have to be careful about whom you associate with. Your friend seems to have led you down . . ."

"Vanessa, this is between Drew and me. I don't want to talk about it with you."

"I am his mother, Amelia. . . ."

"And I'm going to be his wife!"

She looked startled. "Don't raise your voice in my home, young lady," she said, clenching her fists.

"Fine. I was just leaving," I said, and picked up my bag. "Just one more thing, Vanessa. Drew and I are going to be married and you're going to have to learn to stay out of our business," I said, wanting to bolt for the door, but she wasn't done yet.

"I'd gladly stay out of your business, Amelia, but you don't seem to know how to conduct yourself. All my friends are talking about you. . . . How do you think that makes me feel?"

"I don't care how you or your friends feel, Vanessa. The only person's feelings I care about is Drew's, and I need to go find him. Good-bye."

I fled the house as quickly as possible, waving good-bye to Mr. James, who was standing amid a hibiscus bush looking perplexed. Did I handle that right? Should I have cussed her out? Whitney would have. What right did she have talking to me like that, anyway? My own mother didn't use that condescending, patronizing tone on me. Freaking Vanessa. Oh, I hated her smug, bejeweled, overly made-up, prissy . . . Oh, God. This woman's going to be my mother-in-law. *Amelia, you really need to think about this!*

I slowed down as the traffic got heavier as I neared Roseau. This was a lot, I realized. A lot to take on: A new place full of land mines. The gossip. The watchful eyes wherever I went. The feeling that I really couldn't come and go as I pleased. Vanessa. Vanessa. I thumbed my engagement ring, and it felt so good. So right. If it were just Drew and me. In Boston. It would be perfect. But would it? I'd have to go back to my crappy job and the crappy weather. And taking care of Ma and Gerard. Well, maybe it wouldn't be perfect, but it wouldn't be as bad as this. Or would it? I didn't know. All I knew was that I wasn't sure.

When I drove up the path leading to the house my heart was pounding. I knew what I was going to tell Drew would change everything. I fingered my ring again. I didn't want to part with it. But there was just too much uncertainty. It wasn't fair to him if I was only going to keep waffling like this. I'd ask him for more time. Maybe another six months to get used to the idea and get some closure, if possible, between myself and Boston. I couldn't pretend that I was 100 percent sure that a wedding was going to happen in December. And he needed to know that.

I heard hammering sounds as I opened the gate leading into the house.

"Drew?"

"In the back!"

I walked out back and he was on a ladder hammering plywood to a window.

"What's going on?"

"Storm's on the way. A big one."

"Like a hurricane?"

"It won't be like one, it could be one. . . ."

He must be in a good mood if he's teasing me like this.

"But it's so sunny and clear." I looked at the sky. I couldn't see a cloud for miles.

"Doesn't mean anything."

He was right about that. The weather swung between tropical extremes by the minute.

"Are you going to do all the windows?"

"Nah, just these three. If the forecast gets worse I'll do the others."

I went inside to wait. Sonny was all jumpy and excited. I hadn't taken him out in three days so he'd been running around on his own. "You missed me, babe?" I asked him, scratching his ears. "Bet you miss Whitney more, huh?" His ears pricked up when I said Whitney's name. "Sonny, you're such a playa."

Drew came in looking sweaty and exhausted as I played with Sonny. It was barely noon, but the sun was already baking hot. The air conditioner was blasting, though.

"Let's go cool off under the waterfall," he said.

"What?" I wanted to talk.

"Come on, let's go."

But I thought we were fighting? "Don't we have to talk about what happened?"

He shrugged. "Do we have to?"

I had things to say. But the waterfall idea sounded good. Maybe I could work up my courage while I was under the rushing water.

"Okay, I'll grab my swimsuit."

"Orange bikini," he said.

"I don't have one."

"You do now," he said. "My gift . . . I got it in Barbados."

"Drew!" I ran to the bedroom and sure enough, lying on the bed was the skimpiest thing I'd ever seen.

"I can't wear that!"

"You have to!" he yelled back.

I got undressed and put the thing on and looked at myself in the mirror. I had stretch marks, but I still looked good. My tummy, if I turned to the right, almost looked flat. I didn't look horrible. I didn't look like Naomi Campbell. But I didn't look like Monique.

He walked in the room. "Oh, yeah. That's what I'm talking about." He grabbed me.

"Stop. Let's go before the hurricane starts," I giggled.

"Fine. But I'll get you when we come back. If I can wait that long."

We walked the quarter-mile from the house to the waterfall, through a thicket of guava trees, other wild plants, and those mercenary weeds that scratched at my legs every day I went walking with Sonny.

"I'm gonna miss this place," I said as we heard the waterfall crashing down on the rocks below.

He looked at me, surprised. "Why? You're coming back, aren't you?"

"Yes, I am. But I mean, when I go home to get my stuff. . . ." I sounded lame and I knew it.

His jaw clenched and he grew quiet. We stood and watched the water, falling in a majestic straight line as if from the sky.

"Last one in cooks dinner," I said and ran into the pool underneath the fall. He walked in after me.

We didn't talk about it for the rest of the day, but I couldn't say that it wasn't there. The fight that had never gotten resolved. The waterfall didn't wash it away. The dinner that he cooked didn't make us forget. Even staying up half the night making love didn't change that we were ignoring the fact that something had changed.

I woke up to the wind howling and the rain pelting the roof. Drew was not in the bed next to me. I turned on the lights and saw that it was seven A.M., yet the house was as dark as if it were midnight. Where was he? I heard a banging outside so I went to investigate.

I poked my head out the back door and Drew was pounding a hammer into a slab of wood against the window frame.

"What's going on?" I called out over the sound of the wind.

"Hurricane changed course again. It's heading this way."

"Are you serious?" Oh, crap! So it wasn't a storm anymore? They'd talked about it on the news the night before, but it was supposedly going to change course and go somewhere else. It had hit a few other islands, but all we'd gotten was rain. Last night before we went to bed, the weatherman said it had been downgraded into a tropical storm. Had it regrouped itself overnight? Darn! One week left here and I had to experience a hurricane.

"Do you need help?"

He paused for a second and then said, "Yeah, I've got most of the windows but the three side ones. Know how to use a hammer?"

"Of course." I was lying but I couldn't just stand there and leave him out in the wind and rain doing all the work. Especially after my "I am woman, hear me roar" speech the other night. I'd better put up or shut up.

Besides, I thought, as I climbed the wobbly stepladder, I was no longer fat Amelia Wilson. I was athletic Amelia Wilson, who knew her way around a hammer. God, help me, please.

"You all right?" he yelled. The wind was picking up, and the rain was blowing into my eyes.

"Yup," I yelled back. I couldn't really see what I was doing but I decided to try anyway. I held the board against the window and placed the nail against it. As I raised the hammer, a wind gust whooshed against me. I felt the step-ladder wobble and next thing I knew I was on the ground. I had landed in a patch of grass, flat on my butt, which hurt like hell. My hand was throbbing because I'd tried to break the fall. Drew came running.

"You okay?"

I nodded. My hand felt like it was broken and some bone in my behind was pounding. I bit my lip and held back the urge to cry. He helped me up, and my butt hurt even more when I stood. "I'm fine," I said.

"You sure?"

"Yeah, I'm sure." The rain was coming down in sheets now and we were both soaked. The wind was so fierce I could hardly keep my eyes open.

"Go inside," he said. "I'll be done in a few minutes."

I limped in the back door, flexing my wrist back and forth. I didn't think it was broken, but it really hurt. Oh, me and my bravado.

Ten minutes later, Drew was inside, wet as a dog.

"Your hand okay?"

I nodded. I'd taken some Tylenol and the pain had decreased to a dull throb. But the weather had gotten worse. The wind had gotten stronger and I thought I heard a thud, like a tree falling outside. I didn't even want to ask.

"It's bad out there," he said, changing into dry clothes.

"What do people do during a hurricane?"

"Wait it out. The power's gonna go out pretty soon. I have lamps and a few candles in the kitchen. We'll save the generator for the days ahead. I need to go check on Mom."

"What?" I couldn't believe what I'd just heard.

He looked at me and tied up his shoelaces. "She's by herself up there, Amelia."

"She's not by herself. The maid's with her. The driver's with her."

"That old man can't do anything . . ."

"What . . . What about me? You're leaving me here all by myself?"

He stopped and sighed. "I'll be back as soon as I check things out up there. You'll be fine."

"No, I won't be fine, Drew!" I sounded hysterical but I didn't care. "I'm freaking scared. I've never been in a hurricane before and I'm not staying here all alone!"

He looked at me as if he'd never seen me before, and that's when something occurred to me. He didn't know. He had no idea. He just didn't know what he was supposed to do. It's like he was stuck in between being his own man and Vanessa's son. He looked torn and confused.

"Drew, I'm going to be your wife," I said in a voice I usually reserved for my thickest-headed students. "You can't just leave me and go to her, okay?"

He looked stunned, the same way Vanessa had looked when I told her that she needed to butt out of our business. They had no idea how codependent they were on each other.

"Can't one of your brothers-in-law go over there? They're only a few minutes away from her house."

He hesitated. "I guess they could. I'll call."

But the phone rang before he could pick it up. It was Vanessa calling to see if we were okay.

"We're fine," I told her. She sounded oddly calm. "How are you holding up?" I asked her.

"Oh, I'm fine. My friend James is here. He even helped the gardener board up the windows last night."

Mr. James was there? She sure moved fast. "That's good news, Vanessa. We were worried about you. . . ."

"That's why I called, sweetheart," she said. "There's no need to worry about me."

"Do you need to speak to Drew?"

"No, tell him I'm fine. I'll see him tomorrow."

I looked at Drew, who stood there expectantly, waiting for the phone.

"Oh, and Amelia, don't worry about this storm. I've been through hundreds of these. It's just a little wind and rain."

"Thanks, Vanessa," I said and hung up. She acted like we had not even had our heated discussion. Did she forget or was Mr. James that good?

"She didn't want to talk to me?" Drew looked hurt.

"No, I think Mr. James is over there." I searched his face for his reaction. I could tell he was disappointed. But I was ecstatic! Thank you, Mr. James!

Then the wind howled and the house went black. I ran to Drew. "Calm down," he laughed.

We lit a few lamps and candles all over the house and sat on the couch, listening to the wind and the rain outside.

"I didn't mean to yell earlier. About your mom."

He shrugged. "It's okay. I wish you'd said something earlier. I didn't know it bothered you that much."

Was he that dense?

"After my dad died, my mom had a really hard time. I was the only person she could lean on. My sisters were busy with their families, and they never really got along with her." That didn't surprise me.

"I understand," I said. "But you can't always be there for her forever. You have to live your own life, Drew." As I said those words I felt that I was speaking them to myself. We were the same, Drew and me. We were both being pulled in all directions by possessive, manipulative mothers who forced us into thinking we owed them so much.

"I can't turn my back on her."

"I'm not asking you to. Just don't forget I need you, too."

"Okay. Oh, and since we're talking . . . Why don't you tell me exactly what happened during that weekend with Whitney?"

I told him everything.

"You need some new girlfriends," he said.

"Yeah? Like Shauna maybe?"

He shook his head. "I was wondering when you'd bring that up."

"Why didn't you tell me you guys had been involved?"

"There's nothing to tell. That was a long time ago."

"Really? I find it hard to believe that there's nothing to tell. I mean, Shauna's a smart, gorgeous sister . . ."

"And so are you. . . . We dated for three months, then it just didn't work out. I was too busy working. And Shauna's a handful."

"That's all there is to it?"

"That's all there is to it, Amelia."

Okay. I would accept that. "And since we're in confession mode, Drew, I need to ask you something."

"Okay. Shoot."

I told him that I'd found the passports while I was looking for drawer space for my new clothes. He tensed when I mentioned the name Steve Harrison.

"You weren't supposed to see that," he said.

"I want to know . . . What's the story behind all that?"

He stood up and for a second I thought he'd end the conversation and run off to Vanessa in the middle of the storm. Instead, he went to one of his bookshelves and rifled through a stack of books and pulled out a yellowing newspaper.

"Here." He handed it to me.

It was an *Atlanta Journal Constitution* from seven years ago. The headline read: DOT-COM ENTREPRENEUR FLEES COUNTRY WITH $32 MILLION. I looked at his face and it was passive. "Read it," he said.

The story wasn't very long. It said that Drew and his partners had sold their company to GE for sixty million dollars and that there'd been a dispute among the five partners about how the money would be divvied up. Before the lawsuit was settled, Drew left the United States, moving thirty-two million dollars into overseas accounts that his partners couldn't touch. He was considered a fugitive by the FBI and the authorities in the state of Georgia.

I took several deep breaths as I read the story. This couldn't be true. There was something missing. That still did not explain who Steve Harrison was.

"Is all of this true?" I asked.

He looked at me seriously. "What do you think?"

"I don't know, Drew. Why don't you tell me your side of it?"

"I started that company, Amelia. On my own. Those guys . . . my partners came in after I'd built it into something worth selling. What I did was stupid, I know. I'd just lost my father and I just wanted to be away from the States. So I took what I thought rightfully belonged to me and I left."

I tried to streamline my thoughts. So the story was true. He had stolen—or taken—the money. Except that he was saying that it was his to begin with.

"Who is Steve Harrison?" I asked, trying to put all the pieces together.

He sat down again. "When you came down to visit me that first time . . . I . . . knew I wanted to marry you to be with you forever. But I couldn't travel to the States using my own documents. I'd get arrested the minute I hit U.S. soil. So I had the passport made up so I could come and visit you."

I stood and scratched my head. He'd broken the law. For me. "What if you'd gotten caught?"

He shrugged. "It was worth it."

"Drew, I'm so . . . I can't believe all of this."

"I know. I'm sorry I didn't tell you."

"Does Vanessa know?"

"Yes."

"Who else knows?"

"Rumors have been going around on the island, but only

a few of my associates know the whole story. We look out for each other."

"So where's the money?" I had to ask.

"It's being put to good use," he said. "It's helping people."

I sat down again. Who did he think he was? Robin Hood?

"I'll understand if you . . . if this changes things for you." He let his arms drop by his side and a space formed between us on the couch.

Was he a criminal? I believed him; his version fit in more with the Drew Anderson I knew. But according to the FBI, he was a fugitive. He could never visit the States without worrying about getting caught and probably sent off to prison. Was there a way to make this right? And could I be with someone who had something so big hanging over his head? Did that make me an accessory?

We didn't talk much more; we just let the howling wind punctuate the silence and we watched the candles flicker. Eventually, he fell asleep, but I stayed awake listening to the wind and thinking how at that point I didn't care about what happened eleven years ago. I didn't want to go back home, even with the scary hurricane tearing up the world outside, even with Drew not being the perfect man that I thought he was.

Chapter 31

Hurricane Erica left a few twisted trees and torn-off roofs in her wake, but no lives were lost. The day had risen with clear skies and sparkling seas; it was like the hurricane had not even been here at all.

I was awakened by voices outside. It was nearly six A.M. I looked out the window and Drew was in an animated conversation with his two lawyers, Phillip and Jason. What were they doing here so early? And on the day after a hurricane? I had to find out.

"Hi, guys," I said, from the back porch. All three seemed surprised by the interruption.

"Why are you up so early?" Drew asked.

"I heard you guys talking. What's going on?"

Jason spoke up. "We just wanted to make sure everything was fine up here." There was something so smarmy about that guy. I wondered if he was tied to that whole embezzling mess. What was a rich white guy doing living down here anyway?

"I'll be in in just a second," Drew said, dismissing me with his expression.

Fine. I went inside and began to make breakfast. *Some-*

thing else is going on, I thought. *Has to be. Those guys are really upset about something.* A minute later, Drew came in from outside.

"Where are your friends?"

"They left."

We ate breakfast silently at first. I tried to find the right words. "I believe you, Drew," I said.

"I'm glad you do," he said.

"Those guys, Jason and Phillip, do they know? Is something else going on?"

"They know. They're my lawyers, Amelia. And, no, nothing else is going on. We shouldn't talk about this anymore."

I wasn't all the way convinced, but I'd accept this for now. "How can you make this right, Drew?"

"Turn myself in. Have a trial and convince a jury that I didn't do anything wrong."

The way he said it made it sound impossible. "Don't you want it to go away sometimes?"

He shrugged. "I don't think about it often. I'm happy here; I don't want to live anywhere else. And I didn't do anything wrong, Amelia."

"I know," I said. "But they think you did."

"They're wrong. And I don't care what they think."

"Can they come and arrest you here?"

"No, they don't have jurisdiction, and there's no way our government would extradite me."

Of course. He was their great hope. Then I thought, he bought this place. This entire country was his because he could afford it. Thirty-two million U.S. dollars was a gold mine here. No wonder he was being groomed for greatness. He'd bought his way in on his father's reputation and his thirty-two million dollars. But this is what politicians do, a voice in my head said. It had nothing to do with Drew as a person. Or did it? Could I separate him from the practical, scheming politician who I was beginning to see emerge? I didn't ask any more questions. I pretended that everything was back to normal.

We went outside to survey the damage and it seemed that the entire island had undergone a cleansing. Even with all the debris laying about there was purity in the air and crispness to the colors under the blazing sun. Our jacaranda tree would have to be cut down; it leaned dangerously to the side as if straining to hear some conversation with the earth, and some of its branches were touching the ground. I couldn't even see the hammock. I wanted to cry when I saw its forlorn, twisted trunk.

From the front porch the calm ocean glistened blue, miles and miles away in the distance, and seagulls swooped overhead. A wren landed on a calabash tree and twittered. Once again, I felt that I was in the Dominica of *Wide Sargasso Sea.* This place was insanely beautiful and I couldn't imagine going back to cold, gray, old Boston.

Drew came up behind me with the dog. "Wanna go walk with us?"

My hand was still achy and my butt still hurt from my fall, but I was curious to see how the rest of Castle Comfort had fared in the storm. Sonny ran ahead of us, sniffing the ground. Branches were strewn across the narrow road and some of the trees listed dangerously as if they would break at the slightest breeze. We'd been so lucky. My favorite tree was gone, but at least the house had been spared.

Jimmy Wilkes and his parents were clearing branches from their huge front yard. Drew waved and Jimmy came running toward us. He went straight for Sonny, who promptly began to lick his face.

"Sonny, your breath stinks!" Jimmy said.

"Hi, Jimmy," I said, making the first move.

"Were you scared last night?" He stared hard at me as if he dared me to tell the truth. But I was not competing for a medal of courage with a seven-year-old.

"A little bit," I said. "Were you?"

"Nope," he said. "I'm not a girl."

"Boys get scared, too," I said. Sheesh! What were his parents teaching him?

"Not during hurricanes."

Fine. Whatever, Jimmy.

"When are you leaving?" he asked.

"Soon. But I'm coming back," I said.

His face fell. That kid just hated me and I didn't know why.

"Jimmy, we gotta go. See you later, man," Drew said.

"All right, man," Jimmy said, sounding as grown up as a 7-year-old could.

"Why does he hate me?" I groaned.

"He doesn't hate you. I think he has a big crush on you. That's just his way of showing it."

"Uh-huh. Whatever."

I could hear the river raging louder than usual, and I wanted to see it. When we crossed the grove of guava trees that led to it we stopped as the ground began to sag under our feet. I could feel water seeping into my sneakers. Silly me had decided not to wear socks. "It's too dangerous," Drew said. "We shouldn't go any farther."

"Why not?" I was disappointed. I'd never seen an overflowing river up close.

"Don't even think about the waterfall," he said, a warning look in his eyes. I pouted dramatically.

"You think this is really cool, don't you?"

I didn't sense where he was going so I glibly said, "Yeah. No one got hurt, right?"

He shook his head. "Do you know how much money this storm is going to cost the government? Power lines are down all across the country. People lost their homes. And a lot of animals died. That's people's livelihood."

Oh, shoot! I remembered the family of goats that lived up

in the hills. Did they make it out alive? "Drew . . . I . . ." What I should have said was that I hadn't thought of it that way, but saying that would make me sound even more pathetically naïve and selfish.

"It's okay," he said. "It's your first time. Enjoy the view. Just keep in mind that a lot of people are not going to just bounce back from this storm like magic. Our government doesn't send relief teams to help the folks out in the country like they do in Florida."

"Sorry, I didn't mean to sound insensitive." I was sorry, but I was also growing tired of apologizing all the time. How am I supposed to just *know* all these things?

"It's all right," he said. And we walked back onto the main road, which was now fairly busy with traffic and people walking down the road toward the capital. Others were cleaning up their yards, cutting down trees, and clearing debris from their porches. A few called out to him and he waved. They didn't even look at me. He asked about their families and whether everyone was okay. He knew so many of these people by name. One man came up to him and told him that a tree had totally destroyed his house and everything he had. Drew fished into his wallet and gave the man all the cash that he had. I was so touched I wanted to cry. I did not deserve this man. But then I thought that was just a drop in the bucket for him. What was a couple hundred out of thirty-two million? Ugh! I had to stop thinking like this, else it would destroy what I was desperately trying to preserve: my image of Drew.

The more people he talked to, listening to their problems and giving them advice, the more insignificant I felt. I tried to make eye contact with them, to smile, to show them that I cared, too. That I would try to be someone they could trust. But was I faking it? Would they ever accept me? I felt like an interloper. Here was the entire community bonding together after a natural disaster, and all I wanted to do was take pictures. I cared that they had lost so much, but another part of me was amazed and fascinated. I had gone through the storm with them, but it still seemed like their problem and not mine. But the voice in the back of my head told me that I was wearing a ring on my finger that pretty much said that this place, with its wild weather, was to be my new home. I'd better start thinking of this as my problem, too.

Later, Drew went to check on Vanessa, and I watched TV. We were running on generator power because the electricity had not come back on, and according to Drew, it might be a week before it did. A news report from Barbados was showing pictures of the damage the storm had wreaked. The reporter said that Dominica was entirely without power. It would cost millions of dollars to repair the damage, plus it would hurt the tourism industry for the rest of the year. The pictures showed houses razed to the ground in villages I'd never heard of. People were replacing corrugated iron roofs and sifting through battered belongings that had flown out of their homes into the streets. I wanted to smack myself. Drew was so right. I hadn't even thought of these other people who didn't have generators or solar-powered homes. All I thought about was me, me, me. I figured that would always be a huge difference between Drew and me. He cared much more for other people than I ever could. I wondered if he was now complaining about my insensitivity to Vanessa.

At least the phones were working. I decided to call Ma just in case she'd heard the news about the storm and was worried.

"What's going on?" she asked, sounding bored.

"Ma, we just had a huge storm. Half the island is totally destroyed." I was exaggerating, but she didn't sound interested in talking to me at all.

"That right? You okay?"

"Yeah, I'm fine. But a lot of people lost their homes."

"Amelia, when you gonna come home, huh?"

"I told you, I'll be home in a couple of weeks."

"Yeah, but you said you gonna marry that, that, Drew. Where you gonna live? Down there?"

"Eventually, yes."

"With all the hurricanes and stuff?"

"They don't have major hurricanes every year, Ma."

"Amelia, I hope you'll come to your senses. Just 'cause a man pays a little attention to you doesn't mean you have to go running after him."

"Ma, Drew is not paying me a little attention. We love each other, and he's going to be my husband."

She snorted. "You're not gonna go through with it. I know you. You can't live on some godforsaken little island in the middle of nowhere."

"Ma, I gotta go."

I hung up before she could say anything else. I wondered just how she'd react if I told her that Drew was rich. Rich and wanted by the law. Boy, she'd have a field day telling me how stupid I was to go running after a man who stole thirty-two million dollars and still lived like any old regular person. God. I had to talk to somebody who could understand; I desperately needed to hear a friendly voice. Thankfully, Whitney sounded cheery.

"Guess who I had dinner with last night?"

"Who?" I didn't care. I wanted to hear from her whether or not I was crazy for still wanting to be with Drew.

"Mr. Stevenson."

"Your dad? How was it?"

"Weird at first, but then he loosened up. We talked for a long time."

"About what?"

"A lot of things," she paused. "He's real nice, you know. Reserved but nice. He said he's proud of everything I've accomplished with my life." Her voice broke.

"Whitney, that's . . . that's so sweet."

She sniffed. "Anyway, I just had to share. . . . What's new with you?"

"A lot," I said. "But I'll tell you another time. I don't want to steal your moment. When are you seeing him again?"

"No. No, tell me now. I get all emotional when I think about that other stuff."

"Okay. Well, I asked Drew about the passports."

"And?"

I told her what Drew told me, what the newspaper story had said about him. She gasped. "Wow. Who does he think he is? Robin Hood?"

"I thought the same thing, girl!"

"So he's using the money he stole, or didn't steal, depending on whom you believe, to develop his little island. Hmmm . . . interesting," Whitney said.

"Interesting? That's all you can say? What should I do?"

"Do? What can you do? You want him to turn himself in and go to prison? 'Cause there's no way in hell an American jury's not going to convict his black, fugitive behind."

"He didn't steal it!" I said. "It was his to begin with. Besides, he's using it to do good. . . . It's his money."

"So he says," Whitney said.

"You're not helping."

She laughed. "All of a sudden I like him a lot more."

"Great. That makes me feel so much better. He has the Whitney-approved criminal edge."

"It's not just that . . . He could be living in some ridiculous mansion with five yachts or something, but he's not. So either he is a Robin Hood or maybe he's just keeping a low profile for now."

"I don't know, Whitney. Sometimes I worry that it's all an act. That he's just buying the government's protection so they won't extradite him. Plus, there's the other stuff with those two guys. Something's just weird."

"Come on! He told you the truth; you saw the news clipping. I'm sure the guy's for real. Hey, and even if he were just buying off the government, that's the way the world works. Especially in politics. You better get used to it."

But it's wrong, a voice in my head said. I needed affirmation. "So, I'm not a bad person for wanting to stay with him?"

"Not really. You guys will be like Bonnie and Clyde."

"Stop it! I'm being serious."

She giggled. "Okay. Okay. I don't know. You have to think about it. Personally, I wouldn't care if I were in your shoes. But then again, you're not me."

"And that's the problem," I said before she could say it.

I leaned back into the sofa and looked up at the ceiling after I'd hung up. As if things weren't complicated enough! Why did I go looking in that drawer? I wish I'd never found out. I didn't want to know this at all. I wanted to go back to the time when I thought the biggest problem between Drew and me was Vanessa. I would try, I told myself. I had to put all these other thoughts about morals, justice, and due process, accessory to the fact, and prison sentences out of my mind.

Chapter 32

The day before I was to return to Boston, Drew was appointed Minister of Education. I sat with Vanessa, Sophie, Stella, and their husbands through the confirmation hearing as other important-looking men old enough to be his grandfather asked him questions, mostly about his allegiance to the political party and the country. Senators referred to him as someone who was "full of integrity" and "devoted to the welfare of his people." I wondered if he saw the irony in those statements, or did his mind just selectively skip over such thoughts?

But I was proud of him. I'd never seen him wear a suit before and it hit me again that this man, my man, was going to be someone really great, and that he wanted to share it all with me. I caressed my engagement ring with my index finger. This was it. No turning back.

We hadn't had much time to talk since the hurricane. He'd toured the country with the prime minister, visiting the villages that had been hardest hit. The new school in the village of Delices had been decimated and would have to be rebuilt. He'd been so devastated over that it felt like Sonny had died. That had finally brought home the impact of the hurricane. I felt like I'd lost something, too. I'd seen the school almost finished; students were ready to start in September. Now it would take at least another six months before it was ready again. It was a huge loss, but Drew was resolute. "We'll just build again," he'd said. "We'll start up next week."

That seemed to be the spirit encompassing the island. Saws were humming, nail guns popping, hammers pounding everywhere. Optimism floated in the air as people replaced roofs, windows, and rebuilt houses from the ground up. They seemed totally unfazed even though they'd lost so much and had to start rebuilding, that was just life on an island.

I watched Drew answer each question calmly and eloquently. He was obviously made for this kind of thing. When I thought of all the plans he had for this place, I couldn't help but think that Dominica was going to be better because of him, whether he had thirty-two million dollars or not. There was no wrong or right in this.

Afterward, Vanessa had planned a huge luncheon in her home, which she said would also be an unofficial good-bye party for me. I tried to stay out of the limelight and let Drew get all the attention he so deserved. Everyone was congratulating us on his appointment and our engagement. I felt like a princess, heady from all the attention and Vanessa's lavishly done outdoor party. There were waiters everywhere with glasses of champagne, an ice sculpture shaped to resemble a map of Dominica, a live jazz band, and plenty of beautiful people.

"You look wonderful," Vanessa purred as I stood in her flower garden trying to remember the names of some of the species. Mr. James was by her side, and it was obvious that he was now her top priority. "Red is a lovely color on you." She smoothed the shoulder of my red silk dress, just like my mother would when I was a little girl. I was so touched. Maybe she cared about me, liked me even, in her own controlling way.

"Thanks, Vanessa. Thanks for everything."

She shrugged. "You'll be my daughter soon, Amelia. You don't have to thank me anymore."

I watched her and Mr. James walk away, his hand gallantly placed on her waist. I was going to have another difficult mother in my life. The thought made me want to laugh and cry at the same time. I missed Ma so much. She would have enjoyed a party like this. I saw her beautiful face in my mind and I imagined her right here, dressed to the nines, giving all the women a good reason to doubt themselves just by virtue of her presence. Beautiful Grace Wilson. I missed her so much.

A trio of men laughed loudly nearby, and I escaped to Vanessa's back porch with its amazing view of the ocean.

"Hi, Amelia." I turned around and looked right into the tanned face of Jason, Drew's lawyer. Phillip was two paces behind him.

"Hello." I hadn't even noticed that they were here. But, of course, they seemed to be everywhere.

"Mind if we go inside and talk for a minute?" Jason asked.

"Why? Is something wrong?"

"No, not at all. Just a couple minutes."

Where was Drew? I was confused but I would go. "Sure. If it's only a couple minutes." I followed him through the kitchen and into one of Vanessa's sitting rooms. Phillip walked behind me.

"Have a seat," Jason gestured.

"I'll stand." I didn't trust that guy.

"Fine," he smiled. "Listen, I don't think I ever congratulated you on the engagement. I'm so excited for my man Drew. He's a lucky guy."

"Thanks," I said, wondering whether this was what he'd called me here for.

He cleared his throat and pulled out a sheaf of papers from inside his suit jacket.

"Okay, let's get right down to business. Now, Amelia, I hardly know you but I already feel like we're friends, so this is hard for me. But I need you to sign a few things. It's just standard . . ."

"A few things?" I was starting to see it now. A prenuptial agreement. I am so stupid!! I hadn't even thought of that.

"Jason, Drew and I haven't talked about any of this yet."

He looked surprised. "He didn't tell you?"

"No, we haven't . . ."

Phillip piped in. "It doesn't matter. You need to sign these today." He grabbed the papers from Jason's hand and handed them to me. I glanced at the stack of about thirty pages. I'd need a week just to read them! One thing caught my eye. The very first sheet of paper did not read like a prenup. According to the heading it was some type of confidentiality agreement.

"What is this?" I asked them.

Jason smiled at me again. "What did you think they were?"

"A prenup?"

He shook his head. "No, this is about what you found out about Drew."

"What do you mean?"

Phillip sighed. "He means that Drew needs to know that you will not tell anyone about what you found. And that you won't stake any claim to his properties."

"Wait a minute!" I said. What the heck was going on here? "I don't want his money! And I'd never do anything to hurt him."

Jason smiled and spread his hands magnanimously. "Of course not. We know that. Drew wouldn't be marrying you if he thought you were that kind of woman. It's just standard legal procedure. He has to protect himself."

"Drew put you up to this?"

"No, it's my idea, actually," Jason said, still smiling. "I'm his lawyer and I want the best for him, same as you do."

"So, you think I'm going to turn him in or something?" I couldn't believe these guys. Where was Drew?

Phillip folded his arms. "When you go back to the States, what exactly are you going to tell people? Your friends?"

"How is that any of your business?" I wanted to smack his smug face; he was becoming more snakelike by the second.

He clenched his jaw. "Listen, you're not the first woman who . . ."

Jason stepped in between Phillip and me. "Amelia, there's no reason to get upset. You're doing this for Drew. For his and your future. You see the work he's doing down here; you don't want anything to get in the way of that."

"Why didn't he ask me to sign them himself?"

They were silent. Then Jason said, "He trusts you. It's me. I'm the one who wants you to do this."

"Well, I'm not signing anything. I'm not signing anything until I talk to Drew."

Jason stepped back; his face grew serious. "Okay. I'll leave you here to think about it for a while."

"No, I'm through with you guys," I said. But Phillip stepped in front of me as I headed for the door.

"Not so fast," he said. "You're going to stay here and think about this. Did you hear him?"

"You can't keep me here!"

"Amelia, please, don't make a scene," Jason said.

"Don't tell me what to do!" I was becoming hysterical and afraid. Where the hell was Drew? What was going on? Then I heard a knock on the door. Phillip and Jason exchanged looks and Jason went to the door. He closed it behind him. I stared at Phillip. He had to be about six-two. I couldn't get past him. Oh my God. Was I in trouble?

The door opened before I could fully map out an escape plan, and to my surprise Vanessa walked in, looking calm as day, a huge smile on her face.

"Can you boys leave us alone?" she told Phillip and Jason, who promptly exited the room.

"We'll be right outside, Ms. Anderson," Phillip said, glaring at me.

"Vanessa, what is going on?"

She smiled, took both my hands in hers, and sighed. "Amelia, you're a good girl. I really wish you hadn't gone snooping around Drew's personal things. And I wish he'd been more careful about protecting himself."

"I didn't go snooping around his things!"

"Calm down." She smiled. "Do you know why I won't have him marry any of those local girls?" She didn't wait for me to answer. "They all think he has this money. They're not sure about the details, but their minds are full of rumors and gossip. When I saw you, I thought: Yes, there's someone who could love my boy just for who he is. And I thought you did."

"I did, Vanessa. I do. You still haven't told me what's going on."

"Isn't it obvious?"

"No, it's not."

She sighed. "I want to make sure that Drew's secret will be safe. That's all. I'm not asking you to do anything illegal. Just put my mind at ease. I don't want you going home to the States and then being overpowered by your moral convictions."

"Why? He didn't do anything wrong. It was his money anyway."

She paused. "Yes, that's right, Amelia. He didn't do anything wrong. So just sign the agreement. I'll sleep better tonight. And so will Drew."

"So he knows about this?"

She didn't answer. "I'll give you all the time you need to

read them, okay?" She smiled at me and walked out of the room. "Phillip will be right outside if you need anything."

I closed my eyes as I sat down. The stack of papers felt heavy, like a set of weights in my hands. What do I do? I paged through them. It was more than just keeping quiet. They also wanted me to agree that I would stake no claim to anything belonging to Drew that was not specifically spelled out in any other agreement. I felt betrayed. Drew must have known about this. I'd been gone from the party almost a half hour; he must have been wondering where I was. I considered my surroundings. There was no window, no trapdoor. Only the door outside where Phillip stood waiting for me. I'd sign their agreement. I didn't have much choice anyway.

I knocked on the door and Phillip opened it. Jason was standing next to him wearing his smarmy smile. I handed him the papers.

"Thank you so much, Amelia," he said. "We'll let you go back to enjoying the party. Sorry to have upset you."

Phillip said nothing as they walked away. I could hear Vanessa laughing out loud in the distance. I had to get some air.

"Why are you standing here all alone?" Drew came up behind me and kissed my neck.

How convenient to appear just now, I thought. But a plan had already formed in my mind. I would play along. "I'm just thinking."

"About me, I hope."

"Yup," I said. "I'm gonna miss you so much."

"So stay. We'll have all your things shipped here."

"I couldn't do that to Ma. And my students. I have to tell them good-bye."

"Whatever makes you happy."

"You make me happy," I said. "And so proud."

"I'm glad I do. You make me happy, too."

"Yeah? How?" I wanted to hear this from him if only to

reassure myself I wasn't crazy. What we had was real until all of this.

"I'm glad we don't have any secrets anymore. . . . Before you came I was doing all of this"—he gestured toward the house where I could hear laughter and music echoing from the front yard—"for everybody else but myself. But once I realized I wanted to spend the rest of my life with you, that all changed. I want this country to be better for the people here now, but also for their kids, and our kids, Amelia. You're not just going to be my silent partner. You're smart, kind, passionate, organized, and you know a lot . . . about education, about literacy . . . We're going to make a great team."

"I think we would, too," I said.

"I want you to help me make Dominica a better place. I think we could do a great job together."

"Drew, do you trust me?"

He pulled me closer. "Of course, I trust you, Amelia. If I didn't I wouldn't be letting you on that plane tomorrow." He shook his head. "Let's not talk about that stuff anymore. You don't have to worry about anything anymore. Okay?"

"How can you be so sure?"

"Just trust me."

I looked in his eyes and all I could see was goodness. I didn't see a thief. I didn't see a scheming, opportunistic politician. I didn't see someone who could hurt me. "Okay. I'll trust you."

That night I lay awake in one of Vanessa's guest rooms, waiting for Drew. He never came in. He'd said he'd drunk too much to drive us all the way home. I was afraid that he didn't want to be alone with me. It was obvious to me that he knew about the papers I'd signed but would never talk about it. The party lasted way into the early hours of the morning and he never did come to my room. And before I knew it, it was time to leave for the airport.

Vanessa was not there to say good-bye this time. She left me a note saying that she had an early appointment but that she wished me well and couldn't wait till December, when we'd begin our relationship as mother and daughter. No mention of the previous night's incident. Drew was bleary eyed as he loaded my bags into his truck.

"The house is so quiet this morning," I said, struggling to make conversation.

"Everyone's wiped out from last night," he said.

"I wish you'd come to bed."

"I wish I had, too," he said.

I did my best to fill the silence as we drove to the airport. I commented on things, like the fact that I could name the trees and flowers growing along the roadside. Drew only nodded or grunted in response.

The winding, hilly roads did not freak me out anymore. I didn't even jump out of my seat when a sports car came roaring out of nowhere and passed us in a 100-mile-per-hour blur. Was I almost a Dominican now? And was it too late?

The airport was busy. A lot of tourists were flying back to the States and the UK, apparently. The airport had been closed for a few days after the hurricane so flights were still backed up. I recognized a couple from the diving trip with Whitney.

"Drew, where you going, man?" A taxi driver, jangling keys in his hand, approached.

Drew told him that he was dropping me off.

"You leaving us?" the man asked, his expression confused. "I thought you was getting married."

"We are," I said. "I'm just going home to tie up some loose ends."

The man looked doubtful. "Don't leave my man here at the altar. You hear me, young lady?"

"I hear you," I laughed. "I'll be back."

"And you think no one likes you," Drew said.

"I'll see you soon," I said as the last boarding call for my flight sounded overhead.

"If I have to come to Boston to get you, I will," he said. He didn't seem to be joking. And I wondered if there was an underlying threat in those words.

"You won't need to do that, Drew." I caught my breath. I didn't even want him joking about that.

"Are you sure? My mother would never forgive you. And remember the stakes are very high. . . ."

"I know, babe. I'll be back."

"Okay, I'll see you in three months. Twelve weeks," he said.

"I think I'm nervous," I said, looking at the last of the passengers entering the gates to board the plane.

"I'm nervous, too, Amelia. But I'll be right here waiting."

"I will be back. You have my word."

"And you're wearing my ring, remember that."

"Yes." I said. And I signed the papers. We kissed long and deeply. And just like that my escape from reality was over.

Chapter 33

The house seemed large and empty when I walked in that afternoon. James and Kelly had already moved most of their furniture out. Only a couch and a bookshelf were left in the living room. Wow. This really was it. Besides my bed and a few more bookshelves, this was all I owned in this world.

James and Kelly were really leaving. And I could either stay here by myself or go back to Dominica and be with Drew. As I looked around the almost-empty apartment, the choice seemed an easy one. There was no way in hell I could swing this rent on my teacher's salary. I guess I could move in with Whitney for a while and then buy a house eventually. But I didn't want to live with Whitney, which reminded me to give her a call.

"I'm back in town, lady."

"Ooooh! Chica, you're back. I'm coming over," she said.

I began to unpack my bags. I opened the closet door and looked at the tops, pants, and dresses that hung there. They looked like they belonged to someone else. They were so . . . big. It then dawned on me that I needed all new clothes. Those size 14 things would hang off me like a sack. I touched the sweaters and wool pants that I loved so much.

And I couldn't imagine any place in my new life for them. I'd never once even thought of a sweater while I was on Dominica.

A few minutes later, Whitney rang the doorbell. We hugged like we hadn't seen each other in a year.

"Whitney, what happened to you?" I asked. Something was different about her. I couldn't put my finger on it.

"What happened to me? Look at you! You look so fabulous, girl."

I followed her into the living room. What was it? It was like her aura had changed from frenetic to serene.

"You seem so calm," I said.

She shrugged. "I decided to take myself off the sauce."

"The sauce? Your meds?"

She nodded. "My doc's not happy about it, but I am. I feel feelings now. It's refreshing, clearer, like I got new glasses or something—for my emotions."

That didn't make much sense. She hadn't mentioned any of this the last time we spoke. "You think you made the right decision?"

"Yup. I'm going to find out what it's like to live like a normal person."

I shook my head. "How are things otherwise?"

"Otherwise?" Whitney asked.

"Yeah. With your dad?"

"It's going well, I think. I met his wife the other day. Still haven't met his daughter."

"Your sister."

"It's going to be a while before I can think about her that way."

"But things are moving along?"

"Yes, I found out why he had a change of heart, though."

"Why?"

"His father, my grandfather, died. I didn't even know I had a grandfather. Apparently they'd never been close. But his sister, my aunt, called him out of the blue and told him that their father had died. He was eighty-nine."

"Wow, Whitney. That's really deep."

"He lived in Pawtucket, Rhode Island. And I have three aunts and one uncle and several cousins. Less than an hour away. Ain't that something?"

I looked at her. She was so calm. Not angry. Not bubbling over. "Are you going to meet any of these people?"

"I don't know. It just feels so weird to know all of this. It's good in a way. I don't feel as lost as I used to. You know? He told me all these stories . . . About why he doesn't speak to the rest of the family anymore and all I'm thinking is: I have aunts and uncles and cousins. I'm not alone in the world. All the drama doesn't bother me at all. I think I'm even starting to forgive him for how things went down before."

"Whitney, I'm so happy . . . I told you everything would work out if you gave him a chance."

"It wasn't easy," she said. "But I . . . I think in time things will work out. His wife is nice, too."

"Whitney, that's just so great. . . . I'm so happy for . . ."

"What are you doing back here anyway? Why didn't you just stay?"

"You knew I was coming back!"

"I was hoping you wouldn't."

"I had to make sure everything and everybody was okay."

She snorted. "Right. We'd just all go to pieces without you, Amelia."

"I didn't say that." How did she know me so well.

"So tell me all about the wedding plans," she said, sipping a Diet Coke.

"Oh, Vanessa's taking care of everything."

"And you're letting her?"

"I don't really have a choice. I wouldn't know how to begin planning a wedding down there anyway. She'll do a much better job than I could."

"But don't you want to add your own personal touch? It's the biggest day of your life."

"Is it?"

"Girl, are you serious?"

I sighed. "It's not that big a deal. Things got kinda strange since we last talked."

"Really? How?"

I told her about the encounter with Jason, Phillip, and Vanessa.

"No way! No way!" Whitney said a few times. "You signed it?"

"What was I supposed to do? They wouldn't have let me go."

"They couldn't have kept you there forever!"

"I wasn't thinking straight, girl."

"What did Drew say when you told him?"

"I didn't."

"What!!!"

"I just couldn't . . . He knows. The whole scene was so choreographed. I think he knows about all of it. He just didn't want to get his hands dirty so he let his lawyers and Vanessa do his dirty work."

"Oh, girlie. What are you gonna do?"

"I don't know. I still feel like something else is missing."

"Like what? You mean there's more to it?"

I nodded.

"Did you ever Google him?"

"No, I never got around to it."

"Girl, where's your laptop?"

Whitney ran to my room and powered up my Dell. I stood over her shoulder as the screen came up. She typed in his name. Within seconds a page full of hits came back.

"Wow," she said. I sat down and peered at the screen.

The first news story we clicked on was the one he'd shown

me. Another one printed five years later by the *Washington Post* was much longer and quite different.

"Oh, shoot!" Whitney said as she read the text. "This is unbelievable."

The more I read the more my suspicions were confirmed. The thirty-two million dollars was just the tip of the iceberg. Drew had been honest about some things; he had built the company from scratch, but once it began to grow he and his partners began to fight over the profits.

An investigation after he'd already left the country found that he'd been siphoning off millions of dollars to various overseas accounts for several years before the company was sold. The *Washington Post* put the total amount at almost 500 million dollars. The IRS was also in on the investigation and claimed that Drew owed them hundreds of millions of dollars.

The story went on to say that Drew's lawyer was also wanted by the FBI for his role in the embezzlement. So that explained why Jason was living on the island and not in the States. They were all a bunch of criminals? My Drew. My perfect Drew.

I bit my lip.

"You okay, girl?" Whitney asked.

"I'm fine."

"Amelia, newspapers get stuff wrong all the time," Whitney said.

"Nah, look at all these other stories," I said, looking at the screen. There were more from the *Boston Globe* and *Philadelphia Inquirer.* The story of the black dot-com millionaire who made off with millions had made national news in the late-nineties. Ugh. Why wasn't I more suspicious? Why hadn't I done this Google search six months ago?

"Don't beat yourself up. You didn't know." Whitney put an arm around my shoulder. "I'll leave you alone if you want?"

"No," I said. "I'm tired of being alone, Whitney. I was so hoping Drew would make that all go away."

"Girlie, we're all alone. Even when you were with him, you were alone. Remember?"

I nodded and tried to hold back the tears. When I was with him? All I could remember were magical, sunny days on mountaintops, in the blue sea, under a shady tree, splashing in a cool waterfall. With him. I wasn't alone then. I was the happiest I'd been my whole life. Until I'd found out about this thing, Drew was the best thing that had ever happened to me.

"I can't believe he didn't tell me."

"He probably didn't want you to know that side of him."

"Freaking coward."

"Hey, babe. Everyone has secrets; some worse than others. There's stuff you didn't want him to know about you at first."

"Yeah, but it was nothing big. . . . I didn't embezzle, or steal from the government."

Whitney sank back into the couch and kicked her skinny legs out in front of her. "I'm sorry, Amelia."

"I can't wait to tell him off next time we talk."

"What are you going to tell him?"

"I'll tell him he's a thief and a freaking coward!"

Whitney sighed. "Normally, Amelia, I would be behind you a hundred percent, but I just don't know."

"What? Didn't you read what those newspapers said?"

"So what? Okay, he took all this money. Is he spending it on powerboats and diamond jewelry? Look at your engagement ring. That thing costs a month's salary for me, and I ain't that rich!"

I looked at the ring and back at her. "So what? He's a cheap millionaire. That doesn't make what he did right."

"He didn't do anything to you."

"He didn't tell me what he did. That's what he did wrong, Whitney. Why are you taking his side?"

"I'm not. I'm just playing devil's advocate. I'm just saying . . . Why would he tell you if he doesn't know what your reaction would be? He could have lost his freedom when he came here to see you."

"I'm sure he did it for some other selfish reason."

Whitney sighed. "Girl, I'm not trying to argue with you. I just don't want you getting all messed up and depressed the way you were over that ugly married guy."

"He wasn't that ugly."

"He was old."

"He was forty-two."

"At the time, that was old."

"Whitney, I'm going through a crisis here."

"Okay. Fine." She hugged me tightly. "I'm gonna go home so you can wallow, okay? All I'm saying is that this stuff happened over ten years ago. The guy is down there trying to do something good for his country. He's not perfect, but neither are you. That's it. I'm done."

"Go," I told her. "I need to straighten out my head."

But before Whitney was full out the door James and Kelly had come in. She waddled toward me, her arms outstretched.

"Girlie, you are so pregnant!"

She looked sheepish as she caressed her belly. "Nice to see you, too, Ames."

"What are you doing out so late? How's the new place?"

"Couldn't sleep. I wanna hear all about it."

I sat in the chair next to her around our old dining table. "How you feeling?" I couldn't stop staring at her stomach. It was so big and round. It seemed almost apart from her. Yikes! Did I ever want this to happen to me?

"I feel fine. I just can't stop eating. The doctor says it's fine. James is having a hard time with it, though."

"How?"

"Well, I snore now, and it drives him crazy. Plus, my belly keeps bumping up against his back and it wakes him up."

"It's his baby, too."

She shrugged. "James is a little boy in a man's body. He doesn't adjust well to grown-up issues, like being a husband to a pregnant woman."

"I'm sorry, girlie," I said. "You guys will get through this."

"We'll be all moved in next week."

"Oh, that's right," I remembered. "I can't wait to see it."

"It's sort of a mess, but at least I can have my own room."

"Your own room?"

"James thinks it will be better if we sleep apart until the baby comes."

"Kelly!"

She raised a hand. "I'm too tired these days to fight him. Actually, I think I'll sleep better, too."

I couldn't think of anything else to say. I mean, those two were the epitome of love and all that stuff. How could things be going so wrong? Especially now with a baby on the way.

"So, you ready to walk down the aisle?" She grabbed my hand and her eyes popped at my ring.

"I think so. I'm so worried. . . ."

"About what?"

"A lot has happened."

"Like what?" She leaned in.

Then I remembered the agreement I'd signed. Ugh. It was bad enough I'd talked to Whitney about it. But Kelly was a whole different story. She was a strict moralist; I couldn't depend on her not to do anything with the information.

"I'm just worried about leaving my life behind."

"What life?" She laughed. "I'm just kidding. But haven't you guys talked about this? What you're giving up to be with him?"

"Yeah. I mean, not really."

She gave me a curious look that said, Are you sure?

"Marriage is a big commitment, Ames. I'll be the first to tell you to go ahead with it—especially since we set you up with him—but I'll also tell you to take your time and think long and hard about it. There's no turning back once you're in it. You have to know that you can live not just with him, but with everything about him."

"Wow, Kelly. Things must be really rough for you guys right now," I said.

"And then some," she said. "Sometimes I wish I'd never decided to have this kid."

I looked at her, hoping she'd say she was kidding. But she didn't.

"I'm serious," she said as if reading my mind. "This pregnancy is bringing out the absolute worst in James."

We heard footsteps approaching and James appeared in the doorway of the kitchen.

"Hey, Ames. Welcome back."

I smiled at him.

"So when's your big day?"

"Sometime in December," I said. I'd stay with this storyline until I could figure out exactly what I was going to do.

"Cool, we'll definitely be there." He walked away, gathering up posters from their old room.

"So clueless," Kelly muttered.

"What?"

"The baby will be here then. We can't go anywhere."

"Oh, Kelly," I said.

Later that night as I tried to sleep I thought back to what Kelly said. Think long and hard. No turning back. Big commitment. Everything about him . . .

I dialed Drew's number, my heart pounding.

"I miss you so much," he said as soon as he heard my voice. My heart betrayed me. "I miss you, too, Drew."

I wanted to yell at him. Scream at him for not telling me

the whole truth, but I couldn't. It didn't seem right. He was too far away. I was hurting too much just being separated from him.

"Listen," he said. "I'm sorry."

"For what."

"For everything . . . I didn't want to involve you in any of this."

"Are you talking about those papers?"

He didn't answer.

"Drew, you can trust me. I'd never let anything happen to you."

"I know that. But will I ever see you again? I just get this feeling that you're gone forever."

I shut my eyes tightly. I wanted to stop seeing his face. It made it that much harder. "I have to think. I don't know."

"Okay," he said. "Whatever you decide, I'll understand."

I held the phone in my hand long after he'd hung up. I didn't know. I really, really didn't know what to do.

Chapter 34

It felt strange being back in school. The building seemed huge compared to the schools back on Dominica. I sat in the lounge, sipping coffee and preparing for my first class.

Lashelle blew in. "I heard you got engaged!" She grabbed my hand and ogled my ring. I didn't mind so much the ogling, it was the grabbing that bothered me. That and the fact that Lashelle had lost a ton of weight, enough that her butt no longer required its own zip code.

"Looks like we both went on a diet," she said, grinning wildly.

"Yeah, you look good, girl!" I said.

"You, too." She laughed. "I had to get in shape for my wedding, chile." That's right, I remembered. She and gangster-looking dude had gotten married in August.

"Too bad you missed it," she said. "But I have pictures." She pulled out a folder of what looked like thousands of photos. This was going to be a long morning.

"So, tell me all about your summer and your new guy," she said.

I told her as much as I could as I leafed through her photos, which were actually quite nice. I noticed that most of the teachers were in attendance, even Mr. Bell. Guess my absence didn't endear me to the school community. Oh, well.

"So, you're leaving?"

I nodded. "This is my last term here."

"Wow! That's a big step."

"Not really," I said. "I'll be back to visit my mom from time to time."

"Yeah, but it's a whole new place. A new culture." I understood where Lashelle was coming from. The look on her face actually said awe and admiration and so I let her go on and on about how "different" my life was going to be. It didn't matter, I thought, there were a million different ways to get out of this. I could always just say that I changed my mind.

There were a few familiar faces in first period. I looked at my list and matched up names and faces. I surveyed the back row and remembered Treyon Dicks. I was surprised that he hadn't been kept back again. Well, he must have done something right, I thought.

The day went surprisingly well. Maybe I'd been more laid-back after my summer on Dominica, or maybe my new kids were just a better group. Or maybe I'd been too emotionally battered to worry about how badly my students were behaving.

I heard a high voice calling me as I walked wearily to the lounge to get my stuff and head home. It was Tina from last period last year. Boy, she sure had filled out. Her boobs were almost as big as mine!

She gave me a big hug and I hugged her back, genuinely happy to see her so bubbly.

"Ms. Wilson, I read all the books you told me to over the summer."

What books? Ooooh!! The list of books I'd given her.

"You did?!"

"Yes, I decided I want to become a writer. I had so much fun reading them, Ms. Wilson. Do you have any more?"

I couldn't believe my ears. "Yes!" I wrote down three more books for her that I thought she might like: *Meriden, Brown Girl, Brownstones,* and *Sula.* I hoped I wouldn't get in trouble for that last one.

"Thanks, Ms. Wilson!"

"Hey, Tina." I stopped her before she could flit away. "Where's Treyon? I haven't seen him all day."

Her face fell. "You didn't hear?"

"What?"

"He got sent away in July. He shot . . . killed . . . some dude down at Four Corners one night."

I stood there stunned. Treyon was in prison?

"They tried him as an adult . . . You all right?" Tina asked.

"Yes," I said. "Thanks." I walked back to the lounge still in shock. How could that be? He was just a kid. A baby, really. His life would be over now.

I saw Lashelle packing up her bag to leave.

"Did you know that Treyon Dicks got sent to prison?"

"Oh, yeah," she said sadly. "A shame, huh? That kid that got killed was his age, too."

"I just can't believe it."

"Yeah, it's too bad," she shrugged. "But he was always out there looking for trouble." And she said her good-byes and was gone.

I sat in the lounge for a long time, thinking about Treyon. And Tina. And the school and myself. I hated it here. I hated the fact that these kinds of things happened to kids like Treyon and that kid he shot. When I'd taught at Meadow Academy it had been difficult but for a whole other set of reasons. The kids there were always challenging me intellectually. Many were rich and either hungry to learn or lazy brats who cared about nothing. But their lives were not this tragic. It sounds corny, but I was excited about teaching at a public school because I expected more fulfillment. I wanted to feel needed after what I'd been through. Last year I hadn't felt anything at all. But today had changed something. That look on Tina's face had given me a feeling that I wanted to feel over and over again. I felt that I'd lost an opportunity with Treyon, one I could never get back. And I wanted to make that right.

It turned out that Treyon Dicks's family lived one street away from the house that I grew up in. I had called his mother earlier in the day and she said I could stop by to visit after school.

I was surprised that his home seemed quite stable and his mother quite normal. Then why had he been so crazy? He'd been in juvenile detention three or four times that I was aware of, and goodness knows what other trouble he'd been involved in.

Treyon's mother was a petite woman with a soft voice. She worked the night shift as a nurse's aide at Boston Medical Center. There were pictures of Treyon all over the living room, on the walls, in frames on the coffee table, spilling out of photo albums. She was obviously still torn up about what had happened. She brought me a cup of tea in a white china cup.

"He was always rebellious," she said softly. "I wasn't around much because I was working all the time. But his older brother was supposed to take care of him." She said this last sentence with enough rage that it told me she held this older brother responsible.

I asked her more questions about him. What did he like to do when he was out of school; who were some of his favorite sports teams, hip-hop groups? She didn't know much, but she showed me his room. I saw that he liked Fifty Cent, the Game, and that he had a lot of old CDs. I opened up his stereo to see the last CD he was playing. It was A Tribe

Called Quest's *Midnight Marauders*. That was one of my favorite CDs of all time, too.

Notebooks cluttered the floor and table next to his bed, along with pieces of paper he'd scribbled on. I knew what they were. All the boys in school had their portfolio of rhymes that they carried around. I gave in to the curiosity and picked up a notebook on his bed. The first song jumped out at me.

Ms. Wilson, I hate you bitch
Fake ass hair, you a snitch
Make a nigger wanna kill somebody
Fat ass ho, make your nose all bloody

I stopped reading and took a deep breath. He must have written that on the day I sent him to Mr. Bell's office. Maybe I deserved that.

I told Ms. Dicks to keep in touch with me and to let me know if she needed anything. She smiled weakly as I closed the door and walked out of the yard. I hoped she knew that I was serious.

"Well, maybe one Sunday you can come up to the prison and visit with us."

I told her okay and gave her my number. But I was sure that Treyon did not want to see me. And I wasn't sure that I really wanted to see him. But I hoped she would tell him that I'd stopped by and that I cared.

I walked to my car and felt the pull. I hadn't seen my mother since I'd returned to the U.S. I had talked to her once, and she was as rude as she'd been the entire summer. The fact that I'd left her alone, and that she'd had to do her own grocery shopping and errand running, had made me even more of an ungrateful daughter in her eyes. But I decided to go over there even though I knew I was making a huge mistake.

I didn't knock. I used my key and let myself in. It was four P.M. She was probably napping anyway. The house seemed very clean, cleaner than usual, and I could smell food. I walked to the kitchen. Could she possibly be cooking?

"Ma?" I called out. No answer.

She wasn't in the kitchen, but there were some takeout bags on the counter.

"Ma?"

The house was still. I walked up the creaky stairs and thought I heard something. I stopped and it was silent. When I got to the top of the stairs, I definitely heard something. Voices. Groaning. "Grace. Oh, goodness, Grace." That was a man's voice in full ecstasy. I guess he was having his way with my mother. Oh, well. I walked down the stairs. And instead of leaving, I decided to wait. Why not? She had to know that I knew that she wasn't as lonely as she liked to let on that she was. She was seeing someone. At least sleeping with someone. And he'd brought her food! Ha! Let's see her pull the "woe is me" act when she comes down here.

I turned on the TV and watched *Oprah.* I turned up the volume loud enough so they'd know that someone was in the house. I loved Oprah. She looked so fabulous now that she'd lost the weight.

A male voice boomed from the top of the stairs. "Who's there?"

Oh, please.

"It's Amelia, her daughter."

"Amelia?" Grace's voice sounded weak and embarrassed.

"Ma, I'm waiting downstairs."

She hurried down the stairs a few minutes later, her hair all over the place, her face flushed and sheepish. She looked great. Young and pretty.

"Look at you," she exclaimed. "You lost all that weight!"

"Who's upstairs with you, Ma?"

She glared at me. "Don't ask me no questions. You hear?"

I rolled my eyes. Sure. Pull the, "I'm the mother" crap.

"I brought you a present, but it's back at the apartment."

"What is it?"

"A dress."

"What kind of dress? Something I can wear to church?"

"In the summer."

She looked at me. "Let me see that ring."

She held my hand, peered at the ring, and looked in my face.

"I missed you," she said.

I nodded. I swallowed a knot of something that was rising in my chest.

"So, my little girl's getting married," she said. She looked a bit sad but there was a little smile on her face.

"I don't know, Ma."

She looked into my eyes. "What happened?"

"It's complicated."

"He got another woman?"

"No," I stood up. "Just other stuff."

"Like what?"

"His business . . . We have some trust issues."

"Trust issues? That's it? Girl, there ain't no man out there who don't have some issues."

"Yes, Ma." Here we go, I thought. She would tell me now how my father drank too much and only gave her a twenty-dollar allowance a week through their entire marriage.

"See, like my friend Dean, upstairs. Now that's a good man. But he got too many kids. He got at least eight kids. But I can live with that. As long as he taking care of them."

"Ma, he has eight kids?"

She nodded.

"I hope you're using protection," I said.

She ignored my comment. "All I'm saying is I already told him you getting married. Gerard thinks you getting married. Amelia, I haven't been on a plane in over ten years."

I sighed. So I had to marry Drew so she could get on a plane again?

"Ma, it's just not that easy. I have some things to think about."

"All right," she said.

"When am I going to meet Dean?"

"Not today," she said. "Call your brother."

Chapter 35

I pulled up to the apartment and a feeling of dread came over me. I didn't want to go in. It was so empty. So cold even though it was early September. I missed the warm sunshine of Dominica. The nosy people. Even crazy Vanessa. And I missed Drew. I didn't want to wait. I wanted to go back now.

As I sat in the car thinking, a tow truck pulled up next to me.

"Hey, sis, I heard you got back." It was Gerard. Wow, he was still working for that tow company. That's the longest he'd ever kept a job in his whole life.

I got out of the car, and he pulled over behind my Beetle.

"Girl, look at you, all skinny and stuff."

I put my hand on my hip. "What do you think?"

"You look good!" Gerard said. "Lemme see your rock."

I held out my hand. "Dude must have some serious dough or that's some good cubic zirconium."

"It's not cubic zirconium!"

"Aiiiight. Slow your roll, Amelia. You not the only one getting married." He looked at me triumphantly.

"Huh?"

"You heard me. D'Andrea asked me to marry her."

"D'Andrea asked you?"

"Something like that," he said.

"Uh-huh," I said dubiously. The last time I saw D'Andrea she sounded as if she wanted him dead.

"I'm serious," he said. "Why you think I kept this job so long. I told that girl I'd do right by her."

He was serious. He wasn't looking all faux brave and defiant anymore.

"Gerard, you're getting married?" I asked incredulously. I was so touched I wanted to cry. I don't know why, either.

"Yeah, you're my inspiration, girl. I can't be up in Ma's house anymore now that she got this mailman dude coming around, and D'Andrea said I can't stay with her unless I put a ring on her finger."

Good for D'Andrea!

"Does D'Andrea know this yet?'

"No, I'm gonna tell her tonight, though. I'm taking her to the Cheesecake Factory."

I held my little brother's head and kissed him on the forehead. "Gerard, congratulations. I'm so happy for you. For us."

"Well, it ain't gonna be no big thing. We'll probably just go to the courthouse."

"And you can honeymoon in Dominica when you come to my wedding. You're giving me away, right?"

"I am?"

"Yes, you are!"

"Do I gotta wear a tuxedo?"

"Probably."

"I wish the old man was here to see us now," Gerard said, and we looked at each other, each feeling a deep loss we never liked to think about, much less talk about.

"He'd be happy . . ."

Gerard reverted to teasing bravado. "When's all this going to be? I gotta get in shape so I can hit the beach."

"In December, but I'm going back before that."

"I thought Ma said you were here till December."

"Nah, I just changed my mind a second ago. I'm gonna get packing now, Gerard."

"You're crazy. All you women are crazy," he said, getting back in the tow truck.

"I'll call you, Gerard," I yelled as he drove away.

I ran into the empty apartment. I had a lot to do: Type up my resignation letter; close my credit card and bank accounts. Wow. So many loose ends to tie up. I felt as if the old Amelia Wilson was dying and a new one was coming to life. I closed my eyes, saw his face, and wondered: Would he really be proud of me? What would my dad think of what I was doing? I remembered him saying once that not even the President of the United States was good enough for me. But even back then I'd known that I didn't want the "president." I didn't even want a perfect man then. I just wanted someone who loved me just half as much as he did. And I'd found that in Drew. He wasn't perfect and the road ahead was full of uncertainty and probably excitement. But that's love. Right?

Epilogue

A majestic, golden sun dominated the horizon framed by a curtain of pink and gray clouds. Amelia watched the marvel of nature, feeling content that at least she now owned some of that beauty. This was her place, a sunset she could call her very own.

"I'm doing the right thing, right, Ma?" She turned to Grace, who looked stunning in her pink satin and tulle dress.

"Yes, Amelia." She straightened her daughter's veil. "I don't have to tell you that."

Grace looked at her daughter. Amelia knew she had never looked more beautiful. Her wedding dress was a chiffon, satin, and crystal beading creation that looked deceptively simple. The spaghetti straps were crystal beaded, the asymmetrically shirred bodice fit her newly trim body perfectly, and the curved dropped waistline that gracefully fell into an A-line skirt showed that despite her weight loss she hadn't loss all of her curves. She'd opted for a chapel train and a simple veil. It had taken a lot of negotiation with Vanessa to achieve this look, but Amelia was happy with what she saw in the mirror.

The guests were waiting for the ceremony to begin on the deck of the Fort Young Hotel, overlooking the cobalt Caribbean

Sea. Amelia caught occasional glimpses of the formally dressed crowd from the window of her suite. She didn't know most of them but she felt comfortable here. Everyone had been so nice in the past few days; they'd welcomed her to Dominica as if she were family.

Vanessa and Grace had done a magnificent job of not tearing each other apart over the last week. Amelia herself had given up months before and let Vanessa plan all the wedding details, but she had to give it to the woman; everything looked perfect, down to the sunset.

The suite was noisy, mostly due to Whitney chatting loudly with her little sister; her newest friend whom she'd brought along for the ride. Even though they were half sisters, Amelia could see the resemblance in their features and their frenetic movements when they were excited. Whitney looked gorgeous in a light pink full-length dress with a white satin sash around her tiny waist. She was the maid of honor, but the way she wore that dress it could have been her day in the spotlight.

Amelia looked at herself again in the mirror and tugged at the beaded straps. The dress had been her choice—the first time in her life she'd ever owned anything so beautiful. Vanessa had chosen another dress, a huge, beaded nightmare with what seemed like every bell and whistle known to the bridal gown industry, but Amelia had put her foot down. It was something she was becoming more and more comfortable with around these parts.

"You look hot, chica," Whitney said, tapping her on the shoulder. "You ready to walk down the aisle?"

"Yes, scared but I'm ready."

"You'd better relax. Don't ruin Vanessa's day now."

They all laughed, even Vanessa giggled as she smoothed the train of Amelia's dress.

"It's not my day, it's hers. And my son's," Vanessa said between the laughter.

The three of them were quite a sight to behold. Grace and Vanessa fussing over Amelia. Whitney and her little sister shooting Amelia mock sympathetic glances. There was a knock on the door.

Gerard poked his head in. "Ya'll ready or what? Dude's been waiting a long time."

"Come on in, Gerard," Grace said.

Whitney whistled as Gerard strode into the room wearing his black tux. He looked like a taller, lighter version of Taye Diggs.

"Gerard, if you weren't already married . . ." Whitney teased.

"Yeah? I look good, huh." He looked at himself in the mirror and adjusted his bow tie.

Grace cleared her throat. "We need to get going, people."

Gerard stepped up to Amelia and she hooked her arm in his. "You ready to go meet your man, little sister?"

Amelia took a deep breath as Grace, Whitney, and Vanessa took up their positions. The men would meet them outside the door, then they'd walk up the aisle; Amelia would be last in the procession.

"I just hope I don't do anything stupid. Like fall or faint."

"Stop it already," Whitney said. "Let's go, girl."

Minutes later, Amelia heard her cue as the wedding song began to play by the quartet Vanessa had commissioned. She walked down the aisle, flanked by tables decorated in pink and silver ribbons. At the tables sat about three hundred of Vanessa's closest friends and a handful of hers. Darkness was falling gently and she inhaled the smell of scented candles from the tables mixed with tropical flowers and the ocean. The sun was setting deeper and deeper. Cameras flashed as she reached the aisle. She stopped, looked up, and there he was.

He smiled at her knowingly. It had taken a lot of trust building and talking to get to this point. The important thing was that she believed in him. He wasn't perfect. He'd done some things she would have never expected of him, but this was Drew. He'd promised her that he would never hurt her, had pledged his fidelity, his very life to her. Where he went that's where she would go. This was how right this felt. She smiled back and walked to meet him.

Would she take the good with the bad, the bitter with the sweet, sickness, health, richer and poorer?

She did.